Harley & Me

Love Means Never Saying Goodbye

Cassandra Parker

Dedication:

To my readers who asked for a romantic story about Harley and the gang. May love see each person through all the ups and downs of your personal journey.

Harley, my angel, this one's for you wherever you might be in the heavens.

Acknowledgements:

To Kim Williams for her proofreading and invaluable opinions that helped me see this book through.

To Jennifer Reginato for her editing and suggestions.

Anne Mangas Smith whose poetry got me through rough times after the loss of R. Harley all those years ago.

To Carsten Degenhardt whose insights, encouragement, and friendship I cherish.

Harley & Me

Prologue

Whoever said, "Love means never having to say you're sorry," didn't know what they were saying. Love means never saying goodbye. Even after all this time, it still holds true for me. You love someone; you never say goodbye. No matter where they are, or what has happened, they are always with you by your side. At least that's how it was with Harley and me.

When he messed up and hurt my feelings, he was fond of saying, "My purpose is to love you. I guess it slipped my mind. I never said I was good, but I hope you can forgive me."

I invariably did forgive him. I never could stay mad at him for very long. Even when I was upset, Harley found a way to make me smile or laugh. He brought such joy into my life. He could be a devil, but he was my devil.

His other favorite line was, "If you share my bed, you must share my name." And he meant it. Boy, did he mean it! But it didn't mean he had never made love only that it was worth waiting for when you finally found that special person.

He also said, "There's more to love than the physical act of making it. If you love someone, you are in it for the long haul. You stay with that person through broken dreams, heartache, love, and everything that goes with a long term relationship. Not even death can separate you because with real love two people become one person."

The mid-1970's in Ohio were a memorable time. The state was still overcoming the aftermath of the Kent State Massacre over five years earlier. Gasoline rationing was in effect. Social Security funding was set to dry up.

Bands such as America, Elton John, Captain & Tennille, Linda Ronstadt, Hamilton, Joe Frank & Reynolds, Neil Sedaka, Jigsaw, Ozark Mountain Daredevils and KC & The Sunshine Band were all on Billboard's top hits chart. Harley's favorite band, Steppenwolf, had just released 'Hour of the Wolf' in July. Two tracks on that album rapidly became Harley's all-time favorite songs, 'Another's Lifetime' and 'Just for Tonight' along with the classic biker anthem 'Born to be Wild' on an earlier album.

The first time I laid eyes on Harley, it in was September on the Commons at Ohio State University-Lima. It was a warm day for Ohio, with temperatures somewhere in the seventies. The noon sun beat down upon the grounds. Clusters of students sat on the grass around the Commons. Some were reading, others talking, and a guy was playing his guitar. He was playing 'Sister Golden Hair' by America.

Friends I met in Freshman Orientation were sitting nearby. Peg was the pragmatic one of our group. Thomas was the dreamer. He loved coming up with schemes to get to the Bermuda Triangle. Maryanne was an innocent, naïve person who attracted a strange guy named Peter March. March was an out and out stoner, but he loved Maryanne, and they both loved children.

Harley was sitting on the hill listening to an anti-war protester. I guess the protester didn't know the Vietnam War was over. It was over for America and our soldiers who had come home almost two years earlier were greeted by boos and jeers instead of pride and thanks.

Harley sat a few feet away from us with his arms wrapped around his legs. He wore worn jeans with patches on the legs and ragged holes in the knees. A black leather jacket, a t-shirt with sleeves rolled up, and black leather boots with chains at the ankles completed the outfit. He was the spitting image of a biker and would have easily fit into the 'Easy Rider' movie. He was a rebel, dangerous, mysterious, and sexy all rolled into one man.

Did I mention he was drop dead gorgeous? He was the stuff of dreams, handsome, tall, self-assured, not an ounce of fat on his body. His hair was an incredible mix of sandy and dark brown that accentuated his blue-gray eyes. When he smiled, you could almost swear he was an innocent saint or a rascally devil.

He had a wicked sense of humor, and most of all he loved me at first sight. He used to tell me that when he first saw me, his world changed forever. He knew I was the one for him. I was the one he wanted to rest his weary body against, and I brought solace to his heart and peace to his soul.

The Devil in him kept him chasing dreams with never-ending abandonment, and yet he managed to run his customizing motorcycle empire on a tight schedule. He even ran a profit when the rest of the country was still fighting to recover from a recession and shortages of gasoline.

He loved motorcycles, and the open road, Steppenwolf, poetry, and me. I used to tease him and ask which number in that lineup I was. The allure of hard rocking Steppenwolf, the poetry of nature, the freedom of traveling the open road via a huge hog is all pretty hard to beat. Invariably he would answer, "You know where you stand in that lineup, right up there in first place."

His beautiful eyes would drift over my body sending tingles all over me, and a slow smile would creep across his face as he pulled me into his arms. Then his lips would fall upon mine for a long, slow, lingering gentle kiss that invariably took my breath away, leaving me wanting more.

Who would have guessed he was my soul mate? I certainly didn't think so and I sure never thought he was a multimillionaire. He was a junior albeit he was a little older than the average junior. He attended classes on a part-time basis and spent the rest of his hours running his empire.

In 1980, almost two years after losing Harley, John Kay came out with a song called 'Say You Will' that perhaps sums up the love Harley and I shared. Even now when I hear that beautiful song, I become emotional.

Tears come to my eyes because of that one song. It fit Harley and me so perfectly, it was almost as though the famous singer knew our love and wrote about it years later.

What I wouldn't give to have Harley next to me right now. To have his arms encircle me and hold me close, and feel his hands massage my back and shoulders. To smell the Irish Spring soap on his skin and sun-kissed hair, as I gaze into his smoldering eyes, to feel the gentle caresses of his lips brushing mine, just one more embrace to last a thousand lifetimes, one last time to feel the sweet agony of his love.

Chapter One

"Hi, mind if I join you guys?" Harley said with a grin as wide as the Ohio River. Without waiting for an answer he sat on the ground and languidly stretched his legs out before him. He leaned back on his elbows and turned his head to look at our little group.

"I'm a transfer from back east." Harley had a pleasant baritone, sweet, and oh so sexy voice that sent shivers down my spine and gave me goosebumps. I could listen to him talk for hours.

"I'm a freshman," I replied looking down at my hands. "I'm Mari."

"Name's Harlan Christian Robert Davis. My folks are big Harley-Davidson fans. I mean big fans. They ride giant hogs." His chuckle was infectious and soon had us all giggling with Maryanne snorting in her odd laugh. "I know, pretentious isn't it? Call me Harley." His deep baritone voice rumbled in his chest making him sound even sexier than imaginable.

So, Harley, it was. It went along nicely with his big Harley-Davidson hog. Sometimes we'd tease him about his middle name Christian and where it may have originated. He'd get righteous and tell us his name was Christian, never explaining if he meant literally or religiously.

"So, you're a Frosh, huh?" His gaze traveled slowly and lingeringly down my body making me blush.

"Frosh?"

"Freshman. That's what we call freshmen, frosh." He grinned and winked at me. "Come sit beside me," he patted the ground next to him. "I promise I won't bite." He smiled, "this time."

"I wouldn't trust that," March laughed. He was the classic hippy of the '60's era with his long brown hair, unshaven beard, lanky frame and holey jeans and tie-dyed shirt.

I gave him the cheesiest face I could muster as I moved to sit next to Harley. Leaning over, I whispered, "You better not bite me."

"Grr..." he growled and smiled.

"Did you just growl at me?"

He grinned and let out a wolf howl that had us all looking at him like he was crazy. "What? You never heard a wolf howl before?"

"Can't say that I have." The giggles were upon me, and I felt mortified this handsome stranger had to endure my fit of teenage embarrassment.

"Guess we'll have to correct that. What are you doing Friday?"

"Working."

"Hmm..." He furrowed his brow, and a grin spread across his face, "where do you work?"

"Kmart."

"Simple solution. Get someone to switch with you."

"I can't do that. No one wants to work Friday, Saturday or Sunday."

"I bet I can get it switched for you."

"You do that, and I'll go with you Friday."

"Thursday night."

"Can't."

"I know. You're working Thursday," he sighed.

"I have a radio show until noon and Anthropology until nine."

"Pick you up after class at nine." He stood and looked down at me. "Wait a minute. Is your show at ten?"

"Yes."

"You're Gypsy Mar! I call in every day at noon with a Steppenwolf request, and you always play some of their best tunes."

"That's me. Progressives, hard rock classics." I grinned. "Never really into much of Steppenwolf until I started getting requests for them."

Somehow it never dawned on me that this hunky man might be interested in me, a shy wallflower adrenaline junkie.

Thursday night, he was waiting at the door on the most dangerous black and chrome hog you ever saw in your life. With the black leather and chains riding gear you would have thought he was some character out of a sex and bondage movie.

"This is our ride for the remainder of our sojourn." Harley indicated with a sweep of his arm as he bowed low. He flipped up the visor, "I never said I was good, or a saint for that matter. Climb on behind me. Put your foot on the pipes and be careful. They can get hot if your leg touches it. When I lean one way, you do the same. Here," he handed me a helmet and his black leather jacket. "Put this on."

"What about you?" The jacket swallowed me and smelled pleasantly of a combination of Irish Spring soap and Old Spice after shave. Even now I get nostalgic for those days whenever I get a whiff of either scent.

"I'll be okay. We're not going far. We'll pick mine up on the way. I left it at home," he shrugged.

I did as he instructed with trepidation. The hog came alive with a great roar. He popped a wheelie, and down the road, we went riding hell bent as though the hounds of Satan were on our heels. It felt wild and freeing to race off into the night on the back of this giant machine. It growled up the road, spitting asphalt and fine gravel back out in a full throttle roar. The wind whipped around and over us. All too soon the adventure ended in front of an enormous mansion.

A tall older man stepped from the doorway to the hog.

"Here's your helmet Master Davis." He handed him a gleaming black and red helmet. "Shall I gas her up for you?"

"Thank you, Garrett."

"My pleasure, sir. Have a safe trip with your lady."

Harley motioned for me to hold on, "we'll be back Sunday night, Mari." He started the engine with a roar.

"Just a minute," I sputtered. "Where are we going?"

"Not far, only about four hours from here." Suddenly he was all business as he conducted his pre-drive inspection.

"You expect me to ride this thing for four hours?" I stared at the handsome man sitting in front of me.

"I think our sitting here answers that question," he smirked. He took the leather jacket Garrett handed him and shrugged into it.

My heart thudded hard like the heavy metal thunder line from the Steppenwolf song, 'Born to be Wild.' I had never ridden in a vehicle more dangerous than my former race car, a Plymouth Satellite, let alone spent hours on the back of a hog.

"Is this thing safe?"

"That's what the checklist is for," Garrett replied as he continued making tick marks on the paper. "Master Davis is very safety conscious."

"Hold on to me, Mari," Harley said as he pointed to his waist. "Turn on your headset. I'm pioneering a communication device that will let us talk comfortably while riding."

With the engine growling like only a genuine Harley-Davidson motorcycle can do, we sped off into the night.

As we went down the road I looked through my visor at the lights of the city; it was breathtaking. Never did so many pinpricks of light look as beautiful as they did that night.

"Lovely, isn't it?" he murmured over the headset.

"Stunning."

"This is going to sound corny," he laughed, "but you intrigue me."

"I do?" I looked at him and felt the heat rising from my neck to my face. He was by far the most handsome man I had ever met.

"Yeah," he spoke shyly. "I noticed you during Orientation. You looked a little lost and then the posse descended upon you, and swept you away."

"March, Maryanne, Bob, and Peg," I bet. "We were all new and just banded together."

"Kept me out," he sighed. "From the way, you guys were kidding around; I didn't know you had a boyfriend. Guess I know now."

His voice sounded wistful and full of longing. I almost placed my hand on his leg. But, I was brought up to be proper. Good girls don't go around putting their hands on guy's knees. For that matter, they didn't go on overnight dates either. I guess I wasn't a proper young lady after all.

The ride lasted just four and a half short hours. We stopped at a restaurant next to the hotel we would stay in. The diner looked like a typical 1950's era eatery complete with faux red leather seats; Formica covered tables, checkerboard flooring, and a jukebox.

Across from the booths was a counter and stools in what I could only describe as pure baby blue.

"Howdy Flo," Harley greeted the waitress.

Yes, her name was Flo, complete with the ruby red lips and piled high beehive hair-do.

"Good to see you again, Harley." She gathered two menus and flatware. "Regular booth?" She turned and sashayed down the aisle to the mid-point.

Harley followed behind her a bit more slowly. He placed his hand on the small of my back and guided me into the booth before sitting across from me.

"Let's see, a ginger ale float, right?" She pulled her pencil from her pocket. "And you, dear?" She smacked her lips before blowing a pink bubble from the wad of gum in her mouth. She turned to face me. "What'll it be?"

"Coke, please."

"Coke, it is. Be right out."

I watched her until she disappeared in the back. "Is she for real?" I whispered.

"A hundred and ten percent," he smiled. "Flo's kind, decent folk even if she dresses like a 50's waitress." He tapped the back of the booth and frowned. "You know, Coke isn't good for you, right?"

"How so? I mean I know it has lots of sugar and salt."

"Caffeine. Hot caffeinated beverages hurt the body."

"I never heard that before."

"Caffeine, especially in a hot beverage, interacts with your body to create toxins."

"So, you don't drink caffeinated beverages?"

"Nope."

"But you have a ginger ale float."

"Ginger ale is naturally caffeine free. Don't worry, and I'm not going to try to force my beliefs on you," he smirked. "I know better than that." His grin was infectious and quirky.

"So, we are in Fort Wayne, Indiana?" I asked, hoping to change the topic. I loved cold Cokes.

"Nope. We're in a town called Lafayette, population around sixty-eight thousand. We'll be going to Battle Ground. They have a place that rescues wolves. It's called Wolf Park."

I scanned the menu. Nothing exotic here, just plain old American food. "What's good here?"

Harley leaned against the booth and spread his arms across the back. "Everything. Just good old home style cooking. I like the burgers and chili."

"Looks like they have mild, moderate and killer hot. Which one do you go for?"

"Killer hot, babe; all the way."

Flo returned with our drinks and pulled out her notepad. "Ready to order?"

"Mari?" Harley looked at me.

"Cheeseburger and fries." I closed the menu and handed it back to her.

"Very good. Well done, I take it?" Flo snapped a piece of gum and blew a pink bubble.

"Yes, please."

"And you, Harley? Killer hot chili?"

"As always, Flo," he grinned.

She took his menu and waltzed down the diner to the kitchen window.

"Don't tell me; I shouldn't eat burgers, right?"

"Not at all. Full of bad fats, but I like them too," Harley laughed. His joy shone through in the way his shoulders shook, and his eyes lighted with a twinkle. "I like all the bad stuff too, hence the chili."

He sauntered over to the jukebox. Within minutes, the familiar gruff voice of John Kay singing 'Just for Tonight' came wafting through the diner.

"You and your Steppenwolf," I giggled and rolled my eyes. "Do you ever get enough?"

"Nope. You can never get enough of the masters. Goldy McJohn is brilliant on keyboards; just listen to him on 'Tenderness,' and you'll gain an appreciation for this underrated band."

We sat listening to the song. I could not believe how beautiful the keyboards sounded and overlooked the very taboo lyrics.

"Now, you see what I'm saying? Moves your soul, doesn't it? I like to think of the song as a young man coming of age and learning how to appreciate the love of a woman."

"I can see that," I sipped my drink.

We spent the next hour chatting and listening to music.

The hotel was an old Victorian style building and very ornate. The lobby has marble flooring, solid wood walls, and a crystal chandelier. Plush chairs dotted the lobby and were dwarfed by a giant fireplace.

"Good to see you again Mister Davis," greeted the bellhop. "Your rooms are on the top floor, as usual."

We stepped into an elevator decked out in brass and wood.

"Thank you, Jermaine," Harley smiled and handed the man some cash. "It's always a pleasure to see you." He waited patiently while the bellhop opened the door and gave him the keys.

The room looked like a suite, complete with a small dining area, living room, and separate bedroom. "Your room is through this door," Harley opened a door off the living room and guided me into a similar suite. "I might sound old-fashioned, but I believe in the law of chastity."

"Huh?" I had heard of being chaste but was unfamiliar with a law of chastity.

"Under the law of chastity, we are commanded that only in marriage are a man and woman to engage in sexual relations."

I could feel a blush creeping into my cheeks. "Are you a virgin?"

"No," he laughed, "but I have come to respect that law and I'm content to wait for marriage." He grinned wolfishly and snapped his teeth at me. "I told you it sounded old-fashioned."

"No problem with that. Old-fashioned is good. No pressure." I could tell from the speculative look in his eyes, he wondered about me. "Well, I," I groaned as I felt my face turning red.

"That's fine, Mari. I don't need to know. It wouldn't matter either way to me." He paused as though studying me. "You intrigue me, Mari Forrester." He shoved his hands into his pockets. "We have an early day tomorrow, so get some rest."

"What time do we need to be up?"

"Let's get breakfast around eight and then we'll look around Battle Ground. How's that sound?"

"Fair enough."

"May I kiss you goodnight?"

"Uh...sure."

He leaned forward, grasping me gently in his arms and placed a tender, chaste kiss on my lips. "Good night mi amour. Sleep well."

"You too." Somehow, even that sweet kiss made me breathless, and my heart pounded.

I leaned against the door and closed my eyes. I felt giddy. How could one man I had only known a few days make me feel like swooning?

Chapter Two

We ate breakfast at the same diner we visited the night before. "Do you want to do the usual tourist thing, or would you prefer something more natural?"

I couldn't tear my eyes from him long enough to concentrate on his question. He looked devilishly handsome in faded jeans, white shirt, and his worn black leather jacket. The ladies in the diner kept glancing at him. I'm confident they wondered what someone such as I was doing with a hunky guy like him.

"Something more natural. I love the outdoors." I responded, wondering just what he had in mind.

"What do you want to see?" He asked as he casually draped an arm around me.

"Can we visit The Farm at Prophetstown?"

"Of course. Then we'll grab a quick lunch and look at the shops."

The farm focuses on sustainable agriculture. Visitors are invited to help feed the livestock, gather eggs, and other chores.

It was intimidating to a city girl like me to collect eggs from the hens. Harley found my squeamishness amusing and chased me around threatening to toss a rotten egg at me.

"Here comes the egg, Mari! Run!" He yelled as he pelted me with the aromatic chicken by-products, always careful to make sure they landed to my side, in front, or behind me. Still, the sumptuous stench was enough to tear up eyes.

We also visited Clegg Gardens. It is a beautiful park that runs alongside Wildcat Creek. It boasted ninety-five acres of prairie, oak savannah restorations, wildflowers and nature trails.

I found the walk through the park somehow the most romantic thing I had done to date. What girl could want more than a casual stroll with the most handsome man around?

Harley had the most sensual walk I had ever seen. The way he placed his feet and the subtle sway of his hips reminded me of big cats like jaguars, cheetahs, and lions, on the prowl. It was provocative and dangerous, and oh so suggestive. It's hard to imagine; he didn't seem to know the sex appeal he had on women. Who could resist the romantic rebel wearing a biker jacket?

After Clegg Gardens, we ventured onward to Battle Ground and a late lunch at a local tavern and grill with the most delicious food I had tasted in awhile.

Battle Ground, Indiana is where the Battle of Tippecanoe took place. We visited all the historical sites we could that day, and after a quick dinner at the local café, we continued to Wolf Park. The gates opened shortly after seven that night.

Dr. Eric Klinghammer started with two wolves from the Brookfield Zoo in 1972. In 1974 Wolf Park had the opportunity to raise their first litter of pups. The organization officially became Wolf Park in 1976.

To see these magnificent creatures cared for by dedicated staff, to view how they had suffered at the hands of man whether by hunting, civilization encroachment, or pollution is humbling at best, and demoralizing at worst. As the sun set, we heard the first faint chorus. Soon, wolf after wolf lent their individual voices to a full-throated choir that haunted me to my very core.

"Sends a shiver down your spine, doesn't it?" Harley whispered as he wrapped his arms around me from behind. "It's a lyrically haunting song."

I could only nod; the wolf song so enraptured me there were no words to express what I was hearing and seeing.

The next day we returned to the diner for breakfast. The waitress was named Vera, yes; Vera and she looked like the character in the television show 'Alice.'

Harley plugged in coins and selected Steppenwolf's 'Annie, Annie Over,' and 'Monster/Suicide/America.'

"What? No Steely Dan?" I chided. "No 'Reelin' in the Years' for you?"

"Not a fan of the band," he huffed.

"How about some Bruce Springsteen? 'Rosalita Come out Tonight' is pretty decent. You know, he's up and coming."

"Mari," he growled.

"There you go, growling at me again." I couldn't resist teasing him.

"Mari," he grumbled.

"Okay, okay!" I laughed. "Don't get your boxers in a knot."

"My what?" his voice got noticeably louder, and his face turned a lovely shade of pink.

"You ready to order?" Vera asked pulling her pencil from her hair.

"I'll have the ham and Swiss omelet, a side of bacon, toast, and a Vernor's."

"Same for me," Harley closed his menu and smiled at me, all signs of temper gone. "I like it that you aren't afraid to eat."

"Huh?" That comment took me by surprise.

"Some of the girls I dated would not eat a thing around me. They claimed they were watching their figures. I often wondered what figures, when they were stick-thin."

He reached out and took my hand. "You, on the contrary, have curves in all the right places." His blush returned. This hot biker had an innocence about him that I found endearing.

I felt the heat rising in my face as I looked anywhere but at him. "I guess, this is what you call a date?"

"What else would you call it?" He looked at me innocently with twinkling eyes.

"An overnight trip?" I squeaked.

"My, my!" He laughed, "Aren't we both a beautiful red?"

"Here ya go sweeties," Vera plopped our plates in front of us. "Enjoy."

"Just how many women have you dated?" I fiddled with my napkin.

"Does it matter?" he asked softly. His thumb gently stroked the top of my hand. "You're the only one I'm interested in."

"Have you looked at yourself?" I sputtered. "Girls are falling all over you at OSU."

"They are?" The innocence in his voice was startling.

Did he not know just how hot he was? "You're a hunk!" I blurted. To my chagrin, his response was to lift an eyebrow and merely smile.

"Well, you are!" I dabbed my face with a napkin.

"Is the temperature getting a little hot in here?" he smirked.

"Eat your breakfast," I snapped and then giggled.

"Do you really want numbers?" He appeared uncomfortable with giving out such personal details.

I shrugged. "No, not really."

"I courted a lot of women, but I've never taken a date on an overnight trip. I've never met anyone that interested me as much as you do." He sat back in his seat and studied me. "One thing you need to know about me, Mari," he talked slowly with a dangerous undercurrent in his tone. "I never lie."

For some reason, I believed him. "What's the plan for today?"

"We go sightseeing and shopping. Dinner and a dance tonight. How's that sound?"

"Sightseeing is great. I'm not much for shopping," I frowned.

"That's okay. We'll have fun picking on the clerks." He grinned wolfishly at me, "I'm teasing. I want to get you something for the ride home tomorrow."

We spent the day browsing antiques. Nestled next to the shops was a bakery. Harley smiled so widely he looked like a five-year-old in a candy store.

"I love this place, Mari!" He grasped my arm and tugged me toward the door. "They have the best honeycomb I've ever tasted."

"Really? Honeycomb, the stuff bees make?"

"No!" he laughed. His laugh sounded like a hearty rumble from deep in his chest. "This is a confection shaped like a honeycomb and is fried. It's made with honey and sprinkled with cinnamon, powdered sugar, and chocolate." He stepped to the counter.

"Back again, Harley?" An older woman dressed in a baker's apron reached for a plate-sized pastry.

"Two, Edna, please," he clasped his hands with glee.

"Brought a young lady, eh?"

"I'm sorry, Edna, where are my manners? This lovely woman is Mari."

"Pleased," she tucked the warm confections in wax paper and handed us a mountain of napkins.

"Do you know everyone in these towns?" I asked as I nibbled the sweet. Harley was right. Honeycomb was a heavenly treat.

"Just about." He cupped his chin with his hand and reached for a napkin to wipe the sticky mess from his face.

Our next stop was a motorcycle shop where Harley insisted on buying me a stylish black leather jacket that belted around the middle. He also purchased a helmet to fit me. Our next stop was a boutique where I picked out a dress with autumn colors, and he selected a silver chain with a pink heart on it.

"This is so you can carry my heart with you wherever you go," he whispered as he hooked the clasp around my neck. "Now, I will never be very far from you." He tilted my face slightly and gently kissed me.

My face flushed, and I could feel my blood pounding as my heart rate increased dramatically. I wanted to grab Harley and anchor his lips to mine forever. What was it about this man that sent me spinning out of control?

Dinner that night was at a swanky Italian restaurant. The muted lights and tables adorned with lighted candle lanterns created a romantic atmosphere. The tables were lined up along the walls in a horseshoe shape with the middle left clear for dancing.

A violinist softly played an instrumental version of 'Speak Softly Love,' the theme song from 'The Godfather,' while an older couple slowly twirled around the floor.

"Harley!" I gasped as I looked through the menu. "I can't order anything; it's too expensive."

"Nonsense, I can afford it. Just order what you like."

"I'm not even sure I know what some of these items are."

"Shall I order for you?"

"Yes, please, but, no mussels, oysters or clams. I'm allergic to them."

"How about a pasta dish?" He signaled the waiter.

"That would be great."

"What will it be tonight, Mister Davis?"

"The lady will have the Mezzaluna Caprese," Harley paused as he glanced through the menu, "and I'll have the Crab Spaghetti. Please leave off the anchovies." He turned toward me and asked, "what do you want to drink?"

"Lemon and water."

"Make that two glasses of waters with lemon, please." He closed the menu and handed both of them back to the waiter.

"Excellent, sir."

The Mezzaluna Caprese was delicious. It was a Ravioli dish comprised of Buffalo ricotta and spinach half moons and was tossed with a homemade tomato sauce with bocconcini and baby basil.

"What, no wine?" I chided as I sliced a half moon and nibbled at it.

"I don't drink alcohol." Harley's meal was angel hair spaghetti with finely sliced garlic, capers, chili, and fennel, parsley doused with lemon and olive oil.

"None?"

"None," he smiled and shrugged.

"Why is that?"

"Alcohol is a poison. It muddles your thought processes." He paused to fork a bite into his mouth. "It makes the brain's communication paths different and leads to changes in mood and behavior."

All playfulness left his voice as he recited a litany of the evils of alcohol. "You can't think clearly or move with any substantial coordination. Long-term consumption can cause irregular heart beats, stroke, high blood pressure, and drooping of the heart muscle. It also damages your liver and pancreas and a bunch of other nasty stuff." He sipped his water and twirled the water goblet as he studied me.

"Wow," was all I could say. "That's quite some list."

"Lecture aside, how is your meal?"

"It's scrumpdillicious."

"What?" he laughed and water spurted from his nose. He hurriedly covered his nose with his hand.

"It's delicious, mouthwateringly good. I love it."

"For a minute there I thought I got lost in some weird version of 'Mary Poppins,'" he smirked and grabbed his napkin to dab the water from his face and clothes. "Scrumpdillicious, I'll have to remember that one."

"How's your food?"

"Great as always. It's one of my favorites. I always order it when I come here." He forked a bite and held it out to me. "Try a taste."

It was wonderful. I've always loved crab, but this combination of crab with the sauce and pasta was exquisite.

We quickly ate our meals. As soon as we finished eating, the waiter approached. "Dessert?"

"Yes, two tiramisu's, please."

After the waiter had left with our order, Harley turned to me and asked, "Care to dance, my Lady?"

"I would love to my Lord," I giggled.

He rose, pulled my chair back, and offered me his hand. "How chivalrous of you," I murmured.

On the dance floor, he pulled me close, holding me in the classic ballroom pose with one hand grasping mine and his other hand lightly on my waist. My heart soared with desire as my hand rested lightly on his muscular shoulder.

His footwork was spectacular while mine was clumsy at best. With gentle sureness, he guided me through each step without making me feel inadequate. His face went from serious to dreamy as we waltzed around the floor. His lips parted in a sensual, provocative manner that made my heart beat even faster.

We alternated between slowly swaying and twirling around the dance floor. The gentle crooning of the violins and the soft twinkle of the table top lanterns lent themselves to an otherworldly feel as we glided around the room.

Occasionally he dipped me so low I was almost bent over backward. When he pulled me back upright, he planted kisses on my cheeks.

"I love you," his voice was silky smooth. He was an angel whispering the language of romance in my ear.

"Don't worry, I know it's too soon for you, but in time, you'll come to love me as much as I do you," Harley whispered in my ear. It sent shivers up and down my spine.

Time seemed to stand still, and everyone and thing faded from view. It felt like we were the only two people in the room as we glided effortlessly across the floor. The soft strains of the violins added to an aura of dreaminess as the melody drifted gently.

His attention was focused solely on me. His gaze never wavered from my face. A beautiful smile spread across his lips.

"I think you are beautiful," he murmured.

He made me feel like a princess as he guided me around the dance floor. Never in my entire life had I ever felt so beautiful as I did that night. He was my fairy tale prince.

Thus ended the perfect road trip date. The next day we headed back to Lima, Ohio.

Chapter Three

"You're listening to WOSL radio on the beautiful campus of the Ohio State University at Lima." I thumbed a record into position.

Back in those days, radio stations had real turntables and songs were cued using a thumb and backward twist motion to get it into the groove just before the music began. Dead air on the radio meant disaster.

The door to the broadcast booth was kept closed while we were talking on the air. There was a light outside the room. If it was red, it meant the disc jockey was on the air. A green light implied it was safe to enter. Inside the booth, the phone never rang. Instead, a light blinked on the telephone alerting the DJ to an incoming call.

"Hi, you're live on WOSL radio," I greeted the caller.

"Hi Gypsy Mar," came the familiar baritone voice. "I have a request. Do you have 'Snowblind Friend' by Steppenwolf?" Harley asked.

"Yes, I do, my Steppenwolf friend. I'll have it on in five minutes."

I spun around in my seat as the door to the booth unexpectedly opened. The broadcast booth at WOSL was painted orange with a broad black arrow that ran across the wall and around to end at the door to the outer office.

Hixson poked his head in and motioned for me to step out for a second. Lori came inside and sat down. From the strained looks on both their faces, I knew something serious was coming down.

The outer office of WOSL was painted a pale yellow and covered in posters for the movie King Kong, the bands Boston, Seger, and Journcy, along with photos of disc jockeys. Gathered in the room were March, Mike, Peg, Flash, Judy and myself.

Standing at the door were three men wearing dark sunglasses. They dressed sharply in what I can only describe as local gangster garb. Gold chains dangled around their necks, matching the gold watch on their wrists. They wore their hair in the slicked back style reminiscent of the 1950's or the television show 'Happy Days.'

They stood, so the shortest of the three was in the middle and slightly in front. From the way the two taller men kept a hand inside their suit coat, I gathered they were carrying guns, which was a felony on state property at the time.

"These gentlemen have a request," Hixson's voice was oddly muted. You could almost taste the rankness of the fear in the station.

"Name's Brzezicki," said the shorter man. "We have a business proposition."

I looked from March to each of the others and paused at Hixson's robust face.

"Please, go on," Hixson beckoned.

"We heard WOSL radio is in need of funding for new equipment and upgrades to reach more listeners."

The radio station was a small two room unit. The outer room was long and slightly L-shaped. Upon entering the station, you immediately faced a long metal cabinet. Next to it was a two seat divan. Looking to the left from the door was a six-foot long vinyl couch and the door to the broadcast booth. A file cabinet and a metal desk filled the back wall. All the furniture and operating equipment came from donations or were purchased dirt cheap.

"You need a new tower bringing you up to fifty megawatts is required to fit that bill." He stepped forward and lifted the shades from his eyes.

The coldness of his gaze sent shivers down my spine. It was as though a greasy, oily snake skinned serpent had entered the room. Standing before us were the types of men the movie, 'The Godfather' glamorized. The real deal was anything except glamorous. The reality was a fear-inducing, scared for your life hardball sitting in the pit of your stomach. Paralyzing terror made you pray you didn't wet your pants.

To say the tension in the room was palpable was putting it mildly. The silence was deafening. I heard the ticking of the clock on the wall succinctly. It is a rhythmic ticking that only added to the nerve-racking strain of having these men in our presence.

It made us all understand that while we thought we were tough, with it college rebels, we were just kids in our late teens and early twenties. I was eighteen. Hixson was twenty, and Mike was twenty-one. The rest fell somewhere in between.

"We have a new club - Slasher," Brzezicki continued. "We want to hire three of you to disc jockey the place in exchange for all the funding you need."

"Who do you have in mind?" I asked.

"I'm glad you asked that, beautiful lady. We want Gypsy Mar, March, and Miss Peg. Pay you ten dollars an hour and all the drinks and food you can consume."

Ten dollars an hour! That was a fortune at a time when the minimum wage hovered around two ten. When combined with the cost of food and drinks the salary went to over twelve dollars per hour. It was very tempting and scary.

"What is the age requirement to work in your club?" Flash asked.

"Do not concern yourself with the legalities," Brzezicki responded. "We'll be back in three days for your answer." He snapped his fingers. The goon closest to the exit opened the door. "Three days," Brzezicki repeated.

In unison, they turned and exited the room. Hixson and Mike both loudly exhaled as though they had been holding their breaths during the entire exchange. "Do you know who those guys are?" Hixson squeaked.

"Polish Mafia?" Mike whispered. Beads of sweat dripped down his face. "Why do I feel like we narrowly escaped death? I need a toke," he mumbled feeling his pockets.

"Here, have a cig. Don't have any pot on me today," March tapped a camel cigarette into his palm. "Maryanne's friend, Wanda calls them cancer sticks. Guess she'd know being a nursing student."

"Thanks, man. Need something stronger."

"How about a slug of ninety proof?" Hixson pulled a silver flask out and passed it around the room.

The door to the station opened, and virtually everyone jumped as though expecting the gangsters to come back through. A collective sigh of relief washed over the room when Harley slipped in carrying a can of Vernor's ginger ale.

"When my song didn't come on, and I heard someone else, is everything okay? You guys look like ghosts."

"Harley," I took his arm and wrapped it around me. "Three men visited us. One identified himself as Brzezicki."

"They look like Mafia types and want March, Peg, and Mari to work at their new club, Slasher, in exchange for funding the station's equipment upgrades and a new tower," Flash added. His normally tanned face was pale.

"Mari?" Harley glanced down at me with concern. "How many were here?" he handed the soft drink to me.

"Three." I took a huge swallow and looked at the can. It resembled a local brewery's brew. I had never tasted ginger ale so good and was hooked.

"One on each side of the guy making the offer?" Consternation filled Harley's voice.

Everyone nodded.

"A drug cartel. I thought they had been run out of town a few years ago. Guess they're back," Harley frowned. "I don't believe you want to get mixed up with these guys.

Mike piped up, "What's a little dope? Getting high is fun."

He looked as though he was trying to lighten the somber atmosphere, or maybe he had drunk more than his share of the liquid in Hixson's flask.

"Not if you're mixed up with a gang." Harley clenched his fist. "Your life is in the balance with those guys. Besides, Mari doesn't do drugs." His eye color went rapidly from steel to a cold slate gray as he struggled to rein in his temper.

"What? No pot?"

"Nope," I shook my head. "I get high on life."

"What a lush," Mike laughed and winked.

"Not funny, smoker boy," Harley snarled. I had never seen him look angry before. "Not everyone gets a kick out of doing drugs."

"Hey! I was just kidding man!" Mike held his hands up and back away laughing.

"Mari, you don't have to accept their offer. At this point, it's just an offer. Neither does Peg, nor March. None of you do. You get mixed up with those guys, and it'll be almost impossible to get out of there." Harley explained.

"I know," I rested against Harley's hard lean body and felt myself relax for the first time in an hour. "I'm not going to do it."

"Neither are we," March stated. "Hell, Maryanne would kill me if I did."

"Maryanne will kill you if she learned you said, hell," Peg giggled.

I re-entered the broadcast booth and tapped Lori on the shoulder. "I'll take it from here," I whispered.

She jumped up and left the room, leaving the door open.

"You're listening to WOSL radio at the top of the hour. Gypsy Mar here bringing you 'Snowblind Friend' by Steppenwolf for our resident wolf head. It's a sad and slow song from the past." I swiveled in the chair as the song came over the air.

"I quit," Lori said. "I'm not going to be Sales Manager when those guys come back. I'll just keep the books."

I stepped to the door and looked around the room. The station staff still wore a shell-shocked look on their faces. Each of us sat quietly contemplating what had just happened. Did we want to jump into the palm of these guys hands? What would they do to us, if we refused? The silence grew unbearable.

"I'll do sales," I volunteered.

"I'll help," Peg chimed in.

The next day Hixson called them and declined their offer on behalf of WOSL and the disc jockeys. Brzezicki and his goons did not accept our answer and stormed into the station.

"You want to reconsider your decision." He said in a manner that made it more of an order than a question.

"I'm sorry, our answer is still no," Hixson replied nervously.

I looked up from logging my playlist. At WOSL we ran an FM progressive format on an AM band. Being a start up college radio station, we had more leeway than our professional counterparts. While we did not have an established playlist, we disc jockeys were required to log in their selected songs. No tune was played twice during a show. I set aside the clipboard and look at the man.

"Mister Brzezicki, no harm intended, but we are college students. Our work at WOSL is an aside that we enjoy. Many of us have classes in the evening. Peg, March and I have discussed your offer, and our answer is still, no." I said.

Brzezicki tried for several days to get us to change our decision. Ultimately campus security had to get involved and issue a cease and desist order as well as barring him and his cronies from campus.

Chapter Four

Our first day as sales staff for WOSL was chilly and dreary. Peg and I decided to hit the local boutiques to try out our sales pitch. Our success there led us to head back toward the campus.

"Hey, Mari, want to go look for aliens?" Peg asked as she took off her jacket. My car heater had ramped up to a toasty warmth.

"Aliens?" I laughed. "Aliens?"

"The SETI Big Ear is near Columbus. And we can look at the Schoonover Observatory on Jefferson Street first."

"Sure," I shrugged, "I don't have any classes until seven tonight."

We passed the campus turn off and headed toward the Schoonover Observatory on Jefferson in Lima. After a brief break to look at the Observatory, we headed down Findlay Road which becomes Ada Road and 81 into Dunkirk.

"We should try to sell ads in Dunkirk. Isn't that where you live?" I asked Peg.

"Yeah."

"Maybe they'll buy some ads from a hometown girl."

We sold a few ads in Dunkirk then headed north on 68 and 15 into Findlay.

After a couple of hours of selling advertising to businesses, we decided it was time to check out the Big Ear, The Ohio State University's contribution to the SETI project. The Big Ear SETI project was fascinating. A large number of giant satellites filled a football field. Each was calibrated to detect signals from space. The search for extraterrestrial life was on in earnest. A few years later, in August 1977, Big Ear would become the first array to detect a non-random signal from space.

Peg and I spent about an hour looking at the facilities and marveling over the technology required to operate such machines.

"I heard there was a haunted castle in Houckton. Want to check it out?"

"I didn't know you were into the paranormal stuff." I glanced at her.

"I'm crazy about ghost stories and always wanted to see one. What do you say, Mari?"

"What do you plan to do if you see a ghost, Peg?"

"I'd ask it why it was hanging around?"

"Yeah, I just bet you would."

It was off to Houckton and the reputed haunted castle. To our disappointment, it turned out to be just the ruins of an old farmhouse, chapel and servants' quarters. I drew my 1969 Plymouth Satellite with a 400 series Hemi engine to a stop.

We stared at the ruins with just a bit of trepidation. It was as though the world had turned brown and gray. The ground, the house, the sky all looked like the color of lead. The grass and trees were all brown. It was a though a blight had descended upon just this one place. The surrounding landscape beyond the property was green, yellow, red, and all the colors of a bright fall day. But not here; where we stood everything looked like death.

"Well, now what?" Peg sounded disheartened as though she depended on finding ghosts.

"Might as well poke around the ruins and snap a few pictures to prove we were here," I shrugged and got out of the car.

Peg pulled her coat closer around her. It was a little nippy even for Ohio. I reached in back and pulled out my windbreaker.

With camera in hand, we began the trek toward the main house. Stepping onto the porch, Peg screeched and turned around.

"What?" I aimed the camera and snapped a photo of the house.

"I heard something!" She cried excitedly.

"What did you hear?" I turned and looked back the way we had come. There was nothing behind us but my car. I snapped a picture just in case. Cameras are known to pick up images the human eye can't see.

"It sounded like a footstep," she whispered and pulled her coat tighter as though to ward off a sudden chill.

"Hmm," I turned back to the front of the house and tugged on the screen door. It clanged open with a rusty holler which elicited another shriek from Peg.

"Peg," I faced her with my hands on my hips, "if you keep screaming like that, you are bound to scare away any ghosts that might be here."

"Whooo..." the sound drifted toward us followed by eerie moans.

"What was that?" We looked at each other. I grabbed Peg by the arm and tugged her in the direction of the sound, "C'mon! Let's find it!"

We ran around the side of the house and came to a sliding stop. Behind the house was a small graveyard with a single tombstone standing cantilever. Two or three other headstones lay toppled over. Past the cemetery was what we believed to be a chapel. It was a Hindu temple with statuary of Shiva. Behind it was a stone wall with a cannon. Looking past the fence, we could see the cupola of what might have been a castle.

As we tried to find a way around the rock barrier, a cold breeze sprang up. I wished I had worn a coat instead of my favorite windbreaker. We could hear the faint whispering of a voice telling us to leave this place.

"Go away!" Peg screamed. "Leave us alone!"

"Way to go, Peg," I chided. "I thought the whole purpose of being here was to see a ghost."

"I've changed my mind," she huffed.

"GO!" The hollow voice drifted to us.

I swung around and caught a slight motion from the corner of my eye. I turned and ran to the dilapidated barn. "Come out here right now!"

A chuckle rose from behind a pile of wood planks. "Harley! I know that laugh! It's not funny!"

Peg came up beside me. "Are you sure it's Harley?"

"Harley, you get out here, right this minute!" I stomped around fuming mad. How dare he scare us like we were children!

"Yes ma'am," he meekly replied and stepped from the pile of wood. His hands were shoved deep into the pockets of his leather jacket. "Hi," he sheepishly mumbled, his left foot making sweeping gestures over the ground.

"How did you know we were coming here?" Peg demanded.

"I followed you."

"All day?" I asked incredulously.

"Yeah. When I heard you guys were planning to find the castle I thought I'd tag along. You know, just in case you needed a man to help you out of trouble."

"We are not some willy nilly weak women," Peg snapped.

"Could have fooled me, the way you screamed," he smiled his impish grin.

"I'm going to get you for scaring us," I frowned, but couldn't help laughing.

Harley took one look at me and ran toward the field. "You have to catch me first, Mari," he hollered over his shoulder.

We ran around the field and the house with Peg yelling at us to stop and wait for her. I finally took a flying leap and tackled him. We rolled to a stop on the ground with me sitting on him.

"Okay, okay!" he laughed as I started tickling him anywhere I could. "I give!"

I stood up and looked down at him. "Learn your lesson?"

"Yeah. Don't mess with you and Peg," he gasped.

"Need a hand up?" I reached down toward him.

"Yes I do," he grabbed my hand and yanked me down.

I landed on top of him with our lips mere inches apart. The merriment in his eyes and his smile took my breath away. I found myself leaning down toward his luscious lips.

He lifted his head, so our lips met. He had the most deliciously soft lips I had ever kissed, not that I had kissed many guys.

Harley pressed his mouth harder against mine as though he was starving. He finally pulled back and whispered, "Mari, if we keep kissing like this I might forget my vow of chastity and do something utterly ungentlemanly."

"Hmm?" I mumbled closing my eyes.

I was totally lost in the moment. I think I was starting to fall for this sexy motorcycle riding, Steppenwolf loving man. The emotions coursing through me brought to mind the 1969 Roberta Flack rendition of 'The First Time Ever I Saw Your Face,' and Percy Sledge's 'When A Man Loves A Woman.'

Both songs are tender, full of desire, and poignant love. I had never been in love before, had numerous crushes but never in love. It gave me a heady feeling that left me feeling warm with fondness and confused at the same time.

"Mari, have mercy," he moaned, "I am just a man after all."

"Ahem," Peg interrupted, "When you guys are done playing house, I'd like to get some lunch. I'm starving."

"You owe us, big time, Harley," I said.

"How about I buy us all lunch in Columbus?"

"Our choosing," I replied.

"Agreed. Lead the way ladies."

We trudged back to my car. Harley went into the ruins of the barn and wheeled his hog out.

Peg suggested a steakhouse she'd heard about. When we got there, I almost took pity on Harley. The prices were sky high.

"Go ahead ladies and order anything you want. I'm having the steak and shrimp dinner."

That combination was easily the most expensive item on the menu. So, Peg and I followed along and ordered the same thing with a baked potato and a side salad.

We enjoyed the food and ate at a leisurely pace. "Will there be anything else?" The waiter pointedly looked at his watch.

"Yes, there will," Harley grinned wickedly. "We'll each have dessert. Ladies?"

"Cheesecake for me," I smiled.

"Vanilla ice cream," Peg looked at the waiter and grinned coquettishly.

"I'll have the apple pie," Harley said, "with a scoop of ice cream."

"You are evil," I laughed after the waiter left to place our orders.

"He was rude," Harley grinned. "You never indicate to a customer that they are taking too much time. The customer pays your salary. You treat them with respect. Never make them feel like they are wasting your time."

"Wow, you know a lot about customers," Peg looked speculatively at Harley.

"I'd better. If I treated my clients rudely, I lose business."

"What business are you in?" I asked.

"I customize motorcycles and create accessories such as the communication system in the helmet I showed you."

"And you make a good living doing that?" Peg asked.

"I make more than a decent living."

"He lives in a mansion and has a butler, Peg."

"So, you're rich?" Peg quirked her eyebrow at Harley.

Harley just smiled. "Wealth is what you make of it. You can be loaded with money and be poor, or you can be penniless and be the richest person in the world."

Dessert arrived, and we dug in, relishing the delicious treats. All too soon, lunch was over, and it was time to head back to Lima. To show his displeasure with the waiter, Harley left a penny tip.

"Thank you for an excellent lunch, Harley," I kissed him on the cheek and briefly hugged him.

"Yes, thanks," Peg nudged him.

"You're welcome, ladies," he straddled his hog and leaned forward for another kiss.

"Drive safely." He put his helmet on and waited until I started my car before pulling in behind us.

Chapter Five

Once or twice a quarter the campus radio station WOSL held a concert in the circle near the Student Activities Building also known as SAB. It was commonly referred to as the 'Beer Blast' with plenty of kegs being sold by the glass.

"Did we get all the kegs we ordered?" Hixson asked.

"One short," Mike shoved his hand through his short Afro. "The distributor ran out." He glanced at his clipboard, "What we got should be enough."

Every disc jockey had to learn how to correctly pull beer from the tap so as to minimize the head of foam. College students want beer, not foam. The trick was to tilt the glass at a particular angle while filling it.

Flash, a sandy red-haired, disc jockey who thought he was every woman's dream of the perfect man jumped onto the stage.

"Howdy!" He shouted, "Are you ready to Party?"

"Party! Party!" the crowd chanted.

"Let's give a giant Ohio State University-Lima welcome to Incan Lines. I'm sure they're gonna rock your socks off."

'Incan Lines' was a local hard rocking progressive band. A huge crowd came out to see them and the headline act 'Psyche.'

The lines at the beer and refreshment stands were horrendous.

"Give me a Miller," a student said.

"We only have kegs." I grabbed a glass and began pouring.

"I want a pitcher."

"That'll be two fifty."

I was busy filling cup after cup when Harley approached me and offered to help.

"I'm not a drinker, but I can see you guys are swamped." His smile was infectious and soon had Hixson, the station manager, waving him behind the tables into the booth.

"You tilt the glass like so to keep the foam down," I showed him the proper angle.

"What's wrong with foam?" Harley frowned.

"Too much foam means less beer," I handed him a Styrofoam glass.

Harley pulled on the tap of the keg and promptly over filled the glass. Beer gushed over his hand onto the ground.

"I guess there's more to pouring beer than I thought," he mumbled as he took the rag I gave him and wiped off his hands and dabbed at his jeans.

"You lightly pull the tab part way," I showed him.

It wasn't long before he was pulling tap beer like a professional bartender. He grinned and did a dance step. His hip bumped me, and I bumped him back. Soon we were dancing and bumping hips all while pouring beer like crazy.

"Why don't you guys take a break?" Hixson said as he stepped behind the counter.

"Good idea. My sister is around here somewhere." I grabbed Harley's hand, and we left the booth.

Somehow in the crush of the crowd I lost Harley. I wandered around the crowd and bumped into a guy with a girl sitting on his shoulders. Looking up, I saw that she was shirtless and flaunting her body. I hurried away feeling embarrassed and resumed scanning the group. I found my sister dancing to the hard rock of the band near the front of the stage.

"You okay, Sis?"

"Yeah, having a great time," she laughed. "Don't worry about me. I saw you working the booth." We felt the driving beat of loud rock music as college kids chugged the beer in the electric atmosphere of the outdoor concert. From the packed crowd to the long lines at the beer tables WOSL succeeded in reaching our fundraising goals.

There was a break in the music as the bands changed.

"Okay, I have to find someone," I said as I scanned the wave of people.

"Let's give a hardy welcome to Psyche!" Mike announced as he took over from Flash.

Soon the SAB was filled with the ethereal sounds of the band for which they were becoming famous. To say the least, Incan Lines with their hard beat stole the show from the lackluster Psyche.

I spotted Harley chatting with the members of Incan Lines and made my way toward him.

"Dance with me," I tugged on his arm.

"I have a better idea. After you take your sister home, meet me back here, and I will take you dancing. In fact, all the disc jockeys are going."

"Sounds like fun."

We headed back to the refreshment booth and resumed pouring beer until the kegs ran out. By then Psyche was winding down, and I went to get my sister.

After taking her home, I met Harley and the disc jockeys in the parking lot. "So, where are we going?" I asked as I rolled down the window of my 1969 Plymouth. Harley opened the passenger door and climbed in.

"Best Western Dance Hall," Mike said as he piled into Hixson's Chevy.

The Best Western in most places is known as a hotel chain. Near Lima, Ohio there was a place where college students took their dates dancing. It was also called the Best Western. There you could dance to all kinds of music including Country and Western, Rock, and Ballroom. You could also buy just about whatever alcohol you wanted.

It looked like the typical honky-tonk with a wood floor, sawdust scattered around to sop up spills. Giant amplifiers and speakers adorned the stage. A jukebox was plugged in and spinning a variety of music. We had to shout to hear each other over the loud music.

"Care to dance, my Lady?" Harley held out his hand and bowed low.

"Certainly, my Lord," I smiled and took his hand.

Soon we were rocking to the music. Harley swayed his hip to bump mine gently, and I returned the favor. He pulled me close and twirled me around.

Mike and March were playing a drinking game when we returned to the table after dancing.

"Who's next?" March slurred, "How about you Mari?"

"She doesn't want to," Harley responded for me much to my irritation. He looked at me, "What?"

"I can speak for myself. I do have a mouth."

"Mari," he groused.

"Bring it on, March. What do you do?"

"You ever played?" Mike asked.

"Nope."

"It's simple. You each down shots until one of you can't drink anymore. The last person left wins a hundred dollars."

"March! March!" half the disc jockeys chanted while the others called my name, "Mari, you can do it!"

And so it went, until much to my surprise, I was the only one left, besides Harley, who refused to participate, "I win!"

"Yeah, and I'm driving," he mumbled. "Give me your keys."

The drive back to campus was quiet. Once we got there, Harley got out of the car, and I slid over to the driver's seat. To my delight, he got into the passenger seat.

"So, are you too drunk to drive home?" he asked, his voice filling with concern.

"Nope. I don't feel drunk at all."

"Have you ever been drunk?" He looked me up and down much like a doctor assessing a patient. Harley reached out with long, slender fingers and tilted my face upward.

"Nope."

"Tomorrow you are going to have one heck of a hangover. Don't be shocked if you vomit."

I waved his hand away. "I'll be okay. I don't get drunk."

Just then a flashlight shined into the window followed by a knock. The cop motioned for me to roll down the window.

"Yes, officer?"

"What are you two doing here at two in the morning?"

Harley cleared his throat. "We just got back from the Best Western, sir."

The cop stared long and hard at him. "You just got back from where?" From the way the cop looked at us, it was obvious he was thinking the hotel chain and not the dance hall.

"The Best Western."

The cop stepped back and looked at me. "The girl looks a bit young for that. How old are you, miss?"

"Eighteen."

"The Best Western Dance Hall," Harley hastened to clarify.

"I see." The cop continued to stare at us until we squirmed in discomfort.

"We just went dancing," Harley stated as though he was a young child caught with his hand in the cookie jar.

"Which one of you was drinking?"

"That would be me," I replied.

"Beer," Harley piped up, his voice raising a half octave from the lie. "She had a few beers."

"Okay, miss, I'm going to have to ask you to step out of the car."

I nervously looked at Harley, and he shrugged. I opened the door and got out.

"I want you to touch your nose with your right hand and then your left."

I complied with ease.

"Now, I want you to blow up this balloon without making it pop."

It took a few minutes, but I successfully filled the balloon with air and held it out to the police officer.

He took a piece of chalk and drew a line on the asphalt. "Now I want you to walk this line without leaving it and without stumbling."

"Piece of cake," I muttered.

He pushed his cap up and scratched his head. "Okay, you passed the field sobriety test. Drive safely, young lady." He leaned into the window, "Young man, you make sure she gets home okay."

Harley let out the breath he'd apparently been holding, "Yes, sir."

I climbed back into the car and turned to Harley. "I'm never going to do that again," I sighed.

"Good. Alcohol is not good for you anyway. It destroys the kidneys and liver as well as impairs judgment. But, it didn't seem to have any noticeable effect on you."

"I swear, I never knew you were such a stick in the mud," I snapped.

"Mari," he pursed his lips, staring at me, "I'm just concerned about your health. I care about you." He ran his hand through his hair, "But if you want to drink yourself to death, I can't stand by and watch."

"For your information, I don't usually drink like I did tonight, so you don't have to worry about that."

"All the same, I'm going to follow you home to make sure you get there safely."

"That's not necessary. I'm not drunk." I glared at him. I felt like he was treating me like a naughty child and I resented it.

"Yes. It. Is," Harley growled. "The amount you drank tonight would have most people passed out on the floor. I'm going to make sure you get home okay."

"But," I protested

"No. Argument." He leaned forward as though to kiss me but pulled himself back at the last minute. He was genuinely angry with me.

I drove home with him following me. I stepped out of the car and went over to him. "Harley," I said. "I just want to say. . ."

"Good night, Mari," he muttered and roared off on his hog.

"I'm sorry," I whispered and wiped at the tear running down my cheek.

Would I ever see him again? It's funny how much I had come to care about him, to count on talking to him daily. Now, I didn't know if he would ever come around me again. Had I lost him forever? My heart sank.

Chapter Six

The following Monday I ran into the radio station just barely in time for my show.

"Mari," Hixson called, "You got your playlist?"

"Yeah, yeah," I waved a sheaf of papers at him, "Right here." I glanced at the broadcast light and waited until it turned green before entering the booth.

"Sorry, March," I mumbled as I took over.

"Good day folks, you're listening to the classic rock show on WOSL Radio. This is Gypsy Mar, and request lines are open."

I switched to the song and spun around to cue the next disk. "Coming up this Thursday we have a special guest, Ash Tabor lead singer of Sling. Don't forget the lecture series on classic literature tonight."

The time passed quickly, and soon it was noon. Harley had not called in his Steppenwolf request, so I picked one for him.

"The next song is for my Steppenwolf loyal listener. 'Justice Don't Be Slow' off the 'Slow Flux' album. Harley, this one's for you."

"You and Harley okay?" March asked as he completed updating his list.

"Yeah, I think so. I hope so anyway. Why?" I selected 'More Than a Feeling' by Boston and placed it on the turntable. I rotated the disk a quarter turn and lifted the edge with my thumb, so the song would start playing after I finished my commentary.

"He seemed kind of angry Friday about the drinking contest."

"He was, but he doesn't run my life. I can do things without his permission," I snapped.

"Ouch! Touchy, touchy," March laughed as he tucked a strand of his long brown hair behind his ear.

Every day I waited for Harley to call in his request. The call never came. Oh, there were plenty of calls from other listeners, but not from him. Each day, I selected a Steppenwolf song and dedicated it to him. I finally broke down on Friday and spoke on air to him.

"Harley, if you're out there listening, I'm sorry I made you mad. I miss seeing you in the cafeteria and your song requests. Most of all, I miss you. This one's for you, Harley, 'Another's Lifetime' from the 'Hour Of The Wolf' album. Enjoy, my Steppenwolf loving friend."

My shift ended, and I hurried toward the cafeteria for a late lunch before they closed.

"Wait up," came the familiar baritone. "Miss me?"

"Oh, so now you're talking to me? After I cried about missing you on the air? You have some nerve!" I shouted and stormed off in the direction of the cafeteria.

"Whoa!" He caught up with me. Grabbing my arm, he spun me around to face him. "What are you jabbering on about?"

"Don't play innocent with me, Mister! Go ahead and ignore her until she caves in and apologizes on her radio show."

He scratched his head in confusion. "What's wrong, Mari?"

"What's wrong?" I swirled around to face him, hands on my hips.

"What's wrong? I'll tell you what's wrong! First, you get angry about the drinking game, you follow me home, and then I don't hear from you. You don't even call the radio station for your Steppenwolf fix." My tirade made him wince and duck as though I might take a swing at him. "Ouch! Mari, hold on!"

"What am I supposed to think? I thought you were done with me and now you show up acting like nothing happened?"

"Whoa! Slow down, Mari. I was upset with you Friday but not enough to end things."

"No? Then what? Why haven't I heard from you all week?"

"I had to go out of town unexpectedly." He spoke haltingly, trying to keep his emotions in check. "It was an emergency, and it was too late to call you. I left two hours after seeing you home. I just got back into town."

"An emergency?" I felt the blush creeping into my face. "What happened?"

"My cousin Brad was in an accident. I barely got back to see him before he passed away. We were very close, and I couldn't let him go without saying goodbye." The sorrow on his face was heart wrenching. He dabbed at the moisture in the corner of his eyes. "Bad biker dudes aren't supposed to cry."

"I am so sorry for your loss." I reached out and grasped his hand. "I didn't know." I pulled him into my arms.

"I know," he let out little hiccupping sobs, "I know."

"I'm such an ass," I whispered into his ear. "I am sorry for the way I acted."

"It's okay, Mari. You didn't know. I would have done the same, but thank you." He stopped walking and looked at me. "I'm sorry, I didn't let you know. I should have called you Saturday to assure you I hadn't deserted us."

"Tell me about him," I tugged him in the direction of the cafeteria.

"He was my polar opposite, and we were close, almost like twins. We grew up together, and did everything together." He grabbed a tray and went toward the serving line.

"Polar opposite twins, huh?" I chided, following him.

"I'll have the pork chops with gravy, green beans, and a corn muffin, please." he told Hazel, one of the ladies who ran the cafeteria.

All the food served in the cafeteria is home cooked. It was a popular place to grab lunch. People from town often came there just for the food.

"I'll have the same," I picked up a can of Vernor's ginger ale.

Harley leaned over the serving line and motioned for Hazel to come closer.

"See that guy with the pear?"

"Yes."

"I've seen him in here many times. All he ever gets is one piece of fruit."

"He can't afford anything else. He's homeless, and I throw in the fruit."

"Hazel, I want to set up a tab for him. Let him get any meal he wants and a drink. Find out what skills he has. I might know of a job he can do."

"That's very kind of you Mister Harley."

"Just helping out." Harley winked at her.

After paying, we took a seat at one of the tables. Harley peppered his food. "I was closer to Brad than I was to anyone in my family. It's funny," he cut into his chop and chewed it slowly.

"How so?"

"He embraced the wealthy lifestyle while I was the rebel, yet we meshed. When we were growing up, we loved playing with trains and fishing. He loved country music. You know, Porter Wagoner, Merle Haggard, Johnny Cash and the like. While I dig rock and roll."

"I know," I grinned, "Steppenwolf."

"That came later. I started on the Monkees, and Moby Grape, Creedence Clearwater Revival. Until I heard John Kay growling 'Born to be Wild.' I was hooked. Brad, couldn't stand Steppenwolf. But, I dug them. Their songs seemed to fit me." He closed his eyes as he chewed. His expression made him look like he was in heaven eating pork chops

"So, the country boy and the rocker, huh?"

"Yep," he grinned and winked.

"And then the country boy grew up to be the sophisticated rich dude and the rocker became the biker rebel."

"Something like that. Brad went to MIT and Harvard, I decided to start a business and then go to college."

"How'd you wind up here?"

"I didn't want an Ivy League school. I wanted some place small, intimate where I could grow my business and myself."

"Cool. You are the definition of a self-made man."

"Not really," he grinned, "I do have family inheritance money, but I don't use it. Not my style."

"You like the bad dude look, but you're a good man."

"Excuse me," it was the man with the fruit. "I want to thank you for your kindness."

"No thanks needed," Harley smiled.

"Yes, it is. I'm a Vietnam veteran, and I haven't worked since I got discharged. Post Traumatic Stress."

"Veteran, huh? What's your name? I'm Harley."

"I'm Edward Walters. Pleased to meet you, Mister Harley."

"Just Harley is fine," he smiled as he pulled out a pen and notepad from his folio. "Ever work on vehicles?" Harley's voice was quiet and filled with respect for the former soldier.

"Yes, sir! Jeeps, tanks, and motorcycles. You name it; I worked on it."

"Come to this address at eight tomorrow morning. I'll be waiting. If your skills check out, I might have a job for you."

"I'll be there."

You could see his spirit lifted. "That was kind of you."

Harley shrugged, "Least I could do for someone who fought in what had to be one of the most unpopular wars in history."

"Wow! You amaze me."

Harley smiled at me and leaned forward looking directly into my eyes. "And you are sweet and just as headstrong as I am."

Before I could react, his lips met mine in one of the most delicious kisses I had experienced at that time.

"I have to go. I have to work in a few minutes." I stammered.

"Embarrassed to be kissed in public, Mari?" he chided.

"No, no," I blushed. "I just didn't expect it."

"And you expected the others?" He quirked an eyebrow at me and gave me his lopsided grin. "I'm giving you fair warning, Mari. I'm going to kiss you again."

I jumped up and ran from the cafeteria with him hot on my heels and snickers from the diners. He caught me, twirled me around and pulled me close. His lips met mine in a hungry kind of way, and I found myself responding by wrapping my arms around him.

There we stood on the grounds of the Ohio State University Lima campus kissing with arms wrapped around each other completely oblivious to the other students detouring around us.

"Mari?"

"Hmm?" I said dreamily.

"I thought you had to go to work."

"Work!" I gasped, "I'm going to be late!"

"I'll walk you to your car. We'd better hurry."

My vehicle could reach 60 mph in seconds. It was a gas-guzzling muscle car. Harley leaned in the window for one last kiss.

"No speeding, Mari," he waggled a finger at me. "I don't want to hear about you being splattered all over the road."

"I promise," I started the engine.

I sat in my car and hugged myself. I closed my eyes for a moment, relishing the memory of his sweet kisses.

He rapped sharply on the hood of my Plymouth, "Mari? Work?" He said and stepped back as he watched me drive away.

I was deliriously happy. My handsome Steppenwolf loving fan, leather wearing biker, had not dumped me after all.

Chapter Seven

"Hey, Mari, wait up!" Harley yelled as he jogged toward me.

I turned and watched him hustle along the sidewalk. He wore faded denim jeans, matching shirt, and his leather jacket. A pair of aviator sunglasses perched on the top of his head.

"What are you doing on the seventh?" He grasped my hand and quickly raised it to his lips.

"Nothing. I have the entire week off. Why?"

"I was thinking about Christmas. I typically go home for the holidays. I'll be gone a week before Christmas to after New Year's Day."

He spoke with uncharacteristic nervousness. "I thought instead of getting you a gift; I'd take you to a Steppenwolf concert. What do you say?"

He fidgeted, shoving his hands into his pockets and bounced from foot to foot.

"Harley, what's wrong? You sound agitated."

"I am," he admitted. "I hate that I'm going to be all the way back east and you're going to be here. I hate that I won't be able to see you for a few weeks."

He grabbed my hand and held it to his heart. "I want to be here with you. I even suggested they come over here. But, oh no, they couldn't have all their stuck up friends over to show off their latest acquisitions."

"That's so sad. I would have loved to meet your parents," I pulled his hand away and kissed it while I ran my other hand through his hair. It was soft like the fur of a kitten, or the fuzz of a baby.

"No, you wouldn't. I won't put you through that. My folks are vicious, especially if you aren't in their status."

"Meaning, I'm not good enough for you."

The pain was incredibly sharp. I felt as though my fairy tale could end over the holiday. How could I possibly hope to keep him when I wasn't even in the same classification as he was? I felt I had been judged and found wanting. It was an eye-opening experience.

"Ah, no, Mari!" He exclaimed. "I knew you'd feel that way. That's why I didn't want to say anything. It's them, not you. Mari, you're perfect for me. You are beautiful; you get me."

He earnestly stared into my eyes. "Most of all, you are my soul mate, and I love you. Never think I'm ashamed of you, or you aren't good enough. Okay?"

"Okay," I choked back tears.

I thought about the reasons I never mentioned him to my family. Mom would have said that he came from a high-class family. What would he want with a middle-class girl, except sex? She would have nagged me constantly about whether we were sleeping together. When told no, she'd want to know what was wrong with him.

The most irritating question would pertain to his sexuality. How do you explain to your Mom that this gorgeous hunk of man practiced the law of chastity?

Dad, on the other hand, would have been cool about the relationship. He'd want to meet Harley and see if he measured up to Marine Corp's standards. Either he would say he liked him, or you aren't dating him anymore. Somehow, the idea Dad would disapprove of Harley was more daunting than Mom nagging me about him.

My sister was wrapped up in her world. She was into the Rolling Stones, makeup, clothes and shopping. She wouldn't have paid any attention. Harley was not her type.

"I just don't want to put you through their petty meanness. So, will you go with me to the concert?" Harley pulled me into his arms for a comforting hug.

"A Steppenwolf concert? They're touring?"

"Yep. It's out of state, so it'd be an overnighter. You could say, a mini vacation."

"On, your hog? In winter?" I wondered how that would work out in snowy and icy weather. "Are you crazy? We'll freeze to death!"

"Sure, it'll be okay. The leather jacket will keep you warm. Wear a sweatshirt, and thermal underwear beneath, and denim jeans. Throw on some leather gloves, and you'll be fine."

"Not sure how I can get away with an overnight trip only a couple months since the last one."

"Tell your folks; you're going to a concert with a friend." Harley bounced from one foot to the other. "C'mon, Mari. It'll be fun."

"When would we leave?"

"It's about twelve hours from here. With stops for food and gas, I would say it'd take about sixteen hours. We'd need to leave around noon on the sixth. The concert is on the eighth. We'd return home on the tenth."

"That's a long overnight trip." I hesitated thinking over the plan. "My classes will be finished for the quarter. My finals will be over. I'll try. When do I need to let you know?" I asked as I thought about having to buy thermal underwear and leather gloves.

"In two weeks. I need time to make arrangements."

December 6th was a mild 40 degrees when we left Harley's home. I bundled myself in two pairs of socks, thermal underwear, sweatpants, denim jeans, a plaid shirt, a sweatshirt, leather jacket, and matching gloves. My coat was stretched tight because of the other garments and made me look like a toasted marshmallow. Harley took one look at me and burst out laughing. He laughed so hard he had to sit down on the steps leading into his home.

"Sorry, Mari, but you look silly!" His eyes crinkled with merriment.

Try as I might, I couldn't be upset with him. Soon, I was smiling wildly. "Yeah? Well, you just wait. When you're frozen like a Popsicle, I'll be warm and comfortable."

"We'll see how you feel when the sweat runs down your clothes," he chortled as he handed me my helmet.

I stuck my tongue out at him as I put the safety gear on my head. I climbed on to the hog and put my arms around his waist. "I'm ready," I said as I lifted my feet.

"Hold on tight. We might run into some icy conditions."

"I will," I replied and cinched my grip on him even tighter.

He revved the engine and off we roared down the driveway headed toward the highway.

We stopped for gas in a small town. From the reaction of the residents, it appeared as though they had never seen a motorcycle. We both knew that wasn't the case, but the stares we got made us extremely uncomfortable. A sign by the pumps said 'pay inside first.'

"Stay close to me," Harley grated as he dismounted. "Looks like they may have had some thefts here."

"Is everyone in this town watching us?"

"Sure looks like it. I wonder if this place had trouble with a biker gang like some towns did along the route to Sturgis." From the tenseness in his voice, I could tell he was worried.

"We don't want any trouble from the likes of you," a cop said as the police car rolled to a stop beside us.

"Neither do we, officer. We just want to gas up, and then we'll be on our way," Harley said politely.

He wrapped his arm around me as we entered the convenience store. "I'd like to fill up," he tossed a credit card onto the counter and returned to the bike. He quickly filled the tank.

"This place gives me the creeps."

"Small town mentality," Harley said. "Let's go inside and pay before we get accused of trying to skip out or of casing this joint."

The cashier looked sullenly at us as we strolled the aisles looking for snacks and drinks. As we approached the checkout stand, he put one hand under the counter.

"Calling the cops, or touching a gun?" Harley asked as he placed our items down. "If you're calling the police, they're right outside by the pump. If you're reaching for a gun, well like I said, the cops are next to my hog. I believe you have my card."

The clerk quickly rang our items up and handed Harley the slip to sign. "Now, get out. We don't cotton to no bikers here."

"Have a nice day," Harley smirked as he tucked his card back into his wallet.

We wasted no time getting out of that place. The police followed us down the main street toward the highway. Apparently, the cops were as eager to get us out of town as we were to leave that unfriendly place. I sighed with relief once we left the village limits.

We stopped for the night in Clearfield, a borough of around 8,000. It had taken a little over seven hours to get to the Victorian Loft. Originally it was built in the 1890's; it was a beautifully adorned bed and breakfast that overlooked a scenic stretch of the Susquehanna River. It featured a lot of gingerbread wrap around porches.

I felt as though I had walked into a summer version of the Vanderbilt mansion. The windows and doors boasted traditional stained glass. The grand staircase inside was elegant and ornately carved from cherry wood. The wainscoting was impeccable.

Harley, being the gentleman he was, staying true to his vow of chastity, had booked two rooms. They both had thick, plush beds with dark wood headboards, a wardrobe, dresser, bookcase, and a rocking chair. My room had a whirlpool tub while Harley's had a regular bath.

"Do you want to get some dinner?" He asked as he dropped my overnight bag onto a plush bed.

"I could do with a little something." I entered the sink area outside the bathroom. I quickly washed my face and brushed my hair.

Harley hung up the phone as I came back into the room. "They suggest we try the Arrowhead. American and Italian food."

"Sounds good to me."

He grasped my hand, and we went down the elaborate stairs.

"Enjoy your dinner," the clerk called out.

The Arrowhead Restaurant looked like a 1950's diner. A plethora of knotty pine covered the interior. The arrangement reminded me of holiday dinner at my grandparents.

Glancing through the menu, I opted for a hot roast beef sandwich on thick toast with mashed potatoes and cream gravy. Harley ordered an Italian Submarine Sandwich made with Pepperoni, Salami Bologna, provolone and American cheese, with house dressing on a long garlic roll. The portions were huge! We could have shared an order and would not have been hungry.

"How's your meal?" I asked as I looked through mine.

"It's good. Want a bite?"

"Only if you'll try mine."

We cut our meals in half and shared them. Harley's was much better than mine, and I quickly devoured it much to his amusement.

"You ate that like you were starving."

"I was hungrier than I thought," I dabbed daintily at my lips. "Harley, the other day you talked as though you don't like your family. Did something happen to cause a rift?"

"Let's just say their values and beliefs and mine are very different." His guarded tone told me he was uncomfortable talking about them.

"How so?" I persisted.

"Well," he spoke slowly. "You know I believe in the law of chastity. I don't approve of alcoholic drinks, or hot caffeinated ones either."

"Yes."

"I don't cotton to unnecessary violence. I don't think anyone is better than other people. Wealth doesn't make a person," he said. "It's what's in here and God that makes you who you are." He placed a hand over his heart.

"If that's true, then you are an angel."

"I have a lot of devil in me too," he grinned. "You bring solace to my heart and peace to my soul, Mari." Harley put down his sandwich. "We're supposed to provide service to our fellow men. We should help those less fortunate."

"I agree."

"Don't get me wrong; I love my family. I just don't subscribe to their hedonistic ways. My parents are about money and maintaining status. Me? While I have money, both inherited and earned, I see it only as a means to an end. Money is used to help make someone's life better whether it is a person or an animal."

"But," I furrowed my brow, "you have a mansion."

"For my parent's comfort. They do visit at times. Besides, I have to have something to keep Garrett busy. I swear that man can clean a house faster than I can make it messy," he laughed.

We finished our food and headed back to our accommodations.

The next morning we were treated to a fantastic breakfast with the hosts. The elegant formal dining area had a crystal chandelier. Places were set with antique silver and china. The food was served family style and consisted of freshly blended juices, homemade baked goods that made your mouth water at the scent. The main course had eggs, pancakes, sausages, and bacon. It was delightful.

We hit the road again shortly after nine. Going down the highway, Harley took a turn too quickly on the icy road, and the hog went into a skid. It teetered to the far right as we slid into the lane going the opposite direction. He hit the brakes which caused the tires to lock. The smell of burning rubber was strong. Harley had to swing out his leg to keep us from tipping over.

A car barreling in our direction laid on the horn as it blasted past and pulled over to the shoulder of the road. My heart was still hammering as a man climbed out of his vehicle and hustled toward us. I felt lightheaded and gasped for breath from fear.

"You folks, okay?" The man inquired while keeping a safe distance from us.

"Yeah," Harley replied. "I just took a turn too fast and sharp." He pulled his helmet off and ran a shaky hand through his hair and back down his face. "Too many hours on the road. A touch of white line fever, you know?"

"Be careful, son. That can get you and your lady dead in a hurry." The man got back in his car and left.

"You okay?" I asked him. "We can stop at the next town and leave early in the morning."

"I'm fine. We have reservations at our destination. Let's push on."

"Alright," I hesitated.

I was not sure if I should push for us to stop early or go on to make our hotel reservations. I certainly didn't want Harley to lose a night's payment and the room just because we failed to show up that night. In the end, financial considerations won, and we continued down the highway.

It was a grueling eight-hour ride with one lunch and two restroom breaks, making it ten hours on the road. The biting wind made us feel cold despite the layers of clothing. We were beyond tired by the time we reached our destination.

We pulled into the hotel parking lot just after seven that night. The room Harley had reserved was a two bedroom suite. The bathroom was to the left. Straight ahead, there was a small sitting area and then a door to each bedroom. We were exhausted.

Harley called room service. He had potato soup, ham sandwiches and drinks delivered. We sat on the sofa. We ate quickly.

"I don't know about you, but I'm tired," he said, stretching. "I think we should get some sleep. Tomorrow is a full day." He leaned over and kissed me.

"Good night, Harley." I stood and gathered our trash, put it on the tray and left it outside our room.

I watched him walk to his room. Harley had this unique stride that can only be described as graceful as a panther. The man was all sex appeal and no conceit. It was as though he was unaware of the effect he had on women.

We spent the next day sightseeing and enjoyed the local fare. We visited a botanical garden, a carousel village, and strolled by numerous shops. Lunch was at a quaint seafood cafe where I had grilled shrimp and scallops. Harley ordered Oyster's Rockefeller which is oysters on the half shell topped with parsley, green herbs, creamy butter sauce, bread crumbs and baked. Dessert was a creamy egg custard topped with honey and sprinkled with cinnamon and chocolate curls.

As the day progressed, Harley became more animated discussing the merits of the different incarnations of the Steppenwolf band.

"I like the original lineup the best with John Kay, Goldy McJohn, Jerry Edmonton, Michael Monarch, and Rushton Moreve. Still, some of the other incarnations have merit. The guys playing on '7' were pretty good too. They put out some of the best and most taboo songs. I also like the members on 'Hour of the Wolf.' Some excellent tunes on that one." He closed his eyes as though listening to the music.

We stopped in a music store. Harley rifled through the numerous albums while I walked around looking at other merchandise. There were several racks filled with band paraphernalia including T-shirts, sweatshirts, belts, and caps. I found a sweatshirt with the Steppenwolf logo on it.

I waited until Harley was engrossed in reading the album jackets of his favorite band before I approached the cashier. I made my purchase and stepped over to him.

"I got you something," I shyly handed him the bag.

"For me?" He looked in wonderment at the bag in his hand as we left the store.

"It's not much," I stammered. "Just a little something, for tonight."

"Oh, wow!" Harley exclaimed as he pulled the shirt out and held it up. "I love it!" He took his jacket off, "Turn around."

I did as he requested, "Boy, you are modest," I laughed.

Harley looked around the front of the shop where we stood. The street and sidewalk were jammed with traffic, both vehicular and pedestrian. Cars, trucks, and people passed by without notice. He untucked his shirt from his pants and unbuttoned it. He shrugged out of the garment.

I couldn't help sneaking a peek at his body by looking at the storefront window. He was built! Muscles rippled across his shoulders as he pulled the sweatshirt over his head. His chest was ripped, not like a body builder, but like a man who was physically fit. When combined with his height, beautiful eyes, and sandy hair streaked with dark highlights, he was quite a hunk.

Who would have ever thought lurking under his shirt was an Adonis? Superman, move over you've been replaced. He was what you would call hot and sexy all rolled into one modest gentleman. All I could think was, Wow! What a turn on!

"Okay, I'm done," Harley said. "Can't be too modest if I just removed my shirt on a busy street," he chuckled, "I saw you looking in the glass. Like what you saw, hmm?" He winked at me.

Now, it was my turn to be embarrassed. I was caught red-handed admiring the view, and what a view it was. "Touché." I felt my cheeks burning.

I turned back to face him. Harley was wearing the sweatshirt and smiling. It took so little to make him happy. I was glad I had bought the gift.

"How do I look?" He held his arms out and did a mock pirouette.

"You look fabulous, just like a Steppenwolf fan."

He hugged me, "thank you so much!" His enthusiasm was addicting.

The anticipation of the upcoming concert grew immeasurably throughout the afternoon and dinner. Finally, it was time to enter the Civic Center for the show. The place held 13,000.

Chapter Eight

Outside, a coalition of women against what they described as macho sexist music, had formed a picket line to protest Steppenwolf's lyrics, their songs, and the culture they portrayed. They advocated boycotting the concert. I later learned this was not their first demonstration they staged against popular bands. A crowd formed around the concert goers, pushing and jostling us as they tried to keep us away from the venue.

"Hey, you sexist pig!" Someone shoved their face into Harley's. "Get manly and join us in boycotting this filthy group!" She screamed while grabbing his jacket.

"Madam, unhand me," Harley plucked her hands from his garment.

"I am not a Madam!" She huffed.

"Really? You are an adult female, are you not?"

"Of course."

"Then by your admission, you are indeed a Madam; a grown woman." Harley looked both bemused and tense as the woman stomped past him.

"I guess they aren't going to be asking for a performance of 'For Ladies Only.' It's only music, for Pete's sake. Listen carefully enough, and you can derive any meaning you want." He watched the protestor move away from us.

"Or 'Tenderness?' Didn't you say the words were taboo?"

"Yeah, but 'Ball Crusher' is worse."

We entered the concert hall. Harley had managed to snag not only front row seats but also backstage passes. Vendor booths had been set up.

We perused the merchandise, and I bought a key chain, a set of embroidered logo patches and a photograph.

The energy in the audience was high. The venue was packed. We joined in the chanting. Savoy Brown, the opening act, performed a solid set of rock and roll.

People stood on their seats waving posters, handmade signs, and album covers as they chanted,

"Steppenwolf!"

"Steppenwolf!"

"Steppenwolf!"

The band ran out on stage with John Kay coming last at a more leisurely pace.

"He's technically blind," Harley leaned toward me and shouted into my ear. "He only sees in black and white. It's called Achromatopsia."

"Wow!"

The band launched into their signature song, 'Born to be Wild' followed by 'Gang War Blues.' The audience went wild. People jumped into the aisles and danced.

A rollicking rendition of 'Hey Lawdy Mama' had people dancing in the aisles while a more somber social commentary 'Children of the Night' brought the crowd to their feet in applause.

"Enjoying the show?" Harley had to shout over the crowd.

"Boy, am I!" I grinned and raised my arms overhead in a wave.

The crowd greeted song with wild abandonment. The show drew to a close with a rousing version of 'Berry Rides Again.'

After the band left the stage, we slowly made our way behind the scenes. Harley clipped our passes on to our shirts. Meeting the band was the highlight of the evening for Harley. As he made his way around the room, I secretly asked each member to sign the photograph I had purchased earlier.

An hour later we left and returned to our hotel suite. I knocked on the door to Harley's bedroom.

"Come on in," he called.

I poked my head in and was shocked at his appearance. He looked wan. It was as though the trip and concert had sucked the life out of him. Harley sat on the edge of his bed with his shoes off. He ran a hand across his brow. Beads of sweat ran down on his face.

"Are you okay?" I gasped and ran to his side. I had never seen him sick before, not even a cold. I was frightened to see Harley looking ill. I touched his forehead.

"You don't feel like you're running a fever." I looked him over carefully. I sat beside him and began rubbing his legs. The calf muscles felt like knots.

"I'm just tired. The long ride and the excitement of the concert did me in." He reached up and stroked my face. "I'll be fine, Mari. I just need some rest."

His hand shook as he started to remove his jacket. He looked like he was going to fall over onto the mattress.

"Here," I said, reaching for his jacket, "let me help."

I gently removed his outer garment and then unbuttoned his shirt. I turned and looked in his bag for his pajamas. When I faced him again, he hadn't moved. I tenderly removed his shirt and put on his nightshirt.

"Do you want to sleep in your jeans or the pajama bottoms?"

"Pajamas," he replied as he struggled to undo his jeans. "Please turn around."

"Kind of hard to help you that way. I'll just close my eyes, okay?" I knelt down and tugged his pants down while he lifted his hips.

"Fine," he panted.

I then assisted him in getting into bed and pulled the covers over him. "Should I call a doctor?"

"No," he shook his head. "I'll be okay in the morning."

"Okay, then. Goodnight." I stood up to leave.

"Mari?" He asked, "Would you stay with me until I fall asleep?" At that moment he resembled an innocent child of three instead of my handsome biker dude.

"Sure, Harley. I'd do anything for you."

He patted the spot next to him on the mattress. I went around and climbed onto the bed. I put my arms around him and held him with all the love I held in my heart. I watched over him as his eyelids fluttered closed as he drifted into sleep.

I rose, went into my room and grabbed my Steppenwolf swag to place in his bag with a brief but heartfelt note. Sleep was long in coming as I worried about Harley. I kept getting up to check on him. Each time he appeared to be slumbering peacefully.

I woke to hear Harley stirring around in his room. "Mari?" Harley knocked on the door.

"It's okay to come in." I zipped my bag shut.

"What's this?" He asked as he ambled in carrying the Steppenwolf merchandise.

"How are you feeling?"

"Fine," he mumbled. "I was just exhausted. He stared at me for a long time before asking, "Did you dress me in my pajamas last night?"

"I did," I nodded, "with your help. You were pretty out of it."

He wiped a hand across his chin. "I guess so. I am so sorry about that. It was improper of me."

"Oh, please! You scared me; you were so sick. You'd have done the same for me." I pulled on my jacket. "I even held you until you fell asleep."

"Well, thanks," he said sheepishly. "So, are you going to tell me what these were doing in my grip?" He held out the concert purchases.

"Uh, they're gifts? Didn't you see my note?" I chided him with a playful poke.

"Yes," he cooed. "You didn't have to spend your hard earned money on me." He gazed at the souvenirs.

"I know. I wanted to." My voice dropped to a near-whisper. "Merry Christmas, my love." I chastely planted kisses on the side of his face, and then his lips. "Mmm...I sure love you."

"You love me?" He sounded hopeful and yet prepared for a negative response.

"Yes, I love you," I spoke.

"Mari! You just made my entire year!" Harley whooped as we left the suite to head back home.

Chapter Nine

Christmas is my favorite holiday. I get into picking out, setting up and placing the decorations on the tree. I spent hours stringing tinsel, cranberries and popcorn, and lights. I intertwined the berries and popcorn with the tinsel. Aside from stringing items together, the lights took the longest amount of time to hang. I had to hide the wires with the tinsel and make sure the plugs were in the back. Holiday classics blared from my stereo, and I drank hot cocoa by the gallon. It was two days before the festive religious holiday when I finally finished draping the tree with ornaments.

I arranged presents underneath the pine boughs. The last one was from Harley. I sat looking at the present, remembering those last few moments I had with him before he went back east.

Harley had stopped by K-Mart the week before. I was working a lot of hours there. That first-year WOSL went on hiatus between Fall and Winter quarters. He was on his way out of town to spend the holidays with his family.

Karen stopped working and let out a wolf whistle that had heads turning as Harley walked past. A couple of co-workers could be heard asking who the handsome looker was. Typical of Harley, he was oblivious to the stares and whispers generated by his appearance in the Ladies Wear department known as Holly Stores.

He gave me a gift wrapped package. "You have to promise not to open it until Christmas," he had said with a hint of shyness.

"I thought the concert was my present." I gazed at the gift in my hands. I shook the package. There was no sound other than the crinkle of the wrapping paper.

"No," he shook his head. "That was our gift together." He looked devilishly excited about giving me a present. "I can't wait until you see it. I hope you like it."

"I'm sure; I'll love it," I reassured him.

"I'll call you on Christmas. I don't know what time. It'll probably be late in the evening if that's okay."

"I don't see why not." I glanced at my watch. "It's almost break time. I was hoping you'd stop by before you left. I have something for you too. It's in my locker. Follow me." I headed to the back of the store. Opening my locker, I pulled out a small parcel wrapped in Santa colors of red, white, and green.

"It's just a little something."

I had given him two silver framed photos. The first one was of us sitting on the Commons grounds. The second one was of Harley, Peg, and Maryanne. I had gotten a camera for my birthday and had snapped both pictures. I signed the backs, "with love, Mari," and had listed each person in the shots and the date I took the photos.

With a sigh, I placed his gift to me under the tree. The plain paper wrap decorated with Christmas trees stenciled on it, silver, gold, and red ribbon looked cheerfully mysterious. He didn't put his name on the gift tag. It simply read, "for Mari."

A deep sadness threatened to overwhelm me. I never knew I could miss someone known only a few months as much as I did Harley.

Christmas day dawned a chilly 25 degrees. Everyone gathered around the tree as I handed out presents. I saved Harley's gift for last. I neatly peeled the paper off and opened an ornate box.

Inside it were two books by Hermann Hesse, 'Steppenwolf,' and 'Siddhartha,' both novels. He included a note about how the book inspired the band's name. It brought a smile to my lips as I thought about him and his love of their music.

Mom served a delicious lunch of turkey, oyster dressing, cornbread dressing, salad, mashed potatoes, corn, squash, candied yams, green beans, dinner rolls, mincemeat pie, and fruitcake soaked in brandy. Wine, coffee, and tea were the drinks available. We had enough food to last weeks. Turkey sandwiches and leftover fixings were the order of the day.

After cleaning up from our midday meal, my parents and sister took a nap. I retreated to my room and dug into the books Harley had given me.

By late afternoon the temperature had risen to a whopping 34 degrees. Mom made sandwiches for us to eat as we played card games such as Rummy and Pinochle well into the evening. It was after eleven when the phone rang. Everyone had gone to bed. My sister was listening to her stereo and trying on some of her presents.

"Hello?"

"Hi there, Gypsy Mar. Have you got any Steppenwolf? Merry Christmas." Harley's beautiful voice came over the line.

"Merry Christmas to you too. I'm listening to 'Skullduggery' on my new stereo. How was your holiday?"

"Ah, good choice. My Christmas was typical for my family. Lots of pomp and one up man ship. We exchanged gifts in the morning, then had lunch."

"What'd you get? Anything good?" I asked, curious about what a wealthy family gave each other.

"A leather wallet, and some silk paisley shirts." From his tone, I could picture him shrugging. "I did get some classical music I like. Schubert, Aaron Copland, Chopin, and some Hungarian Gypsy music."

"I can't see you in silk paisley shirts." I found my imagined sight of him dressed in silk amusing. "At least you got some tunes. You'll have to let me hear them. In music appreciation class we've been listening to Tchaikovsky."

"Deal."

"What'd you eat?" My curiosity got the better of me. I kind of had an idea based on some of the places Harley had taken me. Still, I wondered what rich people did on holidays. What traditions did they have? What did they eat?

"We always have Quiche Lorraine, spinach salad, and fruit parfait, and a huge party with everyone who is anyone in attendance. Lots of tuxedos and evening gowns full of stuffed shirts and trophy wives or girlfriends." Harley sounded bored.

"I take it; that's not your style."

"You got that right," he groused. "Don't get me wrong; I enjoy the classical music. It's being hounded by starry-eyed women just dying to become my trophy wife that I can't stand."

"They hound you?" I asked basking in the joy of hearing his voice. I could picture scheming, pampered, spoiled debutantes surrounding Harley causing him discomfort. It was not something he would like.

"That's putting it mildly. More like the women are flaunting their wares at me," he grumbled.

I could almost picture these women wearing full corsets that made their cleavage more visible as they leaned over Harley and tried to caress his chest. I could imagine him blushing and trying gently to remove their tentacles.

"They don't know you very well, do they?"

"Not at all. How's your Christmas going?"

"We opened gifts. Mom made her usual turkey dinner with enough leftovers to see us until after New Years. She's got a pot of turkey and vegetable soup made for tomorrow along with biscuits and cornbread. I'm reading the 'Steppenwolf' novel you gave me."

"And?" He prompted.

"It's excellent, but it was kind of hard to get into at first."

"But, you like it?" Harley sounded anxious.

"So far, yes." I looked at the books and smiled. "I've read half of the Harvard Classics. The books you gave me fit right in with them. I'm enjoying 'Steppenwolf,' and I can see why the band picked that name."

"Good. I'm glad you like it," Harley sighed with relief. "Now I have someone other than Garrett to talk with about it."

"You can talk books with me anytime. I'm an avid reader."

"Another thing we can enjoy together," he spoke enthusiastically.

"We can take turns selecting books." I warmed up to the idea. "We each get to pick a book, and the other has to read it. That way we can broaden our horizons."

"You need to see my library. It and the living room are where I spend my time at home."

I hesitated before saying, "I write stories."

"What kind? Romance? Adventure? Horror? Mystery? Have you tried to publish any?" he sounded very intrigued.

"I write mainly paranormal romance and horror. Right now, I'm working on a story about how a swamp witch saves a town."

"You should try to publish. Who knows? You might be the next Stephen King or Nora Roberts."

"I'm not that good." I was beginning to feel embarrassed over his enthusiasm for my hobby.

"You never know until you attempt it." Harley encouraged me. "I think you should try. Get an agent and see what happens."

"That's true."

"Do it. Then when you're famous, I can say I loved you first. I had known you before the books came out," Harley laughed. "What's the worst that can happen? You get turned down. So what? At least you tried which is probably more than ninety percent of would-be writers."

"And got my ego bruised," I mumbled. "Will you be back for New Year's Day?" I asked to change the subject.

"I doubt it. My folks are having a giant New Year's Eve dinner party and want me to attend."

A wistfulness filled his voice. "I miss you." He sounded lonely. "You are my light that keeps me grounded. Just thinking about you makes all this pomp easier to deal with because I know when the holidays are over I'll be able to see you."

"I miss you too, very much. I wish you were here." Tears threatened to choke me.

"Are you okay?" He asked with concern.

"I'm fine. You grew on me, Bucko. I miss you terribly," I sniffled.

"I miss you more," he teased.

"No, I miss you more," I whispered while holding the receiver close to my ear.

It was almost as though by hugging the phone, I was a little closer to Harley. He stirred emotions in me that were both exciting and intimidating. How could I be feeling so strongly about a man I'd only known since September?

"I miss you," a deep longing filled my voice.

As he disconnected our telephone conversation, he made one last comment that brought another lump into my throat. "I love you," he murmured.

Chapter Ten

At the beginning and end of each quarter, students swamps the campus bookstore buying and returning course materials. The store was the perfect place for theft. The lines were long at the check out counter. My arms ached from holding three huge anthropology, one English literature, and two large biology books. I jiggled from one foot to the other.

"I hope they hurry up. I'm going to be late for lunch with the gang," I mumbled. I had been standing in line for over thirty minutes.

Two men entered the bookstore. They did not look like any students I had seen on campus, not even the ones attending Lima Technical dressed like these guys. It didn't take brains to know these men were trouble.

The tall one was skinny and had a lot of pimples. His brown hair hung down to his shoulders in greasy clumps. He wore a baseball cap backward. His cotton shirt was a blue and purple plaid while his jeans were ripped at the knees and washed out. He had on plain white tennis shoes with holes in the toes. Three strands of cheap costume gold and silver necklaces hung around his neck. Dime store rings were on every finger. He carried a steel baton and tapped it rhythmically against his leg.

The shorter guy was swarthy and had a foul odor that can only be described as unwashed or he had messed his pants. His black hair was filthy and tied in a ponytail. He wore a windbreaker. His white shirt had food stains on the front and sweat marks at his armpits. His fingers crusted with dirt, and he wore brass knuckles on his left hand. When he grinned, his teeth were yellow, green, and black. He kept his right hand inside his jacket, possibly hiding a gun.

"Everyone on the floor," bad guy number one ordered. "Not you, babe," he said to the clerk.

"Do as you're told, and no one needs to get hurt," number two sneered.

I sat cross-legged and hugged my books to my chest. I wanted to close my eyes but was too scared to do so. I needed to know exactly where they were and what they were doing. I wished Harley was there. He'd know what to do.

The girl sitting next to me began rocking back and forth. Her lips moved to the motion of her body. I could barely hear her whispers, "Oh God, oh God! Please get us out of this." On and on her murmurs went.

I leaned toward her, "We'll have better luck if we're quiet," I spoke with a hushed tone. "Don't draw attention to us."

She shook her head but kept rocking and mumbling. I sighed and said a silent prayer the thieves didn't notice.

Our campus community was small. As such, we were not used to violence and robberies.

"Open the register, babe," number one demanded.

The cashier's hands were shaking so badly; she dropped the keys several times. I felt sorry for her. When she didn't respond quickly enough, he hit her across the face with the brass knuckles. The cartilage broke and snapped her nose out of joint.

"I said open it!" he demanded.

"Hey!" I shouted, my anger getting the best of me. "That was unnecessary!"

"You want to get nailed next?" He swung around and stared at me.

"No," I lowered both my voice and my head. Now, I'd done it. I'd gone and drawn his attention. My face paled, and my hands shook as I wrung them in fear.

"Then keep your mouth shut." He towered menacingly over me.

"Bully," I muttered.

The door to the bookstore slammed open. Harley stood in the entrance wearing his leather jacket and matching pants. Chains dangled on both sides of his clothing. He had one hand in a pocket while the other held his helmet. He looked mean and dangerous, a not to be messed with biker thug.

He surveyed the scene for a few seconds before swinging his helmet at bad guy number two. The helmet hit the man so hard in the groin it knocked him to the floor. Harley bent over him and punched him in the stomach. He made sure the man was going to stay down.

He turned his attention to the guy at the checkout counter. He grabbed the person's shirt, swung him around and slammed him against the wall. The man's head hit some shelving, and Harley placed a well-aimed punch to his upper chest, knocking the breath out of him.

"You want action, you got it," he growled. Harley sucker punched the guy again.

I stared at Harley with a huge lump in my throat. I'd only seen hints of his temper. This anger was a full blown rage. His face had transformed into a cruel mockery of his usual countenance. His eyes hardened into a solid cold gray. I had no doubt in my mind, if pushed hard enough, he could kill a person, and it scared me.

He shoved the man again. His left hand disengaged a set of chains on his pants. I never noticed the tiny spikes at the ends. They added an aura of viciousness. With a flick of his wrist, the chains wrapped around his hand. He jabbed an upper snap. Everyone in the shop could hear the man's nose break.

"Did anyone call campus security?" He barked as he glanced back at the other thief.

The man remained prone on the floor. He had wrapped his hands protectively in front of himself.

"I'll do it," the clerk said shakily.

"I think the guy over there has a gun. Someone tie him up tightly with a belt," he snapped, indicating the fellow on the floor.

He kept the other man pinned to the wall. "Mari? Could you come here, please?"

"Harley?" My voice squeaked and trembled.

I was shaking so badly my legs on wobbled like gelatin. Fainting was a distinct possibility as I prayed to remain upright and conscious.

"I need you to take my belt off. When I turn this prick around, pull his arms behind him and wrap it around his wrists tightly."

It took a few attempts, but eventually I did as he instructed. I tugged on the belt making sure it was tight but didn't cut off circulation.

"Done," my voice was barely audible.

"Is security coming?" He asked the clerk.

"Should be here shortly,"

"Don't move!" Two men entered the bookstore. "Drop the chains!" He shrieked.

"Drop it!" he screamed.

Harley immediately lets go of the chains around his hand and raised his arms over his head.

"On the floor and spread your legs," the cop commanded. The officer pulled out a pair of handcuffs and placed them on Harley's wrists.

I couldn't believe it! They were going to arrest Harley! "Officer," I called out. "You got it wrong."

"Be quiet, Miss."

"You got it wrong," a student spoke up. "Biker dude is the good guy. He stopped those two from robbing the store and us."

The officers took everyone's statement and let us go as they dragged the suspects out of the building.

"Are you okay?" Harley asked me as he rubbed his wrists.

I didn't know how to answer him, so I kept silent as we walked toward the cafeteria.

"Mari?" He paused and turned me to face him. "What's wrong?" Concern filled his eyes. "You didn't get hurt, did you?"

"No," I mumbled.

"Then, what is it?" Harley continued to look at me.

"So much for 'I don't cotton to unnecessary violence,' Mister Davis," my emotions had gone on a rollercoaster disaster ride from fear, relief, scared, relief, and now anger.

"Uh, oh, you called me Mister Davis," he sighed and hung his head. "Are you upset with me?" Harley frowned.

"You scared me, Harley," I felt tears welling up in my eyes.

"Me?" He squeezed his eyes shut. "I am sorry. That was not my intention."

He pulled me into his arms for a comforting hug. "You said you were going to get your books before joining us for lunch. When you didn't show, I came looking for you. I saw everyone sitting on the floor and these guys robbing the cash register." Harley gently caressed my face.

"My whole concern was stopping them and making sure you were safe. I'd never hurt you, Mari. You do know that, don't you?"

"I know," I sniffed and wiped at my eyes. "It was the violence that frightened me. I never saw you look so capable of killing."

"I wouldn't have," he flashed a lopsided grin. "Not unless you were in danger of dying. I need you, Mari. I can't get through my life without you," he smiled. "You keep me grounded. Without you, I'm just a drifter, lost in this journey of life."

He held the door to the cafeteria open. By some miracle, our friends were still in the cafeteria when we got there.

"Where were you? Out smooching?" Peg asked.

"The bookstore was being robbed. Mari was there. The crooks had the students sitting on the floor." Harley slipped his arm protectively around my waist and guided me to a chair.

I couldn't keep my eyes off him. This man may have just saved the life of everyone in the bookstore, and here he was getting us lunch. I watched him as he headed toward the serving line and ordered us hamburgers, fries, a slice of pie and water with lemon.

"I was waiting in line to pay for my books. I was fretting about missing lunch with you guys when these filthy guys came in." I said as I continued watching Harley as he bought our meals.

"What happened? Did anyone get hurt?" Maryanne asked breathlessly.

Harley set our food on the table and sat beside me. He dug into his burger with relish. "Mmm...Good as usual. Dig in, Mari."

"Anyone get shot?" Maryanne persisted.

"Nope. Harley came in and went all ninja on them," I said.

The entire group turned and stared at him as though he was a bug on a microscope slide. His chewing slowed to a stop. He turned a bright shade of red starting from his collarbone to the top of his head.

"Biker, ninja boy, huh?" Thomas, Harley's best friend teased. "That's some combination there."

"Oh, hush," Harley groused.

"He was awesome." I gushed, all fear gone. Everything was right with the world again.

Two days later a student assistant rushed up to us outside WOSL. "Are you Harley Davis?" He asked as he fidgeted.

"Yes."

"Dean Alexander wants to see you in his office right away."

Harley looked at me and shrugged. "Okay. Mari? Come with?"

"Sure."

With trepidation, we headed to the Dean's office. Getting summoned there was never a good thing. We sat on hard vinyl chairs for an hour. Harley had one knee on the other and kept tapping his fingers on it. Periodically he glanced at his watch.

The secretary peered at us over her plastic-rimmed reading glasses. They were attached to a chain she wore around her neck. She wore a blue skirt, white blouse, and matching sweater. Her silver streaked brown hair was tied neatly in a bun. The boxy black telephone on her desk jingled.

"Dean Alexander will see you now," she said, replacing the receiver.

We both rose. "Not you, Miss."

"She comes in with me," Harley's authoritative tone brooked no nonsense from her.

"Very well," she called the Dean and announced both of us.

"Come in, Mister Davis and Miss Forrester." The Dean stood and walked around his desk.

"Please, be seated." He perched on the edge of his table in a symbolic move meant to intimidate us and show us who was in authority.

"Yes, Sir," Harley said disarmingly.

"I think you know what this is about, Mister Davis." The Dean spoke matter-of-factly.

"Yes, Sir," Harley nodded. "It's about the altercation in the bookstore."

"Then you understand, you can get suspended for your actions." He picked up a pencil and twirled it.

"Yes, Sir." Harley glanced down at his hands.

"Mister Davis, why don't you tell me what happened." The Dean put the pencil back on his desk and crossed his arms.

"In a nutshell, I saw two men robbing the bookstore. They had student customers sitting on the floor. One of them backhanded the cashier. I think one of them may have had a gun." Harley leaned forward in his seat and spoke earnestly. I could tell from his tone and position he was tense and trying to explain his actions.

"These guys meant to not only rob the store but also to hurt people in the process. I saw an opportunity to stop them and did. Security was called, and the men were taken away. Everyone present gave an account of what happened."

"I've read the statements. Mister Davis, we do not condone violence on campus. It is one of the few transgressions that can get a student expelled immediately."

He proceeded to lecture Harley about the assault. I think he used every word in the dictionary to describe the term including fighting, attacking, storming, aggression, disturbing, onslaught, striking, struggling, clashing, and, bloodshed.

Then he progressed to what damage such accused of assault, spend time in jail, goes to trial, gets sent to prison, ruin his reputation, bring shame to his family, lose his career, and wind up on the streets or living a life of crime. The picture Dean Alexander painted was bleak. The talk lasted well over two hours.

"While I could suspend you, I won't. A lot of students came to your defense. So, I'm going to place you on probation instead. No more violence on your part for two months and I'll take this status off your record. Do we have an understanding?"

"Yes, Sir." Harley stood and shook Dean Alexander's hand. "Thank you, Sir."

"Get in trouble much, biker boy?" I chided him as we left the office.

"No," he looked at his watch. "So much for lunch."

"Next time."

Harley faced me and smiled sadly. "Not a chance, you don't have to work, is there?"

"I have to head off to work." I kissed him on the cheek.

"Yeah, yeah," he complained. "Always have to get to work at K-Mart." He tugged me closer and gave me a quick squeeze. "How about I drop in during your break?"

"It's a deal. I'd love that. It'll give me another chance to show you off," I laughed wickedly.

"Mari!" Harley clutched his chest, "I'm shocked! Shocked, I say!" He burst into laughter.

"Be there at seven, ninja biker dude." I lightly kissed him. It seemed to cheer him up a little. "See you tonight, my love."

Chapter Eleven

The only time I celebrated Valentine's Day was in grade school. Harley, on the other hand, acted like it was second only to Christmas. For weeks before the holiday, he pestered me about plans. He hinted around about dinner and kept asking about things I liked.

In 1976, Valentine's Day fell on Saturday. I always worked that holiday so couples could have the night to celebrate.

"Hey, Karen," I called out to my coworker.

"Yes?" She was a tiny slip of a girl with dark raven hair.

"Are you and Jeff going out Saturday?"

"I doubt it. We had a big fight and aren't talking."

"Can you trade days with me? I'll work Friday if I can have Saturday off."

"You never ask for Valentine's Day off. What gives?"

"I have a date. I'll tell you all about it after work," I said.

It was busy in Kmart ladies wear as we assisted clueless husbands in finding the perfect lingerie. Most of them had no idea about sizes.

"Sir," I said, "just put your arms out about how you would hold her." I demonstrated by placing my arms around a mannequin.

"Oh, okay."

"That would be about a size 14. Now, do you want to get your wife a garment in the right size, or would she be flattered if she thought you saw her smaller?"

"Right size. I don't want my wife to have to return it." The husband looked perplexed. "She likes blue."

"Okay, how about a silky blue gown?"

"Perfect."

I handed him several garments, and he left the department with a grin. "Don't forget flowers," I called after him.

"Wow!" Came the husky baritone purr of Harley's sexy voice.

I whirled around. "What are you doing here?" I couldn't help grinning as he pulled me into his arms for a quick hug and nuzzled my ear.

"Stopped by to see if you wanted a ride home."

"I'd like one, but I promised I'd go over to Karen's after work."

"Okay," he looked disappointed.

"I'm sorry."

"It's okay." The look of dejection on his face made my heart ache. "I understand. I just wanted to spend a little time with you. I miss you when you aren't around."

"I miss you too." The lump in my throat made me feel like I was going to cry.

He stood looking at me with longing for a few minutes as though he hoped I would cancel on Karen. With a deep sigh, he said, "see you tomorrow?"

"Absolutely." Impulsively, I gave him a quick peck on the cheek.

"I guess, that'll have to do. Good night Mari." He shoved his hands into his pockets and walked away.

"Night. See you tomorrow."

He lifted a hand in acknowledgment and continued walking toward the door.

"Who was that?" Karen gushed as she leaned forward and watched him walk. "Oh, my! He does have a sexy walk. He is one gorgeous hunk," she sighed. "Wait a minute! Is he the reason you want Saturday off?"

"Yep."

"Girl, you are going to spill the beans tonight!" Karen cackled with glee. "Where have you been hiding him?"

"Under your nose," I laughed. It felt odd having a friend mooning over my guy.

"I mean, really, Mari," she grabbed a nightgown and folded it. "Where did you find him?"

"He found me at OSU."

"Don't tell me he's one of those guys who think he's God's gift to women."

"Far from it. I'll tell you after work."

"Looks like a bad boy to me. Leather jacket with chains, black jeans with studs. Ultimate biker."

"If only you knew."

The hours until 10 pm seemed to crawl. All my coworkers kept shooting me weird looks. I just knew they all wanted to know who the guy was since I never talked about dating or having a boyfriend.

Karen and I carpooled when we were both scheduled to work. We alternated driving. Tonight was Karen's turn. She drove an old tan colored Ford Fairlane. It was her grandmother's car and in nearly mint condition.

When she drove, we always stopped at her place for hot chocolate and a chance to talk. Her apartment on Bellefontaine Avenue was four miles from my home on Harding Highway. She had a second-floor apartment. Entering the rental you stepped into a small kitchen and dining area. Beyond that was the living room and to the left was the bed and bathroom. At best, it could be described as quaint.

Karen busied herself making hot chocolate topped with whipped cream and cinnamon while I got out the cups. "So, what happened between you and Jeff?"

"Oh you know, more of the same," she wrinkled her nose. "Always wanting to spend our dates playing pinball games. Just once I'd like Jeff to take me out to dinner at a real restaurant, not a game room."

"Now, tell me about the hunk." Karen plopped a handful of marshmallows into the cups and handed one to me. She sat on the floor and curled one foot under her.

"What's to tell?" I shrugged and joined her on the floor.

"How'd you meet?"

"We met on the Commons at OSU." I crossed my legs. "And he asked me out. He was irresistibly persistent."

"Where'd you go?"

"He took me to Wolf Park in Battle Ground, Indiana. We spent Friday and Saturday seeing the sights and came back Sunday."

"You spent a weekend together? Did you, you know?" She flushed a brilliant shade of red. "I mean, a guy as gorgeously sexy as he is, well, you know?" She stammered.

I lifted an eyebrow at her. "No, I don't know," I said slowly.

"Did you have sex with him? Did you guys sleep together?"

"Karen!" I gasped.

"Well, did you?"

"Nope. He was the perfect gentleman. I even had my own room."

"Huh!" She huffed in disbelief. "Nobody is that perfect, especially these days. All guys want is sex. You don't do it, and they drop you."

"Harley isn't like that. He's all about being a gentleman, treating people with respect, and helping the less fortunate. He even fed an out of work Vietnam veteran and hired him."

"What'd you mean hired him?"

"Harley has his own business."

"What? Motorcycles? What's with his name anyway? What kind of name is Harley?"

"Yes, motorcycles. Harley customizes them and builds accessories. His name comes from his family's love of the Harley-Davidson motorcycles." I found myself feeling a bit irritated with Karen's view of men.

"What's with the separate rooms bit?"

"As I said, Harley believes in proper behavior. One of those is women and men don't sleep together unless they are married to each other. He called it the law of chastity."

"Sounds old fashioned to me."

"It is. I find it charming." I yawned. "I better get home. I have an eight o'clock lab."

"Okay. If you ever dump Harley let me know. I wouldn't mind a chance at him."

Fat chance, I thought. That's not going to happen. Nope, nada, she was not going to get her claws into him. I was amazed at the jealous feelings welling up. I always considered Karen to be lovely, while I was merely average. The thought she might want him for herself left me feeling cold.

Chapter Twelve

Saturday came quickly. I wasn't prepared for celebrating Valentine's Day. I nervously looked through my wardrobe and realized I only had one dress that might be suitable for such an occasion. It was a simple blue garment that I called a 'Granny dress,' and no teenage or college girl would be caught dead in it. My mother had selected it for my high school graduation the previous May.

I sighed, got out a slip to wear under the dress, pulled out neutral pantyhose and prepared myself for the evening. I wore the pink heart necklace even though it didn't match. I'd worn that piece of jewelry every day since he gave it to me. Sometimes it was under my shirt where I felt he was close to my heart, other times I showed it off.

"I'm off," I shouted down the hall.

"Where are you going?" Mom asked. She came into the living room wiping her hands on a dish towel.

"Out with a friend," I pulled on my shoes. While they weren't exactly heels, they did have a little height and matched my dress.

"Don't be out too late."

"I won't," I sighed when I was safely ensconced in my car. I was still reluctant to tell Mom about Harley. It was probably his bad boy biker image. Mom would never approve of me dating a guy who rode a motorcycle regardless of his financial and moral background. Mom thought every person who rode a bike was in a gang like the Hell's Angels. She wouldn't understand that Harley was nothing like those types of men; he was a true gentleman.

I pulled into the semi-circular drive and killed the engine. I sat looking at the enormous colonial style mansion. Every window in the place was ablaze with light. I could only imagine how much electricity it took and the cost.

Just as I was about to step out of my car, Garrett came rushing through the front doors. "I'm glad you're here Miss Mari. Quickly now, I have to get back inside and attempt to avert a kitchen catastrophe."

We stepped into the foyer. Steppenwolf's 'Magic Carpet Ride' blasted through hidden speakers. I curiously looked around. The entry flooring was Italian marble with inlaid faux gold and silver etchings. Glass framed watercolors of nature painted by local artists adorned the walls. The foyer was elegant and yet tastefully simple.

Garrett grasped my shoulders and removed my coat. He was hanging it in the coat closet when a sonic boom came from the back of the house. An equally loud howl followed suit.

"Oh, dear," Garrett moaned. "I'm afraid I'm too late. Excuse me. I must attempt to rescue the house from Master Harley's culinary expertise." He hurried toward the rear.

I followed Garrett slowly as I peeked inside rooms and looked at the family portraits hanging on the walls lining the hall. Most of them looked stuffy in their starched shirts or Sunday school dresses. Only Harley was casual in his leather jacket. I could not imagine anyone on that wall other than Harley riding a motorcycle. They just didn't fit the biker mold, yet Harley once said he was named after the famous Harley-Davidson motorcycles.

"Master Harley!" Garrett's voice came stridently from the rear of the house. "I wish you had let me cook," he scolded. "Shall I call out for pizza or Chinese?"

"I wanted to make a memorable dinner," Harley said humbly.

"I assure you, that it will be. Look at this mess." Garrett tsked. "Oh, Master Harley, don't look so glum. Miss Mari will be fine with anything served. The important thing is the two of you spend this special evening together."

"Thank you, Garrett. I sure hope Mari will be okay with take-out food. As for this mess, I'll clean it up. Don't worry about it. Make it Chinese, please." Harley sounded sad I wanted to rush in and comfort him. I didn't because I didn't want him to know I had heard their conversation.

I felt like a peeping tom listening to them talk in the kitchen. 'Magic Carpet Ride' had given way to 'Disappointment Number,'

'Lost and Found by Trial and Error,' and Hodge Podge Strained Through a Leslie.' I could hear Garrett talking on the telephone.

He had to repeat the order twice and the address with directions three times. "They need better English speaking workers to take orders."

"Has Mari arrived yet?" Harley sounded forlorn. "I so wanted tonight to be perfect. And now it's a complete disaster. I typically make a mean spaghetti and fresh vegetable sauce. I even make decent meatballs, and a wicked black pepper squash with stuffed mushroom caps."

"Oh, Master Harley," Garrett sounded bemused. "It's not your cooking ability. You are nervous. Trust me; Mari is going to have a perfect evening with you."

"Do you think so?"

"I do," I stepped into the kitchen and gawked.

Harley looked up from the counter and broke into a broad grin. "Quite a mess, huh?"

"I'll say," I giggled as I looked around the room.

"Bet you didn't expect to spend Valentine's Day helping us scrub my kitchen."

"You got that right. Do you have anything I can wear for clean up detail?"

Harley looked me up and down much like other guys would glance at a beautiful woman. "I believe, I do."

I felt myself turning beet red. "Mom picked out the dress. I think I look frumpy in it."

He let out a low wolf whistle, "Not at all, Mari. You look stunningly lovely."

"I'll get the garment," Garrett said. He left the room and returned shortly with a pair of overalls.

To say the kitchen was a mess was putting it politely. It resembled a war zone with noodles hanging from light fixtures, on cabinet door handles, sliding down walls, and even plastered to windows. The red sauce splattered the walls, counters, table, stove, freezer, and the sink. The line of tomato paste clung to the oven, stove, refrigerator, tile flooring, ceiling, and dripped down from the top of Harley's head to his shirt and pants. I couldn't help but laugh at the scene before me.

He stood in the middle of cooking chaos holding a wooden spatula in his hand and grinning wildly. A mess of noodles and sauce was on his head and drizzled down his face. He looked like a mischievous five-year-old.

"I am so glad you're here. Please excuse the mess. I'm usually immaculate when cooking." He looked around and then up when another glob of spaghetti dropped from the ceiling onto his head.

"Garrett has ordered Chinese for us. If we hurry, the kitchen might be presentable by the time the food gets here."

We danced to 'Hey Lawdy Mama' while cleaning the spaghetti bombed kitchen. Harley had a turntable that held five albums at a time. I wiped down the table as the door bell chimed.

"Dinner is here," Garrett announced.

"I'll just clean up a bit," I said and headed back down the hall to a bathroom I had seen on my way to the kitchen.

Harley followed me out of the kitchen and turned left. When I came out of the bathroom, he was leaning against the wall with his thumbs hooked into his black dress pants. He had on a black pinstripe shirt and a ribbon tie.

"You clean up nice," I murmured as my heart started pounding. Was there ever a time when Harley didn't look handsome?

"Come this way, my lady," he bowed and with a sweep of his left hand directed me to a room next to the kitchen.

The room was a formal dining area. In the center were a mahogany table and eight chairs. A sideboard adorned the interior wall. Directly across were floor to ceiling windows and a glass door. There was a splendid view of landscaped gardens and an Olympic-sized swimming pool. In the middle of the gardens were a pagoda and fish pond. The setting sun cast a rosy warm glow making the entire yard look like a Thomas Kinkade painting.

"Wow!" I walked to the windows and stared at the beauty of his place.

"I hoped you'd like the view." He stepped behind me and put his hands on my shoulders. He kissed the top of my head. "Ready for dinner?" His voice grew husky.

"I think so," I whispered, reluctant to end the fantasy. "Will Garrett be joining us?"

"If you don't mind. I hate thinking of Garrett eating alone in the breakfast nook or kitchen."

"I don't mind." I thought it was sweet of Harley to want to include Garrett.

"But, first I want to give you a gift."

I turned to face him. He somehow got a bouquet of red and white roses in his hands during the few minutes I stared at his yard. They nestled into an elegant vase that vaguely looked Oriental in design.

"Roses for my Lady to show her my fondest, most honorable adoration for her."

He reached over to the table and picked up a box. "The finest chocolates from Europe to tell her she is the sweetest person in my life. I will forever cherish our time together because true love means never saying goodbye."

I felt dampness on my cheeks. I am normally not a crier, but his heartfelt words made me choke with emotion.

"Did I do something wrong? Is it the present or the flowers?" Dismay filled his voice. "I am a sap."

"No," I shook my head. "I love your gifts. Your words have made me the happiest girl in the world." I tenderly stroked his face. "I love them, Harley."

He hugged me. The next thing I knew, he was swinging me around. "I am so happy!"

"Ah hem, Master Harley," Garrett poked his head into the room. "Shall I serve dinner now?"

"Absolutely! Just bring it in and join us." Harley went to a counter and pulled out an additional place setting.

"Sir?" Garrett looked back and forth between Harley and me. "I don't . ."

"Please join us," I pleaded.

"Miss Mari, it is Valentine's Day. You and Master Harley should have alone time."

"Oh, nonsense. I insist you join us."

"Garrett, please bring in the food and do as my lady requested." Harley carefully laid out the extra plates and silverware.

"As you wish, Sir."

"I'm never going to break you of calling me Sir or Master Harley, am I?"

"I'm afraid not, Sir."

Garrett brought in plates of Mutton Stew or yáng ròu pào mó. It is made with unleavened bread and served with chili and garlic. It was one of Harley's favorite entrees. My preference was the second dish, Spinach Noodles known as bō cài miàn. It's a savory dish made with spinach noodles in a spicy tomato sauce topped with egg, potato, beef and chili.

The final dish was a mouth watering fried pork dumpling with plum sauce. Steamed rice accompanied each dish. Dessert included coconut bars and egg custard tarts.

We ate until we were stuffed. The conversation was light and filled with stories about Garrett and Harley.

Garrett came from a small Scottish coastal town and dreamed of moving to America. He arrived on Ellis Island when he was twenty. He spent five years working his way down the eastern seaboard until he wound up in Pennsylvania and started employment with Harley's family.

I learned Garrett began working for the family the day Harley was born. His first task was to get his mother to the hospital when she was in labor with him. Garrett found himself growing attached to the baby. When the family hired a Nanny, Harley cried non-stop until Garrett picked him up. He found bruises on the infant and vowed never to leave Harley alone. He presented his findings, and the Nanny was promptly sent away. After that, Garrett became Harley's Nanny, teacher, and mentor. Essentially, Garrett raised Harley to be a generous gentleman.

Harley's second hospital trip was on his fifth birthday. While the other children were engrossed in a magic show, Harley was climbing a brick fence. He misjudged the distance between a low hanging branch and the top of his head. The subsequent collision sent him flying off the wall six feet to the concrete walkway below.

After dinner, Garrett gathered the plates to put into the dishwasher. He returned moments later with a platter filled with pastries. "I made a pot of herbal tea and here's a plate of scones."

"Thank you, Garrett. Would you care to join us?" Harley asked as he reached for a blueberry scone.

"Thank you, Sir, but I think I'll head off to bed unless you need me." Garrett smiled indulgently at Harley and bowed. He looked like a proud father, not a servant.

"Good night, Garrett," both Harley and I said as he headed out of the room.

We enjoyed sipping the tea and munching on the scones in the living room while listening to Steppenwolf's 'Just for Tonight,' and the rest of the 'Hour of the Wolf' album. All too soon the night came to an end.

"I guess you need to get home." Harley stuffed his hands into his pants pocket.

At that moment something about him reminded me of Robert Redford in the film 'The Way We Were,' a movie I adored.

"Yeah," I paused, not wanting the night to end. "I have to work tomorrow, and I just know Mom is waiting up for me." I sighed.

Why did dates with Harley always seem perfect? Was it because he knew how to treat a girl? He spent time finding out what I might enjoy and took great pains to make it happen. He retrieved my coat, then grabbed my gifts.

"I'll see you to your car."

"Harley," I turned to face him. I took his hand in mine and brought it to my lips for a sweet kiss. "Tonight was perfect. I really enjoyed it. I love my gifts. Most importantly I love being with you."

He smiled shyly, "and some day you'll say you love me."

"Oh, I do, Harley, Remember I told you after the Steppenwolf concert?" I whispered. "I do love you, very much."

He gathered me in his arms and kissed my breath away. He held the car door open for me. I slid into the seat. As I was about to pull the door closed, he leaned forward for another kiss. His hand lightly brushed a stray locket of hair from my face. He smiled tenderly and planted a final kiss on my lips. Releasing me, he shut the door.

I started the engine and turned down the drive. As I headed toward the street something made me glance into the rear view mirror. Harley was standing in the driveway. He had tucked his hands back into his pockets. The lights from the house cast him in shadow.

The way he stood staring at the back end of my car reminded me of Gatsby standing all alone while his life unraveled in the movie classic, 'The Great Gatsby.'

Chapter Thirteen

In 1976 there was an up and coming Aerosmith cover band called Blacksmith who occasionally went through Lima on their way to bigger cities. Sometimes they rode in a black car with side panel signage that read, 'Mafia hit car' on the passenger side, and 'Blacksmith hit car' on the driver side.

The first row in the parking lot in front of the building housing WOSL radio was reserved for station staff. As I pulled into a space, I saw the black car parked in the visitor section.

"Guess what, Mari?" Hixson said as I entered the office.

I looked around and saw Tyler Jackson lounging on the couch. Tyler was skinny and wild haired. He wore a lot of jewelry from rings on every finger, bracelets, necklaces, and body piercing. "Let me guess. Blacksmith is here?"

"Correction, Tyler Jackson is here. He wants you to interview him," Hixson beamed like the Cheshire cat.

"Why me?" I asked.

"He heard you at the hotel where we're piped in over our new cable agreement. Said something about you having a sexy voice."

"Me?" I squeaked.

"Yes, you," Mike chimed in.

"Hi there, Sugar," Tyler said as he casually looked me up and down. He winked and pointed his finger in a mock pistol shoot.

"Okay, if we're going to do this I need to establish some ground rules."

"Sure thing, Sugar," he rubbed his nose with one hand, while he set his other on my leg.

"Rule number one, you keep your hands to yourself," I said as I plucked his hand from my thigh. "Number two, no drugs during the interview. Finally, don't call me Sugar. My name is Mari, Gypsy Mar to you."

"Ouch!" He complained. "Where's the fun in that?" He flung his hair behind his shoulders. "No Peruvian powder?"

"None."

"Man, you aren't a fucking task master, are you?" Tyler had quite a potty mouth on him.

"Rule number four, no cussing on the radio. The seven words rule if broken can get us fined, FCC license revoked, and shut down."

The seven words rule applied to radio and television. They were all curse words that are rarely heard today in those venues but are common in movies and literature.

"Okay, you're a little uptight."

"Actually," Hixson cut in, "she's right. The seven words of broadcasting really could do us in."

"Okay, man. I'm cool. Shall we do this gig?"

"Ready when you are," I looked at the broadcast light before entering the studio. The light was green, which meant the disc jockey inside was not talking on the air.

"Hi, March," I greeted as he swiveled around in his chair.

"Mari is here to relieve me. Hurray! I can go to the restroom." His jaw dropped open when Tyler Jackson walked in behind me.

"Hey, Tyler Jackson is behind you. Cool, man." He turned back to the board and thumbed on the microphone.

"Gypsy Mar is up next with a very special guest. This is March signing off. Good music, beautiful day, and get high man. Ciao."

I slid into the chair March vacated and cued the Aerosmith song, 'Dream On.' I grabbed the headset and adjusted the microphone.

"This is Gypsy Mar at the top of the hour. You're listening to WOSL radio on the beautiful campus of OSU-Lima."

Tyler sat in the guest chair and crossed one leg over his knee. His hands grasped his leg as though trying to keep still.

I proceeded to read the news and update the weather. "After the commercial break, we have Tyler Jackson of Blacksmith in the studio. So, call in your questions."

I turned the microphone off as 'Dream On' started playing.

"Got a boyfriend?" Tyler asked and winked.

"Yes."

"Care to step out on him? I'm here until tomorrow."

"No." The call line rang just as the commercial ended. I turned the microphone back on. It seemed we were always keying it on and off.

I reached to my right. "You're listening to Gypsy Mar on WOSL. What's your pleasure?"

Tyler took the headset I handed him and put it on. He adjusted the volume. I signaled to him that his mike was live.

"How about 'The Pusher,' Gypsy Mar?" Harley asked. "So, you have Tyler Jackson in there? Need me to come chaperone?"

"It's not necessary, but you know I always love having you in the booth."

"You must be the lover boy," Tyler quipped. "Tell her to go out with me."

"I'll be right down," Harley growled.

During this exchange, the call board lighted up. "Go ahead caller. You're live with Tyler Jackson of Blacksmith."

"What's it like being in a hit band?" The caller was female. "If Gypsy Mar won't go out with you, I will."

I flushed a bright shade of pink. Peg was the caller, and she was hitting on my guest. It was not unusual for her. She always fell for the wrong boys.

"I just might take you up on that. Are you as luscious as Gypsy Mar is?" Tyler smirked at me. "Meet me at the radio station when this interview is over, and we'll see what's what. I'm in the mood for some fun. Who am I kidding?" He laughed. "I'm always up for fun."

"Anytime you want."

"To answer your question, Blacksmith is great. What's not to love? All the sex, drugs and rock and roll you want. Can't get any better than that."

I cued 'The Pusher' on the turntable. I turned down the microphones to let the Steppenwolf song blare over the air.

Shortly after I switched broadcast light from red to green, the door opened and in walked Harley decked out in his black jeans and biker jacket. His helmet dangled from his hand.

"Hi, love," he bent down to kiss me. Straightening up, he gazed at Tyler as though studying him under a microscope. "So you're Tyler Jackson? You don't look so tough."

"That's 'cause I prefer making love instead of fighting, but I can hold my own."

"You make another move on Mari, and we just might have to test that statement." Harley snarled. He looked Tyler up and down, sizing him up like he was a disgusting bug.

"Harley!" I gasped. "What happened to your manners?"

"Flew out the window when he hit on you."

"Eeeyawow!" Tyler screeched his signature scream. "Down boy, I meant no harm. What'd you say your name is?"

"I didn't. It's Harley Davis."

"Cute. Almost like the motorcycle."

"You said it, I didn't," Harley's voice rumbled.

Callers inundated the station during my entire show. I interspersed Blacksmith songs throughout the interview and ended with Blacksmith's rendition of the Aerosmith hit, 'Sweet Emotion.'

"Flash is up next. This is Gypsy Mar signing out. Keep rocking."

Peg met us in the outer office. The four of us left the station together. I assumed Tyler and Peg headed toward his car. I was wrong. He followed us to the lot where the disc jockeys parked. Harley's hog was next to my car.

I unlocked the door and swung it open just as I felt the car dip and bounce back up. Tyler was sitting on the hood.

"Going somewhere?" He grinned and leaned back, his elbows supported his torso.

"Not with you sitting there," I mumbled.

"Give me a kiss, and I'll get off."

"Forget it," I said as I got into my car. Harley came around and entered the passenger side.

"Guess I'm just going to sit here," he moaned and began humming 'Lord of the Thighs.'

"Mari," Peg poked her head through the window. "What are you doing? Don't ruin it for me. I'm supposed to go out with him tonight."

"I'd rethink that Peg. He's just out for sex. He's bad news for you," Harley told her as gently as he could and still get his point across.

"You think so? It'd be so cool to date a rock star."

"It wouldn't be dating him. More like a one night stand," Harley said. "And he's a doper."

"Hey, what're you guys talking about in there? Me?" Tyler sat up and pulled his legs into a butterfly position with one foot tucked under the other.

"Yeah, right. You're our favorite topic of conversation. We talk about you all the time," I laughed. I couldn't believe it. I was growing fond of Tyler!

"Kiss me, Babe, and I'll go quietly."

"Why not just go?" I started the engine.

"Hey! What're you doing? I'm still on this hulk!"

"I suggest you get off this hulk or it's going to take off with you on it," I hollered out the window.

"You wouldn't dare! After the excellent interview, I gave, following all your silly ass rules and all."

So much for developing a fondness for the musician. "Just try me, Mister."

"Oh, oh," Harley grunted, "she called him Mister."

"I just want one tiny kiss," Tyler persisted.

"Nothing is little with you. I give you until the count of three to get off my car or get dumped off it."

"You wouldn't do that," he flicked his hair. "C'mon Gypsy Mar, give me a kiss." He puckered his lips.

"One."

"Better get going, Tyler," Harley muttered.

"Kiss me, babe. I'm just a lonely guy far from home."

"Two."

"It's just a little kiss to remember you by."

"Three."

"Ah, Gypsy Mar, kiss me."

"You were warned." I put my car into reverse and stepped on the gas peddle, sending the vehicle surging backward.

"Mari!" Harley yelled. "What are you doing?" His voice rose an octave in shock.

"Hey! What the f..." He didn't finish his sentence as he slid across the hood.

He scrambled for something to hold onto while shrieking. "You're crazy!"

He flew off the hood like a sheet of paper caught in a crosswind. One of his shoes came off and smacked him in the face. Hitting the grassy area in front of the parking space, he tumbled over a few times before landing on his back. He reached up and wiped his brow with the back of his hand.

"Well, that was a first for me."

"Mari, I hope you didn't hurt him even if he deserved it," Harley mumbled and ran a hand over his face and through his hair.

I put the car in park and got out. "Are you okay?"

"Yeah, just got my skinny ass beat by a chick. What an ego bruiser." He sat up. "No harm, no foul. Teach me not to listen." He turned to Peg, "Ready to party?"

"I changed my mind," Peg giggled, "Man, that was a sight. Tyler Jackson falling over his ass."

"Ouch! My ass hurts." He cried and then shrugged, "Your loss." He picked up his shoe. He rubbed his butt as he limped toward his car.

Chapter Fourteen

"Hey," Harley called out as he entered the radio station. "What are you guys doing this weekend?" Harley perched on the arm of the sofa. "Did you know that car is parked in your spaces again? It's taking up two slots."

"Again?" Hixson groused. "We have to do something about it. Reporting him doesn't get the message across."

"Those spaces are reserved for us, the media," Mike grumbled. "I know what'll teach him a lesson."

"What?" Peg asked.

"What say we block the sucker in?" Mike rubbed his hands gleefully. "No one is supposed to park in that row except us."

"Let's go see if we can do it." Peg stood up and stretched.

Lori manned the broadcast booth while Hixson, Mike, March, Peg, Judy, Harley, and I trooped out to the parking lot. The tan Oldsmobile was sitting in the middle of two spaces. "Figures," Mike groaned. "Professor Brown's car. He's a real prick."

"We can block him in," Harley said. "Pull a vehicle on each side so close he can't squeeze past. Put a car on the back, so he can't get to the trunk and crawl in that way. Should work. Then we all go to Zag's until closing."

"Genius! You are brilliant, my man," Hixson clapped him on the back.

"You are a devil! I like the way you think," Mike crowed.

Within minutes we had positioned our cars and accomplished the goal. The professor was completely blocked in. There was no way he was going to be leaving campus until we got back unless he called for a taxi.

We went back to the station and hung around until Lori's show ended. Then we put the station on a loop like we normally did each night.

"Harley, you mentioned this weekend. Did you have anything in mind?" March took a drag on his joint before stubbing it out in the parking lot of Zag's Pizzeria. We entered and sat at a booth.

"Yeah, what you got in mind, Harley?" Lori asked.

"A weekend get together at my place?"

"For real?" Peg squeaked. "None of us have ever been there, have we, Mari?" she giggled with excitement.

"I have," I said, looking down at my menu. I don't know why I was examining it. I always went along with what the others wanted.

The silence that ensued was uncanny. I looked up to find everyone staring at me, except Harley. He was intently studying the newly painted checkerboard on the orange wall.

"You have?" Mike asked.

"Yes," I answered slowly and put my menu aside. I looked at Harley. He was fidgety and focused on watching the wall, at the napkin holder, at salt and pepper shakers, at anything other than our group.

"No one has ever been there," Hixson said. "When were you there?"

"The night we went to Indiana to visit Wolf Park." Harley finally chimed in. "We stopped by to get a jacket. It's no big deal,"

He didn't mention our Valentine's Day dinner. I wondered why.

"No big deal?" everyone virtually shouted. "You never take anyone there."

"And now I'm inviting everyone over for a weekend." He lightly drummed his hands on the table.

"What kind of house do you have?"

He shrugged, "A regular run of the mill kind of home, I guess."

"Harley," I pulled him aside and whispered, "Are you sure you want to do this? Have them over once, and they'll expect to get together every weekend."

"Maybe it's time, Mari. Time to let everyone in." He looked at me with his lopsided, boyish grin that always won me over and set my heart pounding.

When we arrived back on campus around nine that night, Professor Brown was hopping mad. He had contacted campus security about our stunt. Instead of us getting citations, the officer was giving him one. It turned out each of us had been calling and complaining about him taking our reserved spaces.

"Well, Professor, you'll have to take it up with my superior. The way I see it, these spots are clearly designated for WOSL personnel. They have a decal on their vehicles. I don't see one on yours."

"Give it here," he shouted as he snatched the paper from the officer. "We'll just see about this!" He stormed toward his car. "Are you going to move your junk heaps?"

Each of us got into our vehicles and moved them out of the way. "Saying please will get you more action from us," Harley said.

"Blithering idiots!" The professor flipped his middle finger in our direction as he stomped away.

"Careful, Professor Brown. I don't think you want to get a citation for behavior unbecoming of a college faculty member." The officer flipped his pad open.

"You can do that?" I asked.

"No, but I let him believe it," the cop said.

"What do I know?" I laughed. "I'm just a Frosh."

"As for you folks, I'd be wary of him. Technically I should give each of you citations for causing a traffic jam by blocking his vehicle. I'm not going to because honestly, I'm hoping this ends the parking war. Hopefully, he will park where the professors are supposed to, and you have your space back."

"Thank you, officer."

"Now, go home." He scratched his head and laughed as he walked to his campus security vehicle.

I was the first to arrive Saturday. It was a beautiful sunny day, perfect for getting together with friends. Harley had asked me to come early. He wanted to make certain he had the right drinks, snacks, and a selection of music other than Steppenwolf. I brought my entire radio station set including some Boston, Journey, Aerosmith, KISS, Grateful Dead, Janis Joplin, Creedence Clearwater Revival, America, Bob Seger, and Steely Dan.

"Do I have enough bedrooms?" Harley wondered out loud as he went over the guest list.

"Harley, you live in a mansion. There's only eight of us, nine including you."

"Ten, eleven including me," he corrected. "I invited Thomas to join us."

"Your best friend? Cool. I hope he likes hanging out with disc jockeys."

"I only have five bedrooms!" He sounded panicky. "Eleven of us and only five bedrooms."

"So, some of us can double up."

"Four girls, six guys, seven if you include Garrett." He looked like he was headed for a full blown meltdown. "I have my room, and Garrett has one. Mari! That leaves only three guest rooms! I didn't think this through very well. Both guys and girls will have to double up."

"Relax, it'll get sorted out. Besides, Lori and Hixson are a couple. So are Judy and Mike."

"Oh, man! I forgot about that. Now, what do I do? I can't have mixed couples sharing a room. It wouldn't be proper! "

"Hmm...five rooms for eleven people. March can sleep on your sofa. So can Flash. That leaves Peg, Lori, Judy, Mike, Hixson, Thomas, and me." I counted on my fingers. "Let Lori, Hixson, Judy and Mike sort out their own arrangements. Peg and I can share a room. You and Thomas can stay in your room. Garrett will have his room."

"Sounds like a plan," he sighed with relief. "I don't like the idea of unmarried people sharing a room."

"Harley, I know you believe in chastity, but not everyone is that way. I say let them pair up if they want."

"And you?"

"I'm fine with chasteness." I smiled at his visible relief.

"Okay. I don't like it, but okay. Do you think March and Flash will mind being on the sofa?"

"They'll deal." I rubbed my hand on his back to soothe his attack of nerves.

I guessed wrong on that one. March was all right with sleeping in the living room. He was a laid back person and would have been okay with laying down anywhere as long as he had something for his head and a blanket.

Flash, on the other hand, was an entirely different matter. I never saw a guy pitch such a hissy fit over where he was going to sleep.

"I don't think it's fair we should be asked to share rooms," he complained.

"Get over it, Flash," I said. "We're here to have fun. If you don't like it, you can go home when you get tired. Then come back in the morning."

"But, then I'll miss out on something."

"Take your chances," Mike chimed in.

Thomas, a slim, light brown haired man, looked around the room, bewildered. "You have a problem with sharing rooms?" He had a melodious voice.

"Hey, guys!" Maryanne greeted as she followed Garrett into the main room. "Peg suggested I join you," she said, looking around.

With the addition of Maryanne, there went our sleeping arrangements. We now had twelve people and four, not counting Garrett's room, bedrooms for all of us.

"Do you have a recliner in one of the rooms?" I asked.

"No, but we can move the one from my library if necessary."

"If we can put it into a bedroom, Peg, Maryanne, and I can share. I'll sleep in the chair."

"I am not sleeping on a sofa in the living room. Don't suggest I go home and come back. I live an hour from here," Flash stomped around the room in a tantrum. "I want a private boudoir."

"Oh, stuff it, Flash," Thomas said. "I don't see why you should be treated any different than the rest of us."

"If he didn't have enough space for all of us, he shouldn't have invited the gang over." Flash pouted like a toddler.

"Flash! That's not fair and is uncalled for!" I had had enough of his temperamental fit. He was one sorry, spoiled guy who thought he was better than everyone else.

Harley looked miserably unhappy. Here he had invited folks to a weekend of food, conversation, and relaxation and this pettiness over sleep space were ruining it for him. Fortunately, the rest of the group didn't agree with Flash.

"Get with the program, or go home." Even laid back March was getting impatient with Flash's attitude.

With sleeping arrangements decided upon, Harley and Garrett left to move the recliner into the bigger guest room.

"Look at the view!" Maryanne gazed out the west facing windows at an elaborate garden and gazebo.

"It's gorgeous," Peg joined her. "Mari, you said you'd been here before?" She looked over her shoulder at me.

"Yep."

"How come you never told us?" Judy, depending on her mood could be sullen, silent, judgmental, or inquisitive.

"The first time was on our first date. The second one was Valentine's Day."

"Was he romantic? I bet he was," Lori sighed. Lori was the heaviest of our group and prone to a highly romantic nature that when combined with a bubbly personality made her a hit in any group.

"Was he ever," I grinned at the memory of Harley's kitchen disaster, and our subsequent take-out Chinese dinner. "He's a gentleman all the way."

"Hey, guys," March sat on the floor thumbing through albums. "Let's fire up this stereo and get some music going."

"He's got some Porter Wagoner. 'Green, Green Grass of Home' is one of my granddad's favorites," Thomas pulled it out of the white sleeve and placed the album on the turntable.

"Here's some old Johnny Cash, 'Folsom Prison Blues' and 'Daddy Sang Bass.' I didn't know he liked Country music." Thomas held up the album.

"There's a lot you guys don't know about him," I muttered. "There's more to his taste in music than Steppenwolf. Did you know he loves Tchaikovsky, Chopin, Aaron Copland, Schubert, or Hungarian gypsy music?"

"He does?" Lori squealed. "I love them too! I knew he was a romantic," she sighed. She almost sounded like a rock band's groupie.

Garrett and Harley returned looking perturbed. "It appears the largest guest room has a narrower door. We couldn't get the recliner in," Harley announced.

"Did you stand it upright?" Hixson asked.

"Take off the back," Thomas suggested.

"We tried everything. It just won't fit. So, Thomas, you and I are going to sleep down here in the recliners."

"That's a good idea, Harley!" Flash enthused. "I can have your room."

"No, Mari will sleep in my room." Harley frowned at him.

"I can't do that, Harley!" I said with dismay at the thought of displacing him.

"Yes, you can, Mari. It's only fair. A gentleman always places the comfort of his lady ahead of his own."

"How archaic," Flash grumbled.

"Get over it," Hixson's voice came out in a snarl worthy of any rabid dog. "He's right. He can pick anyone he wants to use his bedroom. It is his room and his house. He was generous enough to invite us all here."

Hixson had this natural leadership quality that had everyone listening to him. "The sleeping issue is now settled. Anyone who doesn't like it is free to go home. I'm here for a weekend of good fun, relaxation, and company."

"Oh, all right," Flash grudgingly agreed. He looked crestfallen and sad.

A hidden part of me was excited at the thought of spending the night in Harley's bed. I was sorry he wouldn't be in there sharing it with me. At least his scent would surround and comfort me in his king-sized bed.

I was shocked at the unladylike feelings and graphic visions of Harley laying beside me that was running through my head. I had never experienced those before. I had no carnal knowledge, preferring to keep myself pure for marriage. Harley, on the other hand, did have experience and had decided a vow of chastity until marriage was more in keeping with his values.

Glimpses of his bare chest from the time he changed shirts on the street the night of the Steppenwolf concert ran rampant in my mind. The sight of his sculpted muscles and how they rippled when he pulled the shirt over his head sent shivers down my spine. I could picture him lying stretched out on the bed wearing only his pajama bottoms.

Then I remembered helping him undress when he was ill that night. Even then, he looked sexy as all get out. I was having the most improper images of him. He would be ashamed of me if he knew what was in my head at the moment. How unchaste of me! I could feel my face reddening.

Chapter Fifteen

With the sleeping arrangements finally sorted out and a variety of music playing, we grabbed some drinks.

"Would you like a tour?" Harley asked and set off on a grand tour of the mansion.

The first stop on our grand tour was his breathtaking library located next to the living room. It spanned two floors. The windows also reached the second floor and looked out at the gardens and gazebo.

The walls were constructed of cherry wood. In the center of one wall was an enormous, elaborate fireplace with a plush rug centered in front of it. Comfortable chairs, Ottomans, and sofas ringed the woven mat. A crystal coffee table and four end tables completed the sitting area.

Mahogany bookcases went all the way to the ceiling. Midway up there was a walkway along the shelves. Rolling ladders reached from the floor up. Positioned near the shelves were recliners with green Tiffany lamps. Everything was polished to a high sheen; even the brass fire poker gleamed brightly. It all pointed to wealth and a love of literature from the Harvard Classics, history, the sciences to modern horror, romance, and science fiction. It was all there.

"Oh, wow!" Maryanne moaned in ecstasy. "I could live in this room."

Beside the library was the music room. Heavy burgundy drapes adorned the windows creating a muted acoustic effect. Once again, comfortable chairs were scattered throughout shelves of albums and sheet music.

A turntable sat in one corner. The speakers were strategically placed around the room causing a surround sound effect. In the center of the chamber were a Baldwin grand piano and a baroque harpsichord.

"The harpsichord is handmade and Flemish in design," Garrett gently ran his fingers over the keys. "The sound is much lighter than you hear from a piano. It is our newest addition."

"What does something like this cost?" Mike asked.

"Around ten thousand dollars," Harley spoke up.

I almost choked, "Ten thousand?"

"Yep. I imported the harpsichord from Europe."

"Geez, must be nice to have that kind of money laying around," Flash commented.

Harley shrugged. "Anything is possible if you work hard and save for it."

"Yeah, but you come from money," Flash said. He appeared to be trying to goad Harley into a confrontation.

"Don't go there," I warned him.

"It's okay, Mari. He can't hurt me."

"It's not fair how he's treating you," I hissed.

"He's jealous," Harley whispered.

"The violin is also handmade and imported from Germany," Garrett continued.

Next to the violin was a guitar and a flute. "Don't tell me you play all these?" Lori said. "I played the flute in high school."

"Only the piano and the violin," Harley grinned. "The harpsichord is Garrett's passion. Thomas plays the guitar. He brought it over last night. My Mom is the flutist. She likes to show us her latest compositions when she visits."

"You let your Mom visit?" Flash sneered. "What are you, a mama's boy?"

"Enough, Flash!" Hixson bellowed, his hands clenched into fists. "What's with you always picking on Harley? He's always come through for WOSL. He even backed up your request to do a classical show on a progressive rock station."

"So? Mari does an oldies show."

"Yeah, but the bands she plays was progressive rock back in their day," Mike chimed in. "Nothing remotely progressive rock about classical music."

"That's not entirely fair, Mike," Harley spoke up. "Back when classical music was the norm, composers such as Beethoven and Chopin were ahead of others in that grouping. Therefore they were progressive."

Mike admitted after a lengthy pause to consider Harley's comments. "Never thought of it that way."

We left the music room and continued our tour. The next room was a family game room. It was directly across the grand entry from the living room. It was furnished with teak wood tables holding a chess board, checker set, and jigsaw puzzles. There was even a section for board games such as Monopoly and the Game of Life. A tennis table took up one corner, and a billiard table sat across the room from it. Lining one wall was a bank of pinball machines.

"My kind of place," Peg crowed. "I love games."

"Watch out for Mari, Peg. She's a pinball wizard," Harley smirked. He had taken me to a pinball competition in Ada a few weeks ago. I slaughtered the other players. The prize for first place was a hundred dollars.

"We'll have to see about that," she pointed her finger at me. "I challenge you to a game tonight."

"Accepted." I was always up for a good pinball game.

"Don't say I didn't warn you," Harley smirked.

"Anyone play chess?" Flash asked.

"I play chess," March said much to everyone's surprise. "Want to play later?"

"I'll slaughter you."

"We'll see about that," March said in his most lackadaisical manner.

"Harley," Maryanne hesitated, "may I read in the library?"

"Sure, pick any books you want. If you don't finish this weekend, you can borrow them."

"Thank you!" She hopped and clapped her hands joyously. On impulse, she wrapped her arms around him and planted a huge kiss on his lips much to his consternation.

"Uh, Maryanne?" He tried valiantly to untangle himself from her grip. "I don't want to die this weekend over some books. March looks like he wants to murder me."

"March?" She looked around bewildered. "Why would he do that?"

March shrugged his shoulders in a muscle limbering movement similar to Tai Chi. "Really, Maryanne? We've only been dating a couple of months."

"Dating?" Her face turned a lovely shade of pink. "I thought we were...oh, dear! Those were dates, weren't they?"

"Will one of you girls please explain to our dear innocent Maryanne what a date is?" He grumbled good-naturedly.

"Sure thing, March," Judy replied and gently pulled Maryanne away from Harley.

As we continued our tour, Mike dropped behind. Something had caught his attention.

We entered the formal dining area. "We'll eat in here," Harley looked at each guest as though expecting rejection.

"Cool," Thomas said as he rubbed his hands together, "I always wondered what it'd be like to eat in here."

I smiled to myself as once again memories of Valentine's Day dinner ran through my head.

"From the smile on Mari's face, I'd guess she has had a meal in here," Lori grinned wickedly at me and winked.

Harley shot me a panicked glance and shook his head slightly.

"That's for me to know," I arched my eyebrow and shrugged.

Harley sighed with relief. I wondered why he wanted the details of that special day kept a secret. He had mentioned me being here earlier. Then I realized, it was our special day. I felt tingly inside with the knowledge that we had a day shared only with Garrett.

Everyone was suitably impressed with the kitchen. Flash kept wandering around the room touching each appliance. "You could run a restaurant from here." He whirled around, "do we get to cook?"

"If you wish, or Garrett can whip up our meals," Harley studied him carefully.

"Let's do the cooking! It'll be fun! What will we have?"

"I have some steaks in the fridge for tonight. We can grill them and some veggies. Throw in baked potatoes and a tossed salad to round it out."

"Far out!" March peeped. "Flash is going to poison us," he smirked.

"Hey, know what we should do?" Lori laughed. "Let's let the guys cook tonight. We'll clean up. Tomorrow we'll trade."

"I think they're getting the better end of that deal," I groaned, remembering the cleaning Harley, Garrett, and I did after Harley's cooking disaster. "This should be interesting."

"Hey, guys, anyone checked out the bathrooms in this place?" Mike entered, rubbing his hands together. "They are miniature palaces."

"No, way!" Flash was beside himself.

Everyone trooped out to take a gander at the palatial restrooms. I hung back and stopped Harley before he could join them.

"Harley?"

"Hmm?" He shoved his left hand into his pants pocket.

"Do you get the impression Flash came from a poor family?"

"If you mean, poverty-stricken, yeah I do."

"Then, let him enjoy having a private room. I don't mind sleeping in the living room."

"Mari," he began.

I hushed him by putting a finger to his lips. "I know he comes from a large family. He's probably never had a room to himself. Let him have yours this weekend. Give him that."

Harley sighed, "okay. I'll have Garrett get a mattress for you to use."

"No, you won't. There's nothing wrong with me sleeping in a recliner or on the rug."

"You win," a smile lighted up his face. "I knew you were an angel." He kissed the tip of my nose.

"Huh! A lot you know." I grinned. "Now, let's go tell Flash privately."

"You got it, girl."

We caught up to the gang standing outside Harley's room.

"You can take a peek if you want," Harley ushered them inside.

His room was gigantic. A thick, plush, king-sized bed adorned one wall. It faced the fireplace. Windows graced each side of the fireplace giving him a perfect view of the backyard gardens. A mahogany dresser sat along another wall. A brown leather recliner sat in one corner. The entire room was decked out in tastefully dark colors befitting a biker.

His bathroom had chrome fixtures. His tub was a step down into it whirlpool. He had a walk in shower with massaging jets. Stepping from the bathroom, you entered a dressing area with a large closet.

"Flash, may I speak with you a minute?" Harley asked.

"What?"

"Mari and I were thinking, you might like to stay in my room."

"Don't tease me, man!" Flash snapped.

"No teasing. It just seems like you'd appreciate some time to yourself. Mari says you come from a large family."

"I'm the oldest of eight kids. No one has their own room."

"Then, by all means, use mine."

"You really mean it?"

"I do," Harley smiled gently.

"It's not out of pity?"

"Not my style, my man. No worries. I won't tell anyone about this conversation other than to say you persuaded me." Harley clapped him on the back.

Relief showered Flash's face. "Thanks, Harley. You're a decent man."

They both looked like Christmas had come early. Harley was happy because he did a pleasant thing for a fellow human being. Flash was pleased. He would finally have a little privacy even if it were only for a night.

Chapter Sixteen

It turned out Flash was a decent cook. The steaks, veggies, and potatoes came out perfectly. He used home ground flour to make two dozen rolls. We tossed the salad with a raspberry vinaigrette dressing. He had everything timed to be ready at the same time.

We happily took platters of food and put them on the sideboard so we could get seconds if we chose. Flash even made brownies for dessert. We put plates, silverware, glasses, and napkins on the dining table. Each of us took a seat.

"If you don't mind," Harley said, "I'd like to offer a blessing before we eat."

"Okay," Judy replied as she looked at the food on the sideboard. She licked her lips in anticipation of eating the tantalizing food.

"Let's take hands," Harley grasped my hand and reached for Judy's on his other side.

Each person held the hands of the people on their sides. One by one we bowed our heads. I closed my eyes and waited for the prayer.

"Our heavenly Father," Harley bowed his head. "We thank you for all our blessings. We are grateful to the folks who grew the food, for the animals who gave their lives for our consumption, and for the people responsible for getting the food to us. We offer gratitude for the bounty we have that nourishes our bodies. Bless us, Father, as we enjoy a pleasant weekend with friends. In the name of our heavenly Father, amen."

"Amen," each of us said in response.

One by one we picked up our plate and went to the buffet spread. Soon plates were piled high. An assortment of drinks was available including herbal tea, Coke, Ginger Ale, Root Beer, lemon water, Nehi's, Orange Crush, and Dr. Pepper.

"I never thought I'd be sharing a meal in such a grand room," Lori said as she looked around and noticed the glass chandelier overhead. "You have such a lovely home, Harley."

"Thank you. It's a bit big for me, but my family likes it." He smiled and buttered a roll. Biting into it, he closed his eyes and moaned with appreciation. "Excellent rolls, Flash."

Garrett sat on Harley's left side and spread peach marmalade on his roll. "They are good," he agreed. "Better than mine."

Flash relaxed and grinned. He basked in the glory of his delicious meal. "Thank you. I'm glad you like them. I made them from scratch."

"Flash, how did you know how to cook our steaks? Mine is medium rare, just the way I like it," Hixson said, cutting into his meat with gusto.

"I just made some rare, some medium and the rest well done. I figured with a group our size; we're bound to have something for each person."

"You did good," Mike said as he dug into his salad, reveling in the satisfying crunch of the lettuce and raw vegetables.

"Let's play some Steppenwolf," March suggested. He rose and went into the living room where he put on 'Slow Flux.'

When March returned to the dining room, Harley tilted his head back and howled. Soon all the guys were doing their best wolf imitations. They sounded horrible, and the girls couldn't help but laugh. The howls goaded the men into trying to outdo their terrible impersonations of wolves.

"Guys! Guys! Please stop!" Lori giggled, covering her ears with her hands. "My poor ears. I'm going to go deaf!"

After dinner, we made our way back to the kitchen to clean up. Bob Seger's 'Beautiful Loser,' blared over the speaker system. With dishes washed, the dining room cleared, and the kitchen cleaned we headed back to the game room.

By now Journey was blasting over the stereo. Feeling good, we each picked our games with Flash and March setting up the chess set for a match. Maryanne headed to the library. Peg and I wandered over to the pinball machine. The rest sat in the chairs to watch the gamers.

"Ready to be beaten?" Peg asked and bumped me with her hip.

"Bring it on, loser girl," I laughed and bumped her back.

"You just wait and see," Harley came up behind me and placed a kiss on my cheek. "Mari's going to kill her on the pinball game."

Our pinball tournament began with a coin toss. Hixson flipped a quarter into the air.

"I call heads," Peg said excitedly.

"Heads, it is," Hixson said as he looked at the coin on his arm. "Peg goes first."

"Yippee!" She screamed and grabbed the knobs on the machine.

Game after game I scored the highest points. Finally, Peg gave up.

"Man, you are good!" she groaned. "Hey, let's all play Monopoly."

Mike, Hixson, Harley, Judy, Lori, Peg, Thomas, and I gathered around a table and picked out our game pieces. Garrett had gone to his room, Flash and March still played chess, and Maryanne was still ensconced in the library.

Creedence Clearwater Revival's album 'Willy and the Poorboys' was playing with 'Cosmos Factory' cued next. I looked around the room at everyone. I had never seen all of us looking comfortable and having a great time. Most of the time, even though we looked relaxed, we had an air about us that said we were disc jockeys and were serious about our work.

Music was our mantle, and we made sure to keep abreast of the changes in styles, and bands. It was how we remained popular and progressive. Music is a cut throat industry. Not even radio stations were immune.

We played board games late into the night. Occasionally we heard chortling coming from the library as Maryanne immersed herself in the vast variety of books Harley owned. Eventually, the night came to an end with everyone retiring to their respective area.

March picked one sofa, Thomas the other, leaving a recliner for Harley and one for me. I don't like sleeping in recliners, so I planned to sleep on the rug. Harley had other ideas. He insisted on dragging in an air mattress.

"Truly, Harley, I'm okay with the rug. I don't need a mattress." I placed my hand on his forearm.

"I want you to be comfortable, Mari," Harley said earnestly.

"I will be. I liked camping out and sleeping on the ground. The rug will be just fine," I assured Harley.

"Okay, rug it is then." He let the air out of the mattress and folded it back up before leaving to put it away.

"And Mari wins this go round!" March punched the air with his fist while Thomas looked on in amusement.

Harley and I left to get pillows and blankets for the four of us. "Mari, you are one fantastic girl," Harley handed me the covers. "I'm so glad I found you. Now, you're part of my life. You make me happy."

"Aw, shucks, Harley. You make it easy. I'm the lucky one." I blushed with pleasure.

"I'm the lucky one," he replied as he looked at the linens and assorted bedding.

"No, I am," I laughed and stuck my tongue out at him.

"Here we go again," he groaned good-naturedly. He grabbed six pillows and piled two of them on top of the blankets. He then took them from me and pointed to the remaining pillows. "Grab those, please."

We returned to the living room to find the guys had changed into their sleepwear. They had lighted a fire in the hearth. Late spring evening temperatures in Lima can be a chilly 50 degrees.

Harley and I left to change into ours. He knocked on the door to his room. Flash answered, "yes?"

"I'm sorry. I just need to change for the night," Harley said and entered when Flash stepped aside.

I went upstairs to the room Peg and Maryanne shared to change and brush my teeth. I spent a few minutes brushing my hair to a high sheen. "Good night, guys," I called as I left the room.

When I came out, Harley was waiting for me. He held a plush robe and handed it to me. "This might be more comfortable for you."

I lifted an eyebrow at him, and he blushed. "Okay, I admit it. I'd be more comfortable if you wore it around the guys. You know, they'd be leering at you," he smiled shyly.

"No problem. If it makes you feel better, so do I." I had on pajamas with matching top, bottom, and slippers. There was nothing immodest here. I pulled on the bathrobe. It smelled of Irish Spring, and I reveled in the scent. The garment was sinfully soft and warm.

We settled into our spaces. Sleep was hard to come by with three guys in the room. March and Thomas whispered about the events of the day. It was though they were too wired to sleep.

Harley shifted in the recliner and looked down at me. "I can't sleep either. Mind if I sit with you for awhile?"

"Come on down," I patted a spot beside me.

He slid down, and we sat watching the flames dancing in the hearth. He draped an arm around me. I felt comfortable and secure. I rested my head on his shoulder.

"I love watching the flames in the hearth," he murmured. "It's comforting. The way the flames ebb and flow makes me think of gypsies dancing at night."

I closed my eyes and envisioned the scene he described. It was beautiful. I could see the multi-colored dresses swaying as the women danced. The shirts worn by the men billowed as they joined the women twirling around the flames.

We sat silently enjoying the night and the just sitting together. The flames from the fireplace had a hypnotic effect; mesmerizing as they waltzed around the log. At some point, we drifted off to dreamland sitting side by side.

A few hours later I woke up to the haunting strains of a violin. The music evoked feelings of joy that slid into a lilting melancholy as happiness gave way to longing and desire. It lifted, swelled, softened, and quieted in elegance as old as time bringing out a sense of nostalgia, love, foreboding and all the emotions of life fully lived.

I crept down the hall and looked in the doorway of the music room. The drapes were open and provided just enough light to see Harley standing in the moonlight. The shadows cast him in an eerie light making him appear ghost-like as though he stood in a nether land of gypsy magic.

He held a violin firmly with the base tucked under his chin. He closed his eyes as he played. His body swayed to the soft strains emanating from the instrument.

It was the most beautiful sound I had ever heard with just a hint of sadness. The music was pure brilliance sending a cascade of images and sounds to match the lyrical emotions of the song. I could picture a lonely man his wolf head hiking stick swinging from his hand as he walked the grounds of his fog-shrouded estate.

Chapter Seventeen

The next morning we were awakened to the fabulous smells of pancakes, sausage, eggs, fried potatoes, and coffee wafting from the kitchen. Harley ambled into the kitchen to find Flash hard at work cooking. I began pulling out fruit to slice.

"Good morning, Flash," he greeted. He opened the fridge, pulled out a pitcher of orange juice, and another containing apple juice. "Need any help?"

"Nope. I got this. Anyone want an omelet, or will scrambled eggs do?"

"I think scrambled will be just fine," Harley yawned. "How'd you sleep?"

"Like a baby." Flash sopped bread slices in an egg batter to make French Toast. "Mari, can you hand me the cinnamon sugar?"

"Here ya go," I tossed him the container. I took a cantaloupe to the sink and scrubbed it clean.

Lori came in. "I thought the girls were supposed to cook this morning."

"I got this," Flash smiled. He appeared to genuinely enjoy cooking.

"Good. I hate making breakfast." She pulled out bagels and placed them on a platter along with assorted jams and jellies.

I sliced apples, oranges, cantaloupe, melon, grapes, and peaches on another plate.

The others straggled in and gathered dishes, utensils, napkins and food to take into the dining room. March went back into the living room and put on the Carpenter's '(They Long to be) Close to You.' The album was softly romantic and fit the mood of the group.

Once we were in the dining room everyone stared at the spread Flash had put out. Not only were there pancakes, eggs, sausage,

French toast, fruit, potatoes, and bagels. He had baked an assortment of goodies including blackberry muffins, poppy seed cakes, cream cheese Danishes, and biscuits.

"Dang, Flash," March said. "Forget about radio. You should open a restaurant. We'll all come work for you."

"And eat up all the profits?" Flash beamed happily.

Flash was in his element and basking in the compliments. I wondered if he was ever thanked or praised at home. I caught a glance at Harley. He sat with his fingers pressed together as though contemplating Flash's culinary skills.

"Coffee, Harley?" Mike asked as he went around the room pouring the hot beverage.

"None for me. I got it for you guys." Harley poured a glass of orange juice.

"You don't drink coffee?"

"Nope. No hot caffeinated beverages for me other than an occasional herbal tea," Harley popped a grape into his mouth.

"Oh man!" Mike said, "You don't smoke dope, do drugs, drink alcohol or coffee. What do you do to get high?"

"Live life to the fullest," he shrugged. "Take a walk in the forest and listen to the songs of nature."

"You get off on that stuff?" Mike asked.

"Why not?" March said, "I think it's great. I like nature too. There's something mystical about being in the wilderness."

"I agree," Harley cut into his sausage. "I love strolling the beaches, hiking in the mountains, watching wildlife and finding herbal plants."

"I like rock climbing," I added only to have everyone turn and stare at me.

"Rock climbing? Like mountains?" Judy asked.

"No, rocks. I love climbing rocks."

"With safety equipment, right?" Thomas joined in.

"No. I just use my fingers, hands, elbows, feet, and toes. No gear. I climbed Longs Peak and Castle Rock in Colorado and a section of Mount Saint Helens in Washington State."

"You are crazy!" Peg laughed. She put on 'I'm Movin' On,' by John Kay.

Harley looked at me like he might be in agreement with Peg's assessment. "You really did that?"

"Yes," I squirmed uncomfortably under his unwavering gaze. "What? You ride motorcycles!"

"Yeah, but there's one big difference. I use a safety helmet, and I don't have any possibility of falling hundreds of feet."

"You do if you're riding in the mountains," I replied. I didn't understand why I suddenly felt like my hobby was under attack.

"Mari," Harley lifted his hands in a placating gesture. "I'm not saying you shouldn't go rock climbing. In fact, I'd love to learn how to do it myself. I'm just saying you should use safety equipment."

"Like a harness, crampons, Alpine helmet, carabiners and rope. There's no real challenge in that. I'd use them if I were climbing mountains instead of rocks."

"I can't wrap my head around you being a rock climber," March shook his shaggy head. "Whoa! That's like major muscle use." He pumped his arm and squeezed his biceps.

"Don't think you'll make it as a climber, March," Maryanne chortled.

The Carpenters gave way to Moby Grape on the stereo. Hixson sat back in his chair and rapped his hands on the table to the beat of '69' followed by 'Grape Jam,' and 'Wow.'

"This is the life," Hixson sighed with contentment. "Good friends, good food, and great music. What can be better than this weekend?"

"So, what's the plan for today?" Lori asked. "How about a picnic on the grounds?"

"Anyone got a football?" Thomas asked.

"I've got a pool out back," Harley offered.

"We didn't bring our swimwear," Judy wailed.

"You have shorts and a T-shirt, right?" I asked.

"Yeah. Hey! We'll wear shorts in the pool!" Thomas grinned.

"Can we still have a picnic?" Lori sounded disappointed.

"I don't see why not," Harley piled more grapes on his plate. "I have a grill and picnic tables by the pool."

"We'll have hotdogs, hamburgers, chips and stuff." Judy loved junk food. "And more of Flash's brownies."

Soon we were all lounging by the pool. Those of us who went into the water played a rowdy game of Marco Polo. I sat on Harley's shoulders and energetically tried to knock Maryanne off March. Thomas carried Peg, who did her best to dunk me into the water.

Garrett busied himself showing Flash how to work the grill. Hixson and Mike talked about expanding the radio station. Judy and Lori lounged on the chairs and took turns doing their nails.

It was the perfect way to end a weekend that started out ugly but became filled with fun and companionship. Everyone agreed they'd like to do it again, and often. Harley glowed with joy. I think each of us came away with more insight and we came together into a cohesive unit that could only benefit WOSL. We were now an actual team.

Chapter Eighteen

"Let's go see a movie," I said as I climbed on the back of his hog. Little did I know June 7th, was about to become a milestone for us as a couple and the most memorable evening for me. "Dinner and a show."

"Dinner and a movie, it is," Harley said as he started the hog.

He sped through town and pulled into the parking lot of the Ponderosa Steak House. It was near the mall and the movie theater. The Ponderosa Steak House was decorated in the traditional western style. The walls were constructed of highly polished knotty pine. Lassos, and saddles interspersed with paintings of cowboys, and Native Americans adorned one wall. The opposite wall was decorated with rifles, deer heads, and stuffed Trout or Bass. The western theme continued with wood tables, longhorn steer antlers, spurs, paintings of horses and tons of silver jewelry.

"What'll ya have, handsome," the waitress chewed gum and pulled out a pencil.

"I'll have the prime rib, medium rare, a baked potato all the way, creamed corn, and corn bread." Harley closed his menu and handed it back to the waitress.

"And you, Miss?"

"I'll have the same, except substitute a side salad for the creamed corn, and Ranch dressing."

"Drinks?" the waitress asked as she scribbled our orders onto a notepad.

"A Coke," I replied.

"You have any Ginger Ale?" Harley asked.

"Nope. Tea, coffee, Coke, Orange Crush, Mountain Dew, and root beer."

"Make mine a root beer," Harley sighed.

After she had left, Harley leaned over the table and winked at me. "I have something to show you."

"What?" I busied myself with placing my flatware on the table and the napkin in my lap.

Harley didn't answer me. He fidgeted with his flatware, putting each item in a specific order. Then he aligned his water glass with the position of his spoon and fork. Reaching up Harley undid the top button of his shirt. He tugged at the neckline as though he was choking.

"Harley?" I looked at him with concern. It was uncharacteristic of him to exhibit this much nervousness.

"Hmm. . ? Give me a minute," he mumbled.

He rubbed his hands along his jeans and then grabbed his napkin. He dabbed his forehead and wiped his mouth. I couldn't figure out what was making him so nervous.

"Harley, are you okay?"

He looked up at me. He took a deep breath and suddenly the twinkle in his eyes was back. "Sorry," he said sheepishly, a smile crept across his face.

Harley reached into his jacket and pulled out a box. He stared at the box, turning it over in his hands for two or three minutes. With a melodramatic flourish, Harley placed it on the table and scooted it toward me. He peered intently at me, glancing periodically at the table and then back at me. It was as though he was expecting something from me.

I stared at the black and silver jewelry case and asked, "What's this?" now I was the one getting nervous.

The box was simple but elegant. The black wood and inlaid silver only heightened the beauty. It looked old world. The silver swirled in the curls carved into the wood.

"A case for jewelry, silly," Harley smiled, slipped out of his chair, and dropped to one knee.

"Oh, no!" I whispered as shock coursed through me. I felt a tingling sensation starting from the top of my head down to my toes.

"Mari," he reached out and grasped my hand. "You are the most amazing woman I know. I fell in love with you the moment I saw you during orientation." He gently placed his lips on the back of my hand.

He reached up and brushed a stray lock of hair from my face. "Every day, every hour, minute, and second I spend with you only enhances those feelings."

He gazed earnestly into my eyes. "When I see you sitting with friends or all alone with your sketch pad and notebook, I just want to sweep you off your feet and take you away from here." He kissed my hand again.

"I want to leave this world behind and travel to far away places with you." He fumbled with the box. "I want to share the adventure of a lifetime with you, Mari."

I dabbed at my eyes with my napkin. "I want that too, Harley. I want to see the world with you."

"I want you always by my side, forever together. We'll ride my hog seeing the country. We'll expand my business. We'll have a home and all the love and joy in the world."

Harley opened the case. "Mari, will you do the honor of being my partner, my lifelong mate, my wife, my love?"

Nestled inside the box was the most exquisite and unembellished ring I had ever seen. It was not the typical engagement ring. The band was silver karat; the stone shaped like a diamond was a black opal with pink, blue and large green patches. It was the most gorgeous ring I had ever seen.

"I had it designed specifically with you in mind."

My throat closed up, and tears sprang to my eyes. I couldn't speak. I raised a trembling hand to my face and futilely wiped at the tears coursing down my cheeks.

"Are you okay?" he asked, a frown creeping across his handsome face. He looked anxious.

"You don't have to answer me right away. Take your time." He shrugged as though his proposal was just a thought, but I knew better.

I hurt this fabulous, gorgeous man by not giving him an answer. "It's not that. "It's not that. I don't need time. I just didn't expect this so soon."

How anyone could deny him, I didn't understand. He once told me someone had hurt him emotionally in the past. A person as sweet and good as Harley always got stepped on by someone.

These people might be a gold digger or a predator and always homed in on the good ones intent upon getting everything they could. Harley was no exception. How many times had someone played up to his generous spirit and left him empty handed, I wondered? Still, he managed to find some redeeming bit of goodness in them.

I vowed I would never cause him heartfelt pain. I'd always love him. I gulped air and took the plunge, "Harley, you are my heart. You are in my soul. I can not picture life without you. You have come to mean the world to me." I looked him straight in the eyes. "I'd love to marry you."

"But?" he prompted. He held his breath as through afraid of what I might say. "There's a but, isn't there?" He looked scared of my response.

"No buts. My answer is yes. I will marry you." I was scared to death of the commitment so soon after meeting him. I remember how he made me smile. He had come to mean so much to me; I dreamed about him at night. I dreamed about this very moment. There was no way I was going to let my fear get in the way of a lifetime of happiness with this man.

The whoop he screamed could have drowned a jet breaking the sound barrier. He grabbed me, hauling me out of my chair, and swung me around in the air. The people dining in the restaurant broke out in a raucous round of applause.

"Do you like the ring? If not, we can get something different," he said shyly.

"I love it!" I laughed. "It's the most beautiful thing I've ever been given."

"Whew!" he sighed. "I had it designed for you. It took me awhile to get it just right."

'A Star is Born' was playing at the movie theater. Being a Kris Kristofferson fan, we went to see it. Harley sprung for a bucket of buttered popcorn, whoppers for me, Twizzlers for himself and two large 7 Up sodas.

"Let's sit in the back," he suggested. The theater was semi-dark as previews of upcoming movies played across the giant screen. He had to carefully balance the popcorn and drinks so they wouldn't spill. Each soda had a straw in the cup.

"Why? So we can make out?" I winked at him.

Even in the dim lighting, I could see him turn a lovely shade of red before sputtering, "Mari!"

He took a huge gulp of his drink and choked. "No! We can sit back there and talk, or throw popcorn at the screen if the movie sucks."

"Really?" I rolled my eyes. "You do that sort of thing?" Somehow I couldn't quite picture him tossing popped corn at the screen, even though I knew full well his penchant for playing pranks.

We settled on some seats in the balcony. I looked around and noticed we were the only ones sitting there.

"Hey, gotta get some kicks sometimes. Being a good boy gets hard on a biker, Steppenwolf fanatic, you know." He wiggled his eyebrows at me.

"No, really? I always thought you were a rough, tough, bad boy biker. Mister Gentleman was just your alter ego," I chided.

We looked at each other and burst into laughter. "You so get me, Mari. You and I are meant for each other." He smiled and took my hand in his.

I leaned over and rested my head on his shoulder. Harley felt comforting. He made me feel safe and loved. The warmth emanating from him made me tingle. Glancing at the ring on my finger brought tears to my eyes. How did I get so fortunate to land a man like him?

"Harley, can I ask you a question?"

"Of course," he said.

"I have the feeling someone has hurt you in the past." I looked at him and watched as he frowned.

"Yes, I was hurt in the past." His voice grew tense. "At the time I thought I cared very much for her."

"What happened?"

"I was pressured into asking Ashley Vickman to marry me. I was young and foolish. I gave in. She threw my proposal into my face."

"I see," I said sadly. So, I wasn't the first girl he'd proposed marriage.

"Mari," he looked at me. "I didn't love her. I realized later that I never loved her. I love you. You are the girl of my dreams."

"Tonight is perfect," my voice hitched. My heart soared at hearing Harley's words. He never loved Ashley Vickman. He did love me.

"Mari?"

"Hmm?"

"Are you okay?" Concern filled his voice.

I looked up to see him staring at me. His gaze was filled with tenderness.

"I'm fine," I sniffled. "Just wondering how I got so lucky to have you." I knew I'd be dreaming about a future with him at my side tonight.

"I'm the lucky one," he growled softly into my ear. "I have you," his voice came out in a husky whisper. "I love you."

"I love you, too." I grinned at him. "I will always love you, Harley. Nothing will ever come between us."

"You are my heart," Harley replied. He lightly kissed me on the top of my head, taking a long whiff of my lemon scented hair.

Chapter Nineteen

"For the record, this meeting is convened on June 8, 1976, at four o'clock. The purpose of this session," Hixson began, "is to address a shortcoming we have toward progressing with our FCC station license and tower. Currently only Flash holds a first class license. Both Mike and I are planning to get ours."

Harley entered the meeting room and listened. He leaned against the wall with his arms crossing his chest. Only Harley could look so debonair in blue jeans, and chambray work shirt.

"The rest of you need to either get or renew your third class licenses. There is a Colem testing facility near Detroit. They are having exams in three weeks on a Saturday. We need to go and get this done," Hixson continued. "Afterward there's a Bob Seger concert in Pontiac, about thirty minutes northwest of Detroit. We should have time for a quick burger before the show. I'm told as DJs we can have tickets placed on hold for us. I suggest we get hotel rooms in Pontiac. After the concert, we can hit our rooms and leave Sunday morning."

"I have a couple of vehicles that will hold everyone," Harley piped up as he walked over to me and kissed the top of my head. His hands gently massaged my shoulders. It felt heavenly.

"Perfect. The station will pay for gas and hotel rooms. We'll get one for the guys and one for the girls." Hixson pumped his fist into the air.

"We'll need two for the guys. There are six guys and four girls. That makes at least three or four rooms."

"Yeah, okay," Mike said. "Unless the girls want to share with us, guys." He winked saucily.

"Grr..." Harley growled. "Not going to happen."

"It happened at your place," Mike grinned slyly.

"Ok, so it did," Harley admitted. "You, Hixson, Judy, and Lori can share a room. Flash and Garrett can share. Peg and Mari can take one, and that leaves March and me together. Four rooms."

"Prude," Mike joked.

"That's me. Prude and proud of it," Harley grunted.

"Why Garrett?" Hixson asked.

"He's a licensed chauffeur. He'll drive. If we need a second vehicle, I'll drive it."

"Okay," Hixson glanced at his notes. "Looks like that is settled. We'll leave around noon the Friday before the exam. Everyone is responsible for their meals and concert ticket cost. I'll let you know in a few days what that amount will be." He looked at me. "Mari, do you have a sales report?"

"We surpassed our advertising goals by five hundred dollars for the month. I expect sales will be down during the summer as we go into reduced broadcasting hours. So the surplus will be used to maintain our status quo."

"I guess that sums up our situation. We need to get the licenses so we can proceed with additional cabling and a tower." Hixson closed the meeting.

We spent the next two and a half weeks studying for the Colem certificates required to obtain FCC licensing. Harley had Garrett ferry our applications to the Detroit office and pick up sample exams for each level. We spent every free minute at Harley's home or in the radio station cramming for the test. By the time those last few days rolled around, both Harley and Garrett could have gotten certified as broadcasters.

I almost didn't get to go. Mom got it into her head we were only going to Detroit to see the Bob Seger concert. She didn't realize the show was north and west of Detroit in Pontiac. She insisted I had to return home by ten o'clock the night of the show and wanted me to take my sister.

While I love my sister, I didn't want her hanging around the DJ's or Harley not to mention Mike and March. These two guys could be a bad influence on a high school junior with all their talk about sex and smoking pot.

Mom always thought the weekends I spent at Harley's with the gang was actually at my coworker's Karen's apartment. I don't know how she came to that conclusion. I certainly never told her that. She applied that same conclusion to our group study dates. It helped that many of those were at the station.

When she finally understood the concert was going to be in Pontiac, it became a different ballgame. She was convinced we were going to party, get drunk, and stoned. To her rock concerts were the epitome of sin, and disc jockey's promoted that hedonistic lifestyle.

"Mari," at times her Japanese accent was thick, and my name came out sounding like Maru. "You no go Detroit with bunch of boys." She shook her finger at me. "Take sister. Keep eye on you."

Like my younger sister was going to chaperone me. "Mom, the radio station is paying for the broadcaster tests, and the hotel rooms. We have to pay for our meals, and concert tickets. They only got enough tickets for the DJs. Besides, I'm not going with a bunch of boys. Other girls will be there too."

I could hardly believe Mom was doing this at the last minute. Normally she would have been on me when she first heard the plans, not an hour before we were to leave.

"Who? Do I know these girls?"

"Mom, they're Lori, Judy, and Peg. You haven't met them."

"How I know these girls are good girls? No, sleep around with guys." Mom said as she wiped the dining table with a cloth.

"They're good girls, Mom."

"How many boys going?"

"Six," I replied. I just knew what Mom was going to say next.

"Six? Too many boys, not enough girls. You take Dee or you not go."

I groaned. Sometimes convincing Mom took all my patience. "If Dee goes I'd have to get another hotel room, buy another ticket if there are any available. If there are, there's no guarantee she would be sitting anywhere near the rest of us. I don't think you'd want her by herself. Plus, what would she do for nine hours while we're taking the exams?"

"Then, you no go."

Ultimately, I had to get Dad involved. "Dad," I approached him as he sat in his recliner. "I need your help."

"What's wrong, Sweetie?" he asked as he sipped coffee.

"The radio station is taking the disc jockeys to Detroit to take our FCC licensing tests today. After the exam, we're going to see a concert. We will be back on Sunday. Mom says I have to take Dee along or I can't go. We already booked the hotel rooms and bought the concert tickets. It's too late to bring Dee with me."

"Is your young man going to be there?"

"Yes," I replied. "Harley's going to be one of the two drivers. We're going to have four rooms. I'll be sharing a room with Peg."

"Get your stuff ready to go. I'll take care of your Mom," Dad said as he stood up and walked into the kitchen.

"Honey," he held out his hands. "She's going to Detroit to take a test so she can continue doing her radio show. The test starts at nine in the morning and ends at five o'clock. It'd be unrealistic to expect them to go up there that morning and come back that night." He lifted his coffee cup and sipped.

"Besides, the girls are sharing a room. The boys will be in another." Turning toward me, he said, "better get a move on, Mari if you're going to meet them on time."

"Thanks, Dad." I grabbed my overnight bag and hurried out the door before Mom could convince Dad to make me take my sister with me.

"Mari," he leaned in close to me. "You make sure your young man treats you properly with respect."

"Yes, sir," I stammered. How did Dad know about Harley?

"No like it. Baka." I could hear Mom continuing to argue.

"I know, it's stupid, honey," Dad used his most soothing tone of voice.

I jumped into my car and was on my way to Harley's. The traffic was unbelievably heavy for a small town. Instead of taking me twenty minutes, my drive took the better part of an hour. When I reached the bottleneck, I realized an accident involving three vehicles caused the jam. There was a cloth draped body on the side of the road. Cars slowed down to look at the ghastly scene.

"Sorry, I'm a little late," I said as I grabbed my bag and exited the car. "There was a fatal accident on Harding Highway."

"Give me your bag," Mike reached for the handle.

Harley had two vehicles lined up. One was a stretch limousine; the other was a minibus. Mike tossed my bag into the back of the minibus.

"I figured some could ride in the limo on the way up, and others can ride in it coming back." Harley donned a chauffeur's hat.

"Far out!" March cried. "Maryanne is never going to believe this. Who's going first?"

Everyone wanted to be in the first group. We wound up drawing numbers. Peg, Lori, and Flash won. Judy, March, Mike and I got the bus. Garrett drove the limo and Harley drove the bus. I didn't care which vehicle I was in as long as I was with Harley.

The trip would take us approximately two and a half to three hours without stops. We took I-75 north toward Toledo. Garrett had thoughtfully packed an assortment of sandwiches, snacks, and drinks for each vehicle. We pulled into a convenience store just north of Toledo to top off the gas tanks and take restroom breaks before continuing on Pontiac and our hotel for the weekend.

Initially, there was some confusion about the number of rooms we had. Ultimately we wound up with four rooms. Each had two queen sized beds. After taking a half hour to get settled into our accommodations, we decided it was time for dinner.

The hotel clerk directed us to the Rocket Restaurant. The place fit the description of a greasy spoon with some of the best burgers and pizza ever served west of the Mississippi. It had a down home friendly atmosphere and was hopping with clients. We had waited twenty minutes before we found a table big enough to hold our group.

Both Harley and I ordered the Rocket Burger. Hixson and Mike shared a classic pizza. Garrett selected the Philadelphia cheese steak sandwich. March and Flash both picked the spaghetti dinner. Lori, Peg, and Judy all opted for soup and salad.

We ate and talked about the upcoming exams. Flash was relaxed. He had been through this a couple of times to get his third and first class engineers licenses. The fact he had a first class license had helped the station get as far as we did during the primary year.

The rest of us were nervous wrecks. Mike and Hixson had the most on the line. As co-managers, they had to get their first class licenses, or the university might shut the station down. According to FCC regulations at the time, we had to have a first class engineer on site during broadcast hours.

There was a professor who would have been very pleased to shut us down. He was always complaining the music playing over the speaker system in the Commons disrupted his classes. Funny how he was the only professor who thought that.

Having only Flash with a first class engineer's license made it impossible to expand our operating hours. If both Mike and Hixson got theirs, we could broadcast from seven in the morning until ten at night daily. We could also pipe prerecorded shows to our cable subscribers. Back in 1976, we were one of the first cable radio stations. We predated Sirius XM and all the internet stations available now.

"I will be so glad when the tests are done," March said.

"Hope everyone passes," Flash leaned back and stretched. "The failure rate is rather high. About seventy-five percent." He rubbed his stomach, "I'm stuffed."

"That's a pretty high flunk rate," Peg commented. "I hate tests. I never do as well as I should. I know the material and still put in the wrong answer!" She pounded on the table.

"Chill, Peg. Garrett and Harley have been grilling us for weeks now." Judy looked around the table. "I'd be surprised if we fail."

"Of course, you'll do fine," Garrett chimed in. "I didn't learn all this technical, engineering jargon so you could fail."

"Let's return to the hotel and cram for a few hours," Harley suggested.

Mike, Hixson and Flash went to Garrett's room to prepare for the first class licenses. The rest of us trooped into Harley's room. Both groups ultimately studied for both tests.

"Here's the scenario," Harley read from a paper in his hand. "Radio watches for compulsory radiotelephone stations will include what? Peg?"

"Well, it wouldn't be VHF 22.a or 121.5 MHz. So it has to be VHF channel 16 continuous watch." She scrunched her eyes closed as though expecting to be wrong. "I hate tests. I never do well on them."

"That is correct." Harley flipped to another page. "Mari," he paused briefly. "Who has to make entries into a service or maintenance log?"

"Easy. That would be the operator responsible for the station operations or maintenance."

"Very Good. Now Judy, answer this one," he faced her. "Radiotelephone stations are required to maintain specific information in their logs. What are they?" He paced nervously up and down the room.

Judy sucked in a deep breath and counted to ten before responding, "station, date, and time. Additionally, they must include, the name of the operator on duty, and the station call signs or ID with which communication occurred."

"What determines the strength of the magnetic field around a conductor, March?" Harley went to the igloo cooler and plucked out a Vernor's ginger ale.

"The amount of the current." March pulled out a cigarette and started to light it.

"Sorry, not in here, March." Harley plucked the stick from March's hand and stubbed it out.

"Ah, man!" March moaned. "I wanted that cig."

"Lori, what are the two most commonly used specifications for a junction diode?"

"I know this," she scrunched up her face. "I know it." She slapped her hand on her leg, "it's maximum forward current and PIV or peak inverse voltage."

The cramming went on for several hours before we gave in to sleep. By then, we were beyond exhausted.

"Are we done, yet?" Peg asked as she rubbed her eyes. "I'm tired. I need my beauty sleep."

"Yeah, I think I'm done too," March headed for the door. "Thanks for the help, man." He clapped Harley on the back.

"I'm bushed. I think my brain has gone to sleep." I stretched and yawned. "Thanks for grilling us, Harley."

"You're welcome, ladies. Sleep well, good night and don't forget to lock the door behind me." He blew each of us kisses.

I pretended to catch mine and place it over my heart. I blew a kiss back. "Sleep well, Harley."

"You too, Mari." He smiled as he shut the door behind him.

Chapter Twenty

We left to get breakfast at six Saturday morning. Harley insisted we have a nourishing meal in a relaxed atmosphere before we hit the road back to Detroit and a grueling day of testing.

To say the tests were hard was an understatement. It didn't take us long before we realized the statistics on failure were correct. We spent many hours struggling over the exams. Finally, it was over. It was with tremendous relief when we left the facility. By then, I don't think anyone of us cared whether or not we passed. We were just glad it was over. We had a plenty of time to get back to Pontiac and freshen up at our hotel.

Peg pulled out a T-shirt. "Do you think this matches my jeans?"

I eyed the garment. It was a tie-dyed throwback to the sixties with browns, yellows, blues, greens, reds, and purple splattered everywhere.

"That shirt will match any pair of jeans." I pulled on an American Indian print shirt.

"Can we come in?" Lori called through the door adjoining our room.

"It's not locked," Peg replied.

"So," Judy perched on the edge of my bed. "What's with you and Harley?"

"What?" I squeaked. "What about Harley and me?"

"Oh, come on!" Lori laughed. "He's been hanging around you since the Fall Quarter. Then a few weeks ago, we found out you went on an overnighter with him. You'd been to his house when none of us had. Plus we saw you guys kissing."

"So, spill it, sister. We want details," Judy joined in.

"None to give. As you probably surmised, we are dating." I could feel my face heating up.

"Sleeping together yet?" Peg asked, causing me to shoot her a warning glance.

"That's not your business," I smiled.

"If you aren't, then it's not serious," Judy said.

"I think it is," Peg said and grabbed her purse.

"For real?" Lori looked back and forth between Peg and me.

"I'm not saying. That's between Harley and me."

"Oh, man!" Peg groaned. "This makes me the only one here not in a relationship. I better get on the stick."

"Don't go back to Dirk, Peg," Lori said. "He's a full on doper. He'll get you drugged up and dead. Bad news."

"We all know how you're a sucker for the bad ones," I said. "Don't go back to Dirk. Listen to Lori."

"Ladies," Garrett said from the hall. "The gents want to know if you still want to get something to eat before the show."

"We'll be right out."

The group decided a nice leisurely dinner before the Seger concert would fit the bill. We all piled into the vehicles and headed back to the Rocket Restaurant.

This time around, we ordered three pizzas and sodas with a lemon water for Harley.

"Can you believe the lineup on tonight's bill? Point Blank, Elvin Bishop, and Rundgren open for Seger," Mike rubbed his hands together. "I can dig some Rundgren," he reached for a slice of pizza.

"Bishop, man," March said, "now there's a musician."

"I dunno, March," Lori took a sip of diet coke. "I kind of like that Texas band, Point Blank. 'Nichole' is a good one. I hear their newest, 'Distance,' and 'That's the Law' are pretty good, but we don't have a copy yet."

"Actually," Hixson wiped his mouth, "a copy arrived yesterday."

We spent the next hour doing what DJs do best; talking music. Both Harley and Garrett sat quietly munching on pizza.

"Hey!" Judy exclaimed as she looked at her watch. "We better get a move on if we want to see the concert."

We quickly divvied up the bill with Harley insisting on paying mine and Peg's share. Hixson and Mike, not to be outdone took care of Lori and Judy's portion.

"Mari," Harley pulled the minibus into a passenger drop off lane and turned to face me. "Why don't you go inside with the others? I'll find you after I park this thing."

"What and miss a stroll with you? Not on your life, buddy," I playfully poked his arm.

I was greedy. I wanted every spare minute I could snatch with Harley. He found a place to park, and we walked the few blocks to the concert venue.

"I'm beginning to love these overnighters of ours," I snuggled against him. He wrapped his arm around me and kissed my ear.

"You do, do you?" His voice grew husky. "It's not like we do what other couples do."

"You mean, like going on an overnighter for a first date, or sleeping in the same bed?" I teased. I loved making him blush.

"Mari, you know how I feel about that." He turned a lovely shade of red. "You share my bed; you share my name."

"Oh! I get it! Flash is now Flash Davis, not Flash Martin." I giggled and slid his arm from around me so I could hold his hand.

"Argh! You are an impossible minx!"

"And you, sir, are a true gentleman. Any girl would be proud to stand by your side." It was my turn to kiss him. I brought his hand to my lips and smooched him.

"I hope you mean that, Mari. I intend to have you with me always because love means," he began.

"Never saying goodbye," I finished. "And I do mean it. You are a keeper. I wouldn't have agreed to marry you otherwise." I grinned wickedly.

"I love you, Mari!" He pulled me close, lifted me into the air and spun around.

"I love you, too!" I laughed.

He set me back down, "we'd better get inside and join the rest."

The Detroit area had some of the best music in the nation from the blues of Charlie Spand, Speckled Red, Clara Smith to Mamie Smith and later John Lee Hooker. The Detroit region was also home to the likes of Glenn Frey, Sonny Bono, Aretha Franklin, Ted Nugent, Alice Cooper, Commander Cody and His Lost Planet Airmen, Del Shannon, MC 5, and Grand Funk Railroad to list a few.

Of course, who can forget Motown Records was started in the Detroit area?

Before I met Harley and came to appreciate Steppenwolf, my favorite bands were Creedence Clearwater Revival, John Fogerty, Gordon Lightfoot, and Bob Seger and the Silver Bullet band. Seeing Seger live was a big treat for me.

In addition to Bob Seger and the Silver Bullet band, Point Blank, Elvin Bishop, and Todd Rundgren played to a crowd of about 80,000. As the headline act, Seger came on last. He was a regional favorite about to become a national icon in the music world.

He pranced onto the stage in that distinctive side to side rocking stage walk of his. He launched into a rollicking version of 'Bo Diddley' followed by 'Nutbush City Limits' that had the crowd roaring for their Detroit area hometown rocker. His raspy, rusty-sounding voice was perfect for mid-western fans. Seger was ours, and he let us know he didn't forget.

Even Harley got caught up in the festive mood of the attendees. He clapped his hands and stomped his feet to the rhythm of the music.

"He's good," Harley leaned close and spoke into my ear. "No wonder you like his music so much."

It was a night to remember. His highly energetic performance had us on our feet stomping, hopping, clapping, and singing every song as loudly as possible. There were a few times when we drowned out the singer. Seger rocked the crowd with tune after tune until one thirty in the morning and still the audience wanted more.

Chapter Twenty One

Professor Schmidt was a little on the flaky side. He was usually late for class and often appeared to be absent minded. The few things Schmidt was passionate about was biology and the environment. He was a huge proponent of environmental safety as he called it. To most of us students, he was simply a nature lover.

Tecumseh Nature Areas is the largest and most pristine wildlife habitat in Allen County Ohio. The entrance is a short 5,900 feet from Cook Hall. It has over 200 acres of woodland trails and featured a campsite cooking area. It was one of Professor Schmidt's pet projects to make this section wildlife secure. He often talked with Harley after class about how they could make the place safe for animals and people.

"Today is the last day of class before midterms during this eight-week period," Professor Schmidt said as he waltzed into the room.

There were eight or twelve-week courses during the summer term depending on which courses you selected. The biology course Schmidt taught was for eight weeks.

He had a hip-swaying walk that reminded me of a sashay or waltz. Other professors called him a long haired freak because he wore his golden brown hair down to his shoulders along with a neatly trimmed beard. His standard mode of dress was more like a student than a member of the faculty. He could always be seen in a plaid shirt, torn jeans, and leather work boots more befitting a lumberjack than a teacher.

He was easily the most popular Prof on campus. Girls could be found hanging around him which might have contributed to his seven previous divorces. His current wife was jealous of the attention and adoration he received from his students. We had a bet going at the station as to when wife number eight would become an ex.

"I have funding for a summer project. I need twelve volunteers to help me build an environmentally safe cook site at Tecumseh." He flipped a lock of hair back from his face. "Any takers?"

"I volunteer," Harley stood.

"Very good, Mister Davis. Any others?"

Three students joined. Harley nudged me, "c'mon. It'll be fun. Plus, we get to spend time together."

"Professor? Miss Forrester might be interested," Harley tugged on my arm.

"Miss Forrester?"

"Can I let you know on midterm day? I have to check my work schedule." I shot Harley a dirty look.

"Sure. Midterms are Tuesday at eight. I'll expect an answer then."

"C'mon Mari," Harley pleaded. He fairly danced around me as we left class.

"I have to check my work schedule at K-Mart first." while I enjoyed hiking, bicycling, rock climbing, and camping, I was not fond of getting dirty. The campground project sounded suspiciously like hard work and getting filthy.

"Oh, please, Mari!" He begged, "I know you can probably get your schedule changed. Please? Please? Please?"

He gave me his best begging puppy look. He even batted his eyes at me. I think he would have dropped to his knees, clasped his hands and followed me out of the classroom if he thought it would get me to acquiesce. How could I turn him down when he was pulling out all the stops and tugging at my heart?

"Oh, okay," I sighed, pretending his request was an earth shattering one. I theatrically dragged the back of my hand across my forehead. "Since it's so important to you, I'll see what I can do."

He brought such beauty into the lives of so many people. Harley for all his talk about the law of chastity was a very sexy man. He turned heads wherever he went. Such attention would have resulted in an inflated ego in most people, but not him. Harley was about as humble and unassuming as they come.

"Yippee!" He leaped into the air and clicked his heels together.

He hugged me so tightly I could barely breathe. I smiled, and joy filled my heart. It took so little to make this noble man happy. I would gladly do anything for him.

"Harley, I can't breathe," I gasped.

"I'm sorry. You just made my day." His happiness was infectious. "I thank God every day for sending you to me!"

He truly practiced his religion without seeming pushy. Although he never came out and said what Church he belonged to, I had my suspicions. While never one to force his beliefs on a person, if asked, he was more than willing to discuss them.

"As you've probably guessed, religion is important to me. People need to have a real relationship with God."

"Do you attend Church?" I asked, curious about this aspect of my biker dude.

"I do," he nodded. "I can't make every Sunday, but I go wherever possible. Would you like to go with me sometime?"

"I would, but I usually get scheduled to work on Sunday's. The only times I'm off is when I can get someone to switch with me like for the Steppenwolf concert we went to, or when we had a weekend get together."

"I understand," he sighed and shuffled his feet. "I love listening to testimonials and learning about the gospel."

"Does your family belong to the same Church?"

He tilted his head and laughed. "No, they don't. The way they talk about Church, it's as though I joined some outcast cult of devil worshippers instead of a very Christ centered Church based on the Church Jesus established. They teach the ten commandments and how much the importance of family and servitude is to society. We believe in service."

"Why wouldn't they approve of that?" I cocked my head to the side and studied him. "It seems to me this world needs more people who care."

"I don't know," he shrugged. "I'm the black sheep of the family bent on living life the way I believe it should be."

"So, you're a rebel rouser, huh?"

"I guess. Makes for exciting times with family, that's for sure."

"Then, it's a good thing I like rebels, you biker dude, you." I playfully poked his shoulder.

"Mari, haven't you ever wanted to make a difference in another person's life?"

"When I was in high school, I wanted to join the Peace Corps," I told him as we walked across campus toward the radio station. "I wanted to help build schools, medical facilities, water wells for clean drinking water. I wanted to teach people how to better their lives."

"That is service, Mari. Anytime you do something for others it's considered doing service." Harley grasped my hand, and we walked slowly enjoying the warmth of a sunny summer day.

The sun cast highlights on Harley's dark sandy hair making it look like he had put glitter in his locks. His eyes looked bluer than his normal color. He was happy, and that made my heart glad.

"You are really big on service, aren't you?" I asked, swinging our hands back and forth.

"Yes, I am. We should always lend a helping hand." He stopped and looked earnestly at me. "The thing is, we should do it without expectations of recognition or thanks. To expect anything in return negates the good deed because it becomes about you and not about providing a helping hand."

Harley always said he was passing his good fortune to others less lucky than he was. He believed in hope and love and was secure in his religion. Service was tantamount to his Christianity. He waxed philosophically about The Rule of Three. Simply stated, it meant, whatever you put out comes back to you three-fold.

"How about dinner tonight?" He swung me around in an impromptu pirouette.

"I'd love it," I couldn't suppress my giggles. What a wonderful day I was having. Schmidt's biology course was the only class I had with Harley during this summer quarter. I liked the course but loved attending it with Harley more. "What time?"

He pulled out a leather-bound diary and looked up our schedules. "I have a corporate meeting from two to three-thirty. A test drive and showcasing some new accessories to a prospective police office. Other than that I have a meeting with the night staff at seven. Do you have Anthropology tonight?"

"Yes. Before that, my last class gets out at four."

"How about I meet you here at four? We'll get something to eat and be back in time for your evening class. I can still make my staff meeting at seven."

"Sounds like a plan."

"Here we are." He held the door open for me. He waved me into the building with a flourish. He made a sweeping gesture and bowed so low it was comical. "How about playing 'Berry Rides Again' for me?" He pulled me into his arms for a sweet lingering kiss.

"You got it," I mumbled.

The kiss deepened. Passion was present in the way he held me close. An arm encircled me and his hand gently rubbed my back. His lips devoured mind with mind blowing tenderness. His free hand cupped my chin and slid up the side of my face until his thumb caressed my swollen lips. Wow! I have never been kissed with such intense ecstasy. It was heavenly.

"Get a room," March called out as he walked past us. He looked back at our shocked faces and snickered. "What? You don't think we can see you smooching from the doorway?" He juggled a can of Dr. Pepper as he squeezed by us.

Reluctantly Harley let go. "See you at four," he leaned in for a quick peck on the cheek.

"I'll be here." I entered the station and quickly took my spot. "This is Gypsy Mar at the top of the hour. You're listening to WOSL radio on the beautiful campus of The Ohio State University Lima Branch. Next up Steppenwolf's 'Berry Rides Again.' Harley this one's your request. Harley the next one is also for you, another Steppenwolf goody, 'Tenderness.' Enjoy." I busied myself cueing tune after tune, interspersing local, state and national news, weather and advertisements.

I kept looking at my watch all through Creative Writing class. When four o'clock rolled around, I was the first person out the door. I'm typically last out, staying behind to talk with the instructor. I hurried to the radio station.

As soon as I got there, I knew something was wrong. Hixson looked up from the desk and frowned.

"Mari," he said gently. This was an abrupt change for him. He is normally loud and brassy. "Harley asked me to have you call him at this number."

Hixson handed me a slip of paper. "Mari, I don't want to cause any problems between you guys. I think you should know; it sounded like he was in a room with another woman."

"How do you mean?" I could feel a lump growing in my throat.

"I mean it sounded like he was at a party."

"That doesn't sound like him," I reached for the telephone. I closed my eyes and reminded myself Harley had just asked me to be his wife a couple of days ago. There's no way he would be calling from a party; it just wasn't his way. If I knew Harley like I thought I did, he was honest and faithful not a liar or a cheater.

Something must have happened. With trembling fingers, I dialed the number Hixson had given me. I turned away from them, yet I could feel their eyes upon me. I heard their hurried whispers.

"Poor Mari," said Judy.

"How could he do that to her," from Lori.

"We don't know he did anything, yet," said Peg.

The telephone rang four times before anyone answered. "Hello?" Harley's baritone voice came over the line. "Mari? Is that you?"

"Yes, Harley, it's me." I could hear all the chaos of voices in the background. "Where are you? What's going on?"

"Mari, I'm so sorry. I'm going to have to cancel dinner tonight. Something's come up." He spoke tersely.

"What? A party you forgot? Or is it that blonde bimbo people have seen you with recently?"

"Whoa! What blonde bimbo? You mean Elizabeth? She's my sister and is visiting for the summer. She's thinking about transferring to Bowling Green University in the fall."

"Oh," was all I could think of to say.

"As for that party," he sounded upset, "you think I forgot about, it's St. Rita's hospital emergency room."

All thoughts of him lying or cheating flew from my mind. He believed in honesty. There are gentle ways, to be honest with someone without causing undue hurt. He liked the physician's creed of 'first do no harm.' He lived the motto unless people he loved or cared about was going to get hurt such as in the bookstore attempted robbery.

"What happened, Harley?" I felt an urgent need to be there with him.

"Elizabeth's boyfriend, Dale, decided to take one of my hogs for a test drive. I didn't know he was a newbie on hogs. He talked the talk and walked the walk. If I had known, I'd never have let him take it out for a ride. It was my new one, you know, the one I call the Monster."

"Did he crash?"

"That's putting it mildly. Dale wrapped it around a telephone pole. They had to cut the bike off him," Harley sounded mournful and distressed.

"Do you want me to come, Harley?"

"Would you?" He sounded relieved. "Garrett's trying to reach Dale's family in London."

"Of course, I'll come. I'll get there as quickly as possible."

"Thank you, my angel."

"See you in a few." I hung up and turned to face the snoops. "There was an accident at his company test driving a hog. It was not some blonde bimbo or a party."

When I got to the emergency room, I saw a girl matching a photo I had seen of Elizabeth in triage with a young man I assumed was Dale. She was beautiful. I could easily see her winning beauty contests. Her hair was a honey brown that had been carefully coiffed and held in place with a green comb that matched her eyes. She had a willowy body that she carried gracefully.

Harley was pacing the emergency room halls and sitting area. He occasionally stopped to talk quietly with others in the facility waiting for news about their family members. It was typical of him to offer comfort to strangers even when he was worried or suffering. Harley tended to put the needs of others ahead of his own. I found that to be one of the many endearing qualities that made him uniquely lovable.

Harley approached a teary-eyed couple. He squatted in front of them and gently took their hands in his. "Sometimes it helps to talk," he spoke sincerely. "Why is your family member here?"

"Our daughter was working at the convenience store when a robber came in at gun point. The crook shot her. She'd just graduated high school and was planning to go to OSU-Lima in the fall. Now this!" The woman sobbed.

Her husband wrapped his arms around her. It wasn't long before he was crying with his wife. I got some tissues from my backpack and handed it to them.

Harley placed a hand on each of their heads. "God willing, your daughter will be fine. Shall we pray?" Harley asked the couple sitting in the waiting room.

A quick nod from the parents was all he needed. "Heavenly Father, we call upon you in the name of your son Jesus Christ to help this family during their time of crisis. Father, we request healing of their beloved daughter," he paused and looked at them.

"Cynthia," the father whispered, "our daughter's name is Cynthia Wilcox."

"Cynthia Wilcox, that she might live a healthy and happy life if it is your will. We ask for your healing grace to lift this burden from her parents shoulders as we know only you can do. Heavenly Father we thank you for hearing and giving consideration to our prayers in the name of thy son Jesus Christ we pray, amen."

Tears came to my eyes as I watched my wonderful fiancée move from person to person, family to family offering comfort or condolences. Many times all it took was a gentle touch, a hug, or a simple prayer to lift peoples spirits and offer them hope. It hit me hard just how much he believed in benevolence, virtue, and doing good.

Elizabeth stuck her head out of the triage room. She tossed her honey dyed hair. A frown pursed her voluptuous lips. "Harlan, they're taking Dale to surgery. Did you call our parents? If not, what have you been doing all this time? Patronizing the needy?"

"I called them, Liz. They're chartering a plane and should be here in a few hours." Harley said calmly. He watched his sister carefully. "They're probably already on their way here."

"That's not good enough. Mother and Father should be here already." She glared at me. "It's Dale we're talking about, not that two-bit hussy of yours. Mari, is it?"

I watched warily as Harley's fists clenched and unclenched in conjunction with his jaw tightening and loosening. So, his sister thought I was some cheap tramp, did she? I felt my blood pressure skyrocketing and my face turning beet red. Elizabeth was my first experience with a member of Harley's family and it already left a sour taste in my mouth.

"Sorry to disappoint you, but this two-bit hussy is here because Harley wanted me to be," I retorted harshly. "At least, I'm not a Prima Dona."

"Mari," he steered me away. "Why not get Liz some coffee, and a warm blanket. She's going to be here awhile."

"Sure thing, love," I left the room.

As I walked down the hall to the nursing station, I overheard Elizabeth berating Harley. It made my blood boil. Just because she was his sister, did not mean she could treat him so shabbily.

"Honestly, Harlan, I don't understand what you see in that tramp. She's just out for your money."

"Her name is, Mari. I suggest you use it when addressing me about her. She is not a tramp. I better not ever hear you call her that again."

"Harlan, I agree with Mother. You should have worked harder to win over Ashley. She's better suited to you than this Mari person."

"You know nothing about me, do you? Mari understands me perfectly." he hesitated, "I'm going to marry her."

I came back into the room before Elizabeth could react to that tidbit of news "Here's the blanket and a cup of coffee," I said feeling like an ease dropper.

"Does Mother and Father know about this mistake of yours, Harlan?"

"No. There's no mistake, Elizabeth. I've asked, and she accepted. We are engaged."

"Could you get me some water?" Harley turned toward me. He fished his wallet out and handed it to me. "Please go down to the cafeteria and bring back an assortment of sandwiches, chips, and drinks."

"I couldn't possibly eat a thing," Liz said airily. She pulled a compact from her purse and proceeded to apply a fresh layer of lipstick to her pouty lips.

"It's not for you. It's for the folks in the waiting room."

"There you go again, throwing away your money on riff raff."

"Shut your mouth, Liz. It's my money, not family money. If I choose to use it to better someone's life, that's my business. Not your concern," he growled.

I found it admirable Harley was thoughtful enough to provide nourishment to the folks sitting in the waiting room. There was no telling how long they had been there or how much more time would pass before they heard about their loved ones. I rapidly came to the conclusion Elizabeth was a pampered, spoiled brat. Harley would have been mortified at the many uncomplimentary thoughts running through my head.

Dale was taken to surgery. By the time Harley's parents arrived, he was in recovery. He was going to be okay with a few months spent in physical therapy. I wondered if Elizabeth would stick by his side or dump him. Garrett never reached Dale's family.

"Harley?" I tugged on his shirt. I was uncomfortably aware of the stares from his parents. "Do you want me to stay?"

He looked at me and then at his Mom and Dad, "no. It's okay." He kissed me lightly. "I'll see you tomorrow."

"Are you sure?" I asked, not wanting to abandon him to the vultures, but also not wishing to subject myself to their highly dismissive attitudes.

"I'm sure." He whispered in my ear, "I'd leave too if I could."

"Harlan?" His mother asked, "Who is this girl? Is this the Mari you keep talking about?"

"Yes, mother," he said, not bothering to introduce us.

"Why she isn't in our class, is she?" His mother frowned and tsked, "Surely, Ashley is better suited to you."

"Mari is perfect for me, Mother. Now, if you don't mind, we should focus on Elizabeth and Dale."

Harley redirected his parents to his sister who was sitting nearby. She had a full pout going. "Mother, Father, don't you wish to know about Dale? Surely, he is more important than that girl."

"Of course he is, dear," Harley's mother responded. "I just don't want your brother to get mixed up with the wrong person is all."

"Mother...do not go there," Harley warned. "Mari," he whispered to me, "You might want to go ahead and leave before this gets uglier."

As I walked out of the hospital, I marveled at Harley's kind spirit. Generosity was in Harley's DNA. He could not pass by a hungry person without trying to help them. He lived the poem 'The New Colossus' by Emma Lazarus, the motto on the Statue of Liberty, "give me your tired, your poor, your huddled masses.' He once explained to me that it meant we should take care of our brothers and sisters who have nothing.

How can I not love such a generous, thoughtful, and caring man? He gave and gave and never asked for anything in return. How could I deny him such a simple request as working on an environmentally friendly campfire site? Being together, doing things he loves, helping people. Doing things with him made me a better person. I loved him for opening my eyes to a different world, and for loving me unconditionally. How could I do any less?

As luck would have it, the store I worked at had a downturn in sales. Both Karen and I being the newest hired were furloughed for six weeks. Karen wound up moving in with Jeff to make ends meet. I suddenly had a lot of time on my hands to fill.

The volunteers met with Professor Schmidt after mid-terms. He sat perched on the corner of his desk with one leg crossed over the other. "Glad everyone could make it. I'd like to start this weekend."

He stood and handed out two sheets. The first one was a sign-up sheet. "Anyone under twenty one here?"

I looked around and saw no other hands raised. Sheepishly, I lifted my hand, "I'm eighteen."

"You'll need a parent to sign off for you. Bring the consent form with you Saturday."

The second sheet he gave us was a list of supplies and tools to bring. It turns out our favorite professor was a closet doomsday prepper. He had everything you could imagine on his list. Anyone using that fire pit would be able to live there year round as long as they had an insulated waterproofed tent.

As I read the sheet, Harley quietly said, "don't worry about it. I got you covered."

I looked up thankfully. The items on the list would have significantly decreased my funding for the Fall Quarter. "Thanks."

"I know it costs a fortune. I just want to spend time with you, and you are indulging me in one of my passions. It's only four hours a day. Perhaps afterward we can have sandwiches and enjoy my library for a few hours."

"I'd love it. Anything for you, my love."

The widest grin I had ever seen spread across his countenance. "I love it when you say that, my lady."

"What? Anything for you?" I chided.

"My love," he responded with a smile.

Chapter Twenty Two

Saturday started out mild and a bit overcast. We met outside Galvin Hall with a boatload of gear. The volunteers had brought an assortment of shovels, picks, trowels, hammers, spikes, nails, tarps, and blankets. Professor Schmidt brought the mortar, corrugated iron sheets, hardwood cords, fire bricks, river stones, wood planks, saws, and wire mesh bundled into groups.

Some of the stuff such as the mortar, wood, corrugated iron, and bricks were put into the wheelbarrows. The rest of the items, while smaller, were still heavy and we had to lug it by hand into the selected area deep in the woods. We walked around Galvin Hall loaded with equipment towards Mowry Road. At the midpoint, we detoured into a wooded section and headed in the general direction of Thayer Road.

Halfway through this part of wilderness is a flat land perfect for a campfire location. It was our intention to build a secure grilling pit that would both allow people to cook outdoors and still keep wildlife safe when not in use. Additionally, it was to be an environment-friendly site. It was an ambitious project even for college students bent on saving the world from man-made toxins.

Our first task was to clear the area of debris. We started by gathering all the fallen twigs and branches we could find. I soon decided this was not my idea of fun. Rock climbing? Yes. Hiking? Yes. Camping? Yes. Clearing ground and digging holes? No.

"How's Dale doing?" I asked as I dumped an armful of wood onto a designated pile.

"He's recovering nicely, but not fast enough for Elizabeth," Harley said as he dropped his pile. He pulled a handkerchief from his pocket and handed it to me.

"What?" I dabbed my face and neck.

"She doesn't want to wait until he's out of the hospital. She wants him to check himself out. It's just a few more days, so what's her rush?" He pulled his shirt loose and used a corner to wipe the sweat from his brow.

"Do you think they'll make it as a couple?" I asked. "I mean, he seemed nice, and she was, well, um, not so nice."

"I know. Elizabeth's selfish and petty. Do I think they'll make it?" He frowned and shook his head. "I doubt it. It'd be nice if they did, but this isn't her first engagement."

"Really?"

"Yeah. Elizabeth's been engaged three times in four years. So, it wouldn't surprise me if this one doesn't last either." Harley looked at me and pulled his canteen out.

"Kind of humid, isn't it? I thought today was supposed to be sunny." I looked upward to the sky. It was overcast and looked like rain.

"So much for weather forecasting," Harley grimaced. He opened his canteen and held it out to me.

I took a drink. The fresh water tasted delicious. "Oh well, hope it doesn't rain."

"By the way, I don't think we can do the sandwich and books thing today. Not with my folks and Elizabeth there. They'd drive you insane. I was thinking, we can grab some snacks and go to the library." He looked hopeful, almost like a puppy begging for treats.

"Sounds good to me. You duped me." I spoke casually.

"How?" His voice took an incredulous tone as he waited for my answer.

"You said, it'll be fun. This isn't my idea of fun. It's back-breaking, dirty work." I took another sip of the water and handed the canteen back to him.

"Oh," he looked crestfallen.

"The only thing fun about this is being with you." I softened the blow. "I love being with you."

"Does that count for anything?" He spoke slowly, cautiously as though afraid of my answer.

"It counts for a lot," I dumped another load onto the wood pile. "It makes it okay. I'd be happy doing anything with you. But, this isn't fun. It's okay, just not fun."

"Whew! At least all isn't lost," he cast a sneaky glance at me. He started humming as he took a drink from his canteen before putting it away.

"Harley...what are you thinking?" It was my turn to be wary. Harley was an accomplished prankster, and I just knew I was about to become his latest victim.

"Who? Me?" He peeked at me innocently.

"Anyone else here called Harley? Yes, you." I backed away from him. "What are you up to?" I continued moving away from him.

"Nothing, my love." He stepped behind me and placed his hands on my shoulders. He rubbed them, slowly moving down to the small of my back.

"Uh, huh," I closed my eyes. Lulled into a sense of relaxation, I let my guard down. "That feels good."

"I'm glad." In a flash, he bent to the ground and scooped up a handful of dirt. He plopped it on my head.

"Harley!" I squealed.

"Yes, my love?" He gathered another clump and flung it at me. He threw a bunch of dirt balls and dodged away so I couldn't get him.

"Ooh, you are dead!" I grabbed two hands full and threw it at him.

He ran, and I chased after him. Volley for volley we went. At times our aim was off, and we hit the other volunteers, who in turn shot dirt back at us.

"All right, break's over. Let's get back to work, shall we?" Schmidt said only to be clobbered by the entire group.

We laughed so hard we had trouble breathing and collapsed onto the ground. It took another fifteen minutes before everyone settled down and returned to the project at hand.

With twelve students and one professor working nonstop we had the area cleared in no time. Next, we used the wire mesh to lay out a grid. Wooden stakes were hammered to mark the location of both campfire sites. We would remove these later.

The first pit was small at two feet by three feet. The second was much larger at five by six feet. The guys took turns digging while the girls unloaded the bricks. I think the guys got the better end of that deal.

I started singing an old camp song, "Ging gang goolie goolie wash wash."

"What the heck is that?" Harley laughed so hard he sat down in the pit.

"A variation of a Scout song," Professor Schmidt joined in the singing.

Soon everyone was singing as loudly as possible and as off key, as they could get. The pits were dug and ready to be lined with the fire bricks. That's when the first drops of rain fell on us.

Schmidt held his hands' palm up. "The heavens don't like our song."

The sprinkle quickly turned into a deluge. "Well, there goes the weekend," Schmidt chuckled. "Dig a pit, get rain."

"Let it rain!" Harley yelled as he danced a jig in the downpour. He grabbed my hand and twirled me around.

"Harley!" I laughed.

"C'mon everyone!" he beckoned. "When was the last time you played in the rain?"

Soon everyone, much to the amusement of Professor Schmidt, was dancing in the rain. The site rapidly devolved into a mud bath instead of a fire pit. The professor ran around covering the equipment and the wood.

Harley placed his fingers to his lips and crept up on the teacher. I could tell the devil in him was coming out. I just knew the results would be hilarious as they usually are when his wild side comes to the front. With a quick tug on the man's belt, he sent him flying backward into the largest pit.

Schmidt came up sputtering and covered in mud. He looked so silly everyone laughed. Schmidt scooped up a handful of mud and flung it at Harley.

"Oh no, you didn't!" Harley cried out. "Revenge is mine!" He shoveled mud back at the hapless teacher. He threw the wet dirt so fast the professor never had a chance to climb out of the hole.

A stray splash hit me in the face. "You didn't! You just got me!" I hollered at Harley.

He paused, looking like a mischievous toddler about to get himself in trouble. He was covered head to toe in dripping filthy goop. It matted his hair, slid down his face giving him an odd brown complexion, and dropped onto his shirt creating globs of stain. His arms were covered in the mess, and his jeans looked like he'd had a nasty accident in them.

Slowly he shoveled up two handfuls of mud, and casually threw them at me. "Now, you're as much a mess as I am," he crowed in delight.

"Ooh! You are dead, buster!" I threw goop back at him.

"Uh, guys," Schmidt called from the pit. "A little help here?"

We turned to look down at him. He was standing knee deep in brown water. He lifted his arms. "Please help me get out of this."

We reached down, and each of us grabbed one of his hands. As we prepared to heave him up, Schmidt yanked his arms downward. Our feet flew out from under us. We fell in the slippery wetness and to our horror slid face down into the pit on top of the professor.

Dark, loamy mud covered all three of us. It dripped from every orifice, including our mouths. It wedged into cracks I didn't know a body had.

Then the deluge turned into a monsoon. Harley and Schmidt lifted me out of the pit. They, in turn, grabbed hands from volunteers and were hauled out.

"Use the iron sheets to cover the pits! Hurry! We don't want more water in there," Schmidt barked. He slipped as he ran toward the materials. The professor landed on his butt and slid into the pile of supplies.

We hurried to comply. "Put the rest of the stuff around the perimeters with some on the edges of the iron to anchor them in place. Place the tarps over everything and use the lumber and wheelbarrows to hold them down." Schmidt hollered.

"Mari!" Harley called, "Help me move the bricks. We can use them to keep the tarps in place."

I ran over to him. Together we lined the bricks along the edges of the tarps. "What else?" I asked when we finished."

"Let's cover the tools with the last tarp," Harley suggested. He gathered the saws, hammers, and other small items onto a plastic sheet and rolled it into a bundle.

By the time everything was secured, we were soaked. Every pore in our bodies either dripped water or mud.

Thus ended our Saturday construction work. The professor would return later that summer with more volunteers to finish the project.

Chapter Twenty Three

The fourth of July was the Sunday after the Tecumseh fiasco. Harley invited the WOSL gang over to celebrate the day with him. Many of the staff had plans with their families so only, March, Flash, Peg, Maryanne and I came.

Garrett fired up the grill and had hot dogs, burgers, trout, foil wrapped potatoes and shish kabobs cooking. Tubs of coleslaw, three bean salad, and potato salad were next to the buns and rolls. There was a platter filled with cherries, blueberries, strawberries, and grapes. A giant watermelon, partially sliced was on another plate.

Harley had made lemonade for drinks. It was the best lemonade I'd ever had, beating out my grandmother's recipe which always took first place at the Iowa State Fair.

Harley had cued several Steppenwolf albums including, 'For Ladies Only, 'Rest In Peace,' 'Hour of the Wolf,' 'Skullduggery,' followed by Gordon Lightfoot's 'Cold on the Shoulder,' and Bob Seger's album 'Seven.'

"Lightfoot? Seger?" I teased, "what happened to Steppenwolf only?"

"I liked Seger at the concert, and you like Lightfoot. So I bought a couple of their albums. Lightfoot's kind of poetry in song. Cool."

"I knew you'd come around," I laughed.

"Can we see the fireworks from here?" Flash asked as he sampled the fruit.

"Yeah, we'll be able to watch from here. Faurot Park is over there," Harley pointed to the back of the yard.

"Hey," March said, "we can sit in nice comfy seats wrapped in blankets and see everything. No fighting the crowds for us."

"I got us some sparklers, snaps, and smoke bombs to play with."

"Cool!" Flash grinned, "always wanted to play with those."

I was quiet. I hoped Harley didn't notice my lack of enthusiasm for playing with fireworks, even the legal kind. They scared me. Harley didn't notice, but Peg and Maryanne did.

"Why so quiet, Mari?" Peg stepped close and spoke quietly.

Maryanne joined her. We stood in our little huddle while the guys stayed by the grill and talked baseball. If the rankings didn't change, it looked like Cincinnati and New York were headed to the World Series. Of course, the season was still young, and anything could happen.

"Something wrong?" Maryanne asked.

"I'll say," I sighed. "I like watching fireworks, but I don't light or play with them."

"Why not?" Peg looked at me like I was an alien from outer space.

"Anything to do with lighting a fire scares the crap out of me," I admitted.

"But sitting in front of a fire doesn't?" Maryanne frowned.

"As long as someone else starts, maintains, and banks it."

"Does Harley know?"

"Nope, and he's not going to, not if I can help it. Just look at him. He looks happy."

Peg glanced at the guys and back at me. "What is it with you two? You're more than just dating. I knew it!" She exclaimed. "You are sleeping together!"

"That's not any of your business."

"Mari," Harley called out and beckoned to me.

"Yes?"

He whispered, "can we tell them about us, now?" He looked askance, excited but cautious.

"I think it's time we let them in on our secret," I replied.

GASP! Maryanne's hands flew to her mouth. "You're pregnant! Peg was right; you are sleeping together!"

GASP! It was Harley's turn to be shocked. "NO!" His eyes got really enormous as he turned toward me. "Is this what you've had to put up with?"

"Yep," I smirked. "They seem to think we hop into bed every time we're together."

"Crikes! I wished I'd known," he tangled a finger in his locks.

"You do now," I said archly.

"Well, what we have to tell you is nothing so scandalous as an impending birth," he ran his hand through his hair, a gesture he does when flustered or nervous.

"We'd planned on telling all the WOSL staff today, but guess the others will find out later." I jumped on the announcement.

"Please don't tell anyone what we're about to share with you. We haven't told our families yet. So, consider yourselves privileged to be the first to know. Can I get a promise of secrecy?" I asked, glancing at each person. I was gratified to see affirmative nods from everyone.

"I'm happy to tell you," Harley took my hand in his, "on June 7th, Mari consented to be my wife." He lifted my hand to his lips and kissed each finger. "In doing so, she made me the happiest man on earth."

"Awe how sweet," Maryanne's fingers went back to her lips, this time in a gesture of joy.

"Do you have a ring, yet?" Peg asked.

"She certainly does," Garrett piped up.

I was surprised to see moisture at the corner of Garrett's eyes. I always viewed him as friendly, caring, but a little staid in his manner.

"Wow!" Flash said. "I never saw that coming."

"Me either," March said. "I always thought I'd ask Maryanne before Harley ever decided to get married."

"I never saw him as the marrying kind, myself." Flash shook his head. "A lot we knew, huh?"

"I'll say that's for sure."

"Congratulations you two," Flash stuck out his hand.

"Thanks," Harley grasped it and pumped vigorously.

"Where's the ring?" Peg pestered me.

I reached into my shirt and pulled the chain out. I'd been wearing it around my neck except when I was alone with Harley. I took it off the chain and slipped it on my finger, then held my hand out for them to see.

"It's lovely," Maryanne crooned. "Unique. Is that a black opal?"

"Yes," Harley replied, beaming with pleasure.

March jerked his head in her direction. "A what Opal?"

"Black Opal. It symbolizes love and passion." She went into her teacher mode.

I shot a startled look at Harley, who merely shrugged and grinned. He suddenly became very interested in the condition of his fingernails.

"What is a Black Opal?" I asked Maryanne.

"The Black Opal is the rarest of this type of stone. This one looks like it might be solid gemstone." She glanced at Harley for confirmation before continuing. "See how there are tiny specks of color throughout, and how the colors change when you tilt it? This difference in color is called diffraction of light. Is this stone from Australia, Mexico, Peru, the US or Africa?"

"South Australia," Harley mumbled as he looked anywhere but at me.

"The silver setting is unique. I assume you had it designed!"

"Uh...yeah," Harley sounded like he was becoming uncomfortable under the grilling Maryanne was putting him through. "I'm not telling the cost," he grumbled.

"Wasn't going to ask. That'd be rude. However, judging from the quality of this ring, it wasn't cheap. I'd guess it came in on the higher side of five grand. It's a beautiful piece."

"Thanks." Harley continued looking at his nails.

"How much?" Peg gasped. "Mari, want to trade places? Any guy who'd spend that kind of money on a ring is a keeper for sure."

"I know. Harley's a keeper even without a ring," I reached out and hugged Harley.

March mumbled something about having to cut down on his pot supply to save more money if he hoped to get a ring an eighth as nice eventually. I was the only one who noticed his comments.

Instead of commenting about the cost, March said, "well, Maryanne you sure know your jewelry."

"My grandparents own a jewelry store in Ada. When I was in high school, I worked there on the weekends."

"Oh," he sighed with relief, "that explains a lot."

"The food is ready," Garrett announced.

"Awesome! I'm starving," Flash grabbed a paper plate and began loading it with everything.

"Good friends, food, and music, what can be better?" March patted his belly.

"The trout is perfect. It's my favorite," I said, relishing the succulent morsel I had just eaten.

"Master Harley told me you loved trout."

"I do. I've loved it since I first tasted the fish in Idaho. I was fifteen."

We spent the afternoon noshing on Garrett's grilled foods. Periodically one of us would go inside and put on a new selection of albums.

"I love how you've wired your sound system throughout this place," Flash commented. "We can hear music everywhere."

As the day wore on, we began hearing the bands playing in Faurot Park. We turned off the stereo and listened to the local bands. As the sun began to set, Harley brought out the sparklers, snaps, and smoke bombs.

"Mari, which sparklers do you want? I have Morning Glory, Neon, and Gold." Harley was acting like a kid in a toy store.

"None for me," I eyed the assortment he had.

"Okay. How about some snaps? I have Throwdowns and Thunder Firecrackers," he said enthusiastically.

"No, thanks," I suppressed the shivers I felt coming on with difficulty.

"Smoke Bombs? Tsunamis, Grenades, or Parachutes?" He thumbed through the vast assortment of packages.

"Thank you but, no."

"Why not? They're fun," he persisted. "The rest of us are doing them."

"If everyone jumped off a bridge, would you do it too?" I snapped. "I don't want to. I'll watch you guys."

"Is something wrong?" His brow wrinkled with concern.

"No. I just don't want to do fireworks. I prefer to watch." I spoke harshly.

"Mari, can we talk privately?"

"Sure," I shrugged. Now, I was feeling defensive. What was wrong with just being a spectator? I stood up and followed him into the house.

"Uh, oh," I heard Peg say, "trouble in paradise already."

Once inside, I stood with my arms crossed. "You have something to say?"

"Yes. Each time fireworks was mentioned today you seemed to get an attitude. What gives, Mari?" Harley demanded, his hands on his hips.

"I prefer to watch and not participate. I feel like you are trying to force me to play with that stuff." I felt cornered, which is a feeling I don't handle very well.

"I got them because I thought everyone would enjoy them before the fireworks spectacular at the park. Forgive me, if I was wrong!" He huffed.

"Now who has an attitude, huh?" I shouted. "Why do I have to play with them? Why can't I just watch? Why do you have to have it your way?"

"I don't understand what's going on with you today. Hormones?" Harley's attempt at humor failed miserably and only served to make me angrier.

"NO!" I screamed. "It has nothing to do with hormones or PMS. In fact, that's downright inappropriate of you to suggest such a thing!"

"You're right, I'm sorry." Harley appeared taken aback at my outburst. "I just don't understand." Harley spread his hands in supplication.

"You want the truth? I hate them. They scare me." Tears welled up in my eyes.

Why was it Harley seemed to be the only person who could make me cry? When he made me happy, I cried. When he made me sad, or I was missing him, I cried. When I got mad, I cried.

"Don't cry, Mari. I hate it when I make you cry." He reached out and pulled me into his arms.

"I'm terrified of lighting any kind of fire," I sobbed. I played with matches when I was little. One day I let the match flame get really low and burned my fingers. I threw the match and set the curtains on fire. It scared me badly."

"Oh, sweetheart. I wish I'd known. I wouldn't have gotten them." Harley sounded miserable. "I should have talked to you about it first instead of just assuming. I love fireworks and just think everyone feels like I do."

"That's not the problem. I don't mind the others doing them. I like to watch, just don't make me play with them. You were so excited when you were talking about plans for today. How could I deny you that pleasure? I wouldn't be a very good fiancée, if I did that," I hiccupped.

"Shh it's okay," he kissed my hair. "Just tell me next time. I can take it. We can always figure out something we'd both enjoy."

I snuggled deeper into his arms. He was so comforting. "I will. I promise."

"Okay, that's my girl."

He held me until I stopped trembling. He pulled back and looked at me. "Want to go wash up? I'll wait here."

He was leaning against the wall with his thumbs hooked under his belt when I returned. "All better," I smiled tentatively.

"Come here," he held his arms out.

"Why?" I sniffled.

"Just come here, Mari. Indulge me, please?" Harley smiled disarmingly.

I went willingly to him and let myself be ensconced in his embrace. "Better?" He asked as he placed his lips on my head.

"Yes, I'm okay," I smiled through my lingering tears.

Harley cupped my face and lowered his lips to mine. We kissed for several minutes. "Do you want to go out and watch the others play with the fireworks?"

I nodded, "yes. You can do fireworks too." I smiled. I was so lucky to have someone as understanding and accommodating as Harley.

"It's a deal."

Arm in arm we returned to the backyard patio. Harley waited until I was settled in one of the lounge chairs with a blanket draped over my legs before he went to play with the sparklers.

"Cool!" Flash crowed as he swung his fireworks in an arc and watched the trail of lights coming off the stick.

"Everything okay?" Peg asked.

"Just fine."

The fireworks show from the park was truly fantastic. They shot high overhead. A flash of red, white, and blue ended in a flag before shooting even higher and exploding in a shower of golden sparkles raining down. We could hear the crowds cheering with every launch.

March and Maryanne shared a lounge seat, Flash, Peg and Garrett perched on chairs. The day ended with Harley and I sitting together wrapped in a blanket, enjoying companionship almost as much as the Fourth of July spectacular.

Chapter Twenty Four

The Fall Quarter had just begun in mid-September when we learned the results of the FCC licensing tests we had taken back in June.

"Guess what?" Hixson said excitedly, once everyone took their seat for our weekly meeting. "You guys are not going to believe this. I think it must be a record of some kind. We all passed with really high marks. Huge thanks to Harley and Garrett for putting us through the rigorous studying."

"We did?" Peg sounded incredulous.

"Got our licenses right here," Hixson waved the envelope. He pulled them out and handed them to each of us.

"Congratulations on a job well done," Harley fairly beamed with pride. "I can't wait to tell Garrett the good news. He's going to be ecstatic."

"This calls for a celebration!" Mike pounded his fists on the table. "Who's up for a night at Zag's?"

Zag's Pizzeria was just down Harding Highway from the campus. I can only describe Zag's as it was like Arnold's from the television show 'Happy Days' only on steroids. It was in an old red and white metal and brick building that had seen better days. The parking lot was full of potholes and bikers tended to hang out there.

It was also the hot spot of the disc jockeys from WOSL radio. We made it our very own hangout and virtually took over the place every Friday night. Zag was a middle-aged man who loved the college crowd we brought in.

Entering Zag's you saw a stainless steel counter on the right that ran down the back wall. Behind the counter was where the pizzas were made. There was a gap between the cash register station and the food delivery counter. Employees and disc jockeys came and went from the kitchen into the dining area through that space.

"Hey, Zag!" we called out as we entered.

"Hi, guys. You know the drill." Zag was a lean man in his mid-forties. He wore a checkered apron and had a pencil stuck behind his ear.

It was not uncommon to see a disc jockey behind the delivery counter making a pizza for ourselves and often for other customers. At first, I wondered how Zag got away with volunteer labor and why we never paid for our food. Shortly after I joined WOSL radio, I learned about the so-called advertising deal. Disc jockeys' ate free in exchange for ten commercials a month.

Often, visitors saw all the disc jockey's horsing around in the kitchen area as we cooked, many times creating a new pizza to be added to the growing list of favorites. Singing, dancing and tossing pizza dough around was the norm.

Once you tasted a Zag pizza, nothing else would suffice. Zag's favorite line was, "it's all in the dough." No pre-made dough was tolerated. Zag feigned a heart attack at the mere suggestion he used store bought dough. His were completely homemade, and he substituted water with buttermilk and draft beer. Sounded nasty but tasted great.

"What you want on your pizza?" I asked Harley as he shoved enough tables together to accommodate our boisterous gang.

The dining area consisted of booths lining the back wall, and tables lined the windows and across the room near the counter. The tables were highly polished butcher block style about the size of a card table. They were not the lightest to move around. The center was left open for dancing and was decorated with beer tavern lights.

"Everything," he hollered as he strolled to the jukebox and plugged in some coins. Soon we were tossing dough into the air to the tune of 'Ride With Me' by Steppenwolf as he sang along.

It wasn't very long before all of us were singing as loudly as possible while bemused customers looked on and Zag ran around trying to shush us.

"Excuse me," an older woman approached Harley. "Do you work here? I'd like to place an order."

"Certainly," he smirked and stepped behind the register. "What would you like? I recommend the Zag special."

"My husband and I have never been here before. We're new in town," she confided as she nodded in the direction of an older man.

Harley had that effect on people. A couple of minutes with him and people were telling their life story while he listened attentively.

"Then you want the Zag special." He leaned forward over the counter and whispered conspiratorially, "but I would leave off the anchovies. I swear I have no idea what sauce Zag added to them, but they are gross."

"What's a Zag special?" She asked.

"This week, it's a mushroom, pineapple, ham, bell pepper, kalamata olive, apple, onion, egg, pepperoni, pepper jack, cheddar, and Swiss cheese with bacon and coconut sprinkled on top."

"Sounds exotic."

"You won't find it anywhere but here. I promise if you don't like it, we'll make you a pizza of your choosing free of charge and refund the cost of your order."

Zag stood off to the side with his mouth gaping open. It took March, Hixson, and Mike to keep him from yanking Harley out from behind the register. "Relax," I whispered, "they'll love it."

"They better," he muttered and stepped to the jukebox to select another song.

"Okay, we'll try the Zag special," the lady glanced at her husband, "and two beers."

"If you like beer, try the St. Bernardus."

"Is that your favorite?"

"Personally I don't drink beer, but the rest of the disc jockeys here always order it. Or, you could try the house draft, which is another favorite."

"We'll try the house draft." She suddenly spun around and looked at us. "Wait. You're disc jockeys?"

"The Ohio State University at Lima, WOSL radio," Hixson piped up. "We're soon to be the only student-run cable station in the U.S."

WOSL radio started operating in the spring of 1975. I joined the station in the fall quarter. At the time the station ran two-hour shows starting at eight in the morning until sign off at four in the afternoon.

Monday through Friday. Within six months we were broadcasting until six in the evening with plans to be piped to the Lima community via cable. The four to six time slot was designated for recorded lectures. The station did not operate on weekends.

"Good choice on the beer. I hear it's a local favorite." Harley busied himself ringing the order on the cash register. "Okay, guys," he yelled, "We have one Zag Special and two house drafts." Turning to the lady, "That'll be five fifty."

The soft strains of Bob Seger's 'If I Were a Carpenter' drifted over the speaker system. After making change, he took out a rag and wiped his face. I looked at him with concern. He had grown a bit pale. "Are you okay?"

"Just a bit warm is all," he smiled. He stepped from the register to the beer taps and poured two pitchers of draft, being careful to keep the foam head to a minimum. "Will you get me a ginger ale or seven up? My hands are kind if full." He carried the pitchers to the table and looked back at me.

I watched him with concern. It was unlike Harley to look pale and sweaty. I wanted to go to his side and wipe the salty beads from his face and cover him up all warm and cozy. Instead, I got two glasses and filled one with seven up; the other with coke.

"Guys," Hixson called out in his nasal sounding voice. "It's time to dance." He hopped onto a table top and began mimicking a strip tease without the pole. "Va va va boom! Boom cha-la-ca boom!" he shouted as he gyrated his hips and kicked his legs up high.

Hixson is robust and stands six feet tall. Watching him dance on a table to the Daddy Dewdrop song 'Chicka-Boom (Don't Ya Jes' Love It)' was comical at best and downright worrisome at worst. It wasn't long before March and Mike joined him. "C'mon girls," Hixson beckoned as he bent a wiggled his bottom.

"We'd rather watch you guys," Lori was this terminally cheerful, chubby girl who couldn't talk without giggling. Mike loved her and nicknamed her the Pillsbury Dough Girl, which she hated.

She usually had the last show of the day. Lori could never bring herself to get out of bed before ten in the morning and was often late to her classes and WOSL management meetings in the afternoon.

Harley sat at the end of the table and rolled his glass across his face.

"Are you sure, you're okay?" I asked as I reached out and touched the back of my hand to his face. "You are burning up."

"I'm just warm, is all," he mumbled and pulled my hand down to the table, covering it with his. "I'm okay." He gazed into my eyes with all the innocence and earnestness of a small child. His steady mesmerizing gaze almost persuaded me to believe him.

"Harley," I began only to be quickly hushed.

"Let's just enjoy this evening and watch these clowns jiggling. Want to tuck a few bills into their pants and see if they get embarrassed?"

"Who, those guys? Nah...they'd just eat it up."

"We'll see," he grinned like a wolf as he stood and strode over to the dancing guys. "Here ya go, this one's on me," he howled as he stuck bills into the waistband of their jeans.

"Harley!" I laughed, "You do know that made you look so uh, so uh yeah." I snorted, and coke came flying out of my nose. I hurriedly grabbed a napkin and wiped my face.

"Who cares, we both know I'm not," he laughed. "Just look at their faces!"

All three guys wore a look of sheer shock and had turned a brilliant shade of pink. Mike abruptly sat down on the table. "I think I'm getting drunk," he crowed.

"That was fun. How about a dance with me?" Harley stood, holding his hand out to me.

"That I'll do." I walked with him into the middle of the room. Soon we were twirling slowly to the crooning of the Carpenter's 'Close to You.' I snuggled into his arms, "I've always loved that song. Reminds of my berry picking days back in Portland, Oregon."

"I didn't know you were a berry picker. What kind?" He held me close as we swayed gently to and fro.

"Strawberries and blackberries. You had to earn five dollars by noon at ten cents a pound, or you couldn't come back."

"That's a lot of berries. Did you eat any?"

"Everyone did. How did you spend summers?"

"Traveling with my parents. We visited places like Tibet and Paris."

"We were always moving."

"Military brat?" he teased, reaching out to smooth a strand of my hair over my ear.

"Yeah, kind of. Even after Dad got out of the Marines, we moved around. I've been to every state except Alaska. I'd like to go there someday."

"So would I. I'd like to see the whales from a ship, and watch penguins frolicking on the ice or see polar bears fishing."

"If you could go anywhere in the world, where would it be?"

Harley paused as though deep in thought, "Bermuda. Thomas and I want to see if the Bermuda Triangle is paranormal or just a dangerous stretch." Thomas and Harley had the same classes, liked the same movies and books. They could have been twins.

"I'd like to visit the Angkor temples. They've always felt mystical to me, very spiritual, you know?" He looked quizzically at me.

"I've never heard of the place." I could tell I was in for one of Harley's history lessons, but I didn't mind. I loved listening to his wonderful baritone voice. It was hypnotic, and if you weren't careful, you soon fell under its spell.

"I say it's spiritual because the temples are placed in alignment with the stars in the Draco constellation. The demons and gods at the temples indicate the procession of the equinoxes and transition from one astrological age to the next."

"Anyone want another round?" Mike scooped the pitchers and carted them to the tap. Mike was about five foot seven and skinny. We used to call him 'beanpole' but never to his face. He enjoyed music, pot, girls, and beer but not necessarily in that order.

"I'll take another 7 Up, Mike," Harley responded.

"Got ya." Mike grabbed Harley's glass, "What about you Mari? Beer or Coke?"

"Coke, please."

"The temple at Phnom Bakheng uses the Buddhist and Hindu sacred number one hundred and eight." Harley continued with his history lesson. "That number is seventy-two and thirty-six. Seventy-two corresponds with the longitude east and points directly at the Pyramid of Giza."

"Wow," I sighed, but ultimately found myself thinking about the Angkor temples and wondering what it would be like to experience them. "I'd love to see them."

"Maybe we'll go there on our honeymoon," he whispered. "Would you like that or someplace more romantic?"

"Any place as long as we're together."

"We'll travel the world and see all the exotic places we've ever heard of, and end in Paris."

He sounded breathless. I couldn't tell if it was from excitement or not feeling well. "Harley, let's go sit down and eat."

"Yeah, I guess I'm not feeling all that well after all." He sat down and rubbed his left calf.

"Do you want to leave?" I stood behind him, massaging his shoulders. I placed my hand on the back of his neck. "Harley, I think you have a temperature."

"I think I'd better go home." His color turned from a healthy shade to a ghastly white.

I touched his forehead. "Harley! You're burning up!"

"Please, Mari," he rasped. "I want to go home."

"Should I follow you?" I asked as I helped him to his feet. Mike quickly came over to help.

"Yes, please," he moaned.

"Harley, are you sure you can ride your hog?" Mike asked. "Want me to take it to your place?"

"That'd be great. Thanks, Mike."

"If you aren't feeling better by Monday, you should see a doctor," Mike said

"I will," he gasped as though in pain.

"Guys," I said to the other disc jockeys, "We're going to leave."

"Everything okay?" Hixson asked as he bit off a piece of pizza.

"Don't feel well," Harley grunted.

"Be careful man. You want me to have my Mom check in on you?" Hixson asked.

"Nah, I'll be okay. Just something I ate at lunch, I think."

Mike and I got Harley into my car. I took him home. At his insistence, I left him Garrett's care.

That day was the turning point of our romance. It will forever be in my memory as the day I began to lose Harley. In retrospect those times he'd felt ill should have sent warning flags, but the rationale was always sound. This day, however, none of those reasons applied. There was no long road trip resulting in exhaustion. That day at Zag's, he began to leave me, but not by choice.

If I could live that day over, I would have spent it quietly with him and not with a rowdy bunch of disc jockeys at a pizza joint.

Chapter Twenty Five

The following Monday, Harley felt fine but made an appointment to see the doctor.

"My doctor wants me to see a specialist in Toledo. Garrett's going to drive. I hate to ask, but will you go with me?" He looked scared. "When the doctor was examining me, there was a tender spot behind my left leg."

"Of course, I'll go with you." I kissed his brow as though the mere contact would soothe away his fear.

"I hate hospitals."

"I can understand that. You've certainly been in one a lot lately with your cousin and your sister's fiancée."

Garrett let us out at the entrance to the hospital. He asked that we call the car phone when we were done. He was going to run some errands while we were in the doctor's office.

I soon came to hate hospitals almost as much as he did. Why are these health care centers laid out in the most convoluted floor plans I'll never understand. Nothing is ever a straight shot. We walked for what seemed to be miles of bland colored halls just to get to the registration desk for his appointment. Then it's another twenty-minute stroll to the doctor's office where we sat for over an hour.

"My word, they sure want us to walk a lot," Harley grumbled. His breathing was a bit erratic.

"Are you okay?" I turned to look at him.

Since I've known him, he was always into health and in fine form. He could jog five miles and talk the entire time. Today he seemed to be huffing.

"Can't breathe," he stopped and sat on a bench that lined the wall. "Give me a minute."

I sat beside him and watched his chest rising and falling. Within minutes his breathing returned to normal, and we resumed our trek to the doctor's appointment.

The doctor's office was typical with a waiting room, reception area and door to the examination rooms. We sat on hard plastic chairs covered with vinyl.

"Do you want some water?" Harley asked as he stood and ambled over to the water cooler.

"Yes, please."

I watched him as he paced the waiting room. His walk was almost feline in gracefulness. There was no swagger like many bikers had, only a precise placing of his legs one in front of the other. His pacing turned heads as other women ogled him.

"Harley? Come sit with me," I patted the chair beside me.

We had waited over two hours before he was finally called. "Mister Davis?" the nurse opened the door. She held a clipboard in her hand.

"Here," Harley said.

"Follow me," she held the door open for him.

"May I bring my fiancée with me?" Harley grasped my hand.

"Certainly."

We went taken down a hall to a set of scales.

"Step on the scales, please."

Harley smirked at me, "Now you're going to find out how much I weigh."

"One hundred sixty-five, height six feet two inches," the nurse called out. "This way, please." She ushered us into an examination room.

The room held a row of cabinets, a sink, a small hard vinyl table, a stool, a trash can, a step stool, and a chair.

"Up onto the table you go," the nurse said. "Put on this gown with the opening in the back."

"Do I remove my pants?" Harley asked.

"Just leave on your underwear. I'll be back in a couple of minutes to take your vitals." She left the room, closing the door behind her.

"I know the drill," I sighed and turned my back to him.

He laughed, "I guess you do."

He sat on the table dangling his legs. He had a bemused look on his face. "How is it, you keep seeing me in various states of undress? Not very chaste of me, huh?" he teased.

"I guess not," I laughed. "Let's see; there was the sidewalk before the Steppenwolf concert, then your room afterward, and now today. Geez, Harley, I'm beginning to think you like stripping down when I'm around."

"Yeah, right," he laughed, his face turning a nice shade of pink.

We sat almost an hour in that room before the doctor came in.

"I'm sorry for the long wait," he was an older, distinguished looking man with hints of gray in his black hair. He studied the chart in his hand for several minutes before looking at Harley. "Let's find out what's going on with you okay?"

"Sure." Harley fidgeted.

Blood was drawn. Harley was poked and prodded in every possible location from his head, neck, back, arms, torso, legs, and feet. A slight swelling was detected in his left thigh.

"We're going to need to run some tests and possibly a biopsy," the doctor explained. "The goal is to rule out cancer."

There it was the awful 'C' word. There very word cancer strikes fear into many people's hearts.

"The staff will schedule the tests and contact you."

We stopped at the sign out desk to pay for the visit. The nurse signaled for us to take a seat in the waiting room. Once again, we sat quietly waiting. Thirty minutes went by when she called us back in.

"These are the tests you are going to need. They are scheduled for eight am two weeks from today."

When the date for the tests arrived, we learned it wasn't just a one-day event but could take several days. Countless vials of blood were drawn daily. A biopsy was even performed on his thigh.

In all, he spent three days being tested as an outpatient. The biopsy resulted in an overnight stay. The excellent medical staff ran every diagnostic possible only to come up with nothing except a slight deficiency in iron.

"Well," the doctor said. "The biopsy came back negative for cancer. For some reason, Mister Davis, your body deposited fat cells in that one location."

The doctor focused his attention on the charts. "You certainly are not fat by all means. Your weight and height are well within the healthy range." He looked up at Harley and smiled. "I'd say that's good news."

He glanced back at the papers, "The only thing that came back as a possible concern is in your blood work. You are slightly deficient in iron. I suggest you eat foods such as spinach more often. I'm giving you a prescription for iron supplements. Come back and see me in six weeks to test for your iron levels. Here is the order for the lab work. Make sure the lab order is completed ten days before your appointment."

"That's it?" Harley asked, relief showing on his face. "Eat more spinach and take iron supplements?"

"Yes, son, that's it."

This time, the long walk didn't seem so bad. We chatted happily and made plans for lunch at a restaurant in Toledo.

"Garrett!" Harley raced to him. "Good news! It was a fat deposit in my thigh, and I'm low on iron!" He grabbed the older man and hugged him.

Garrett sputtered and grinned with joy, "That is good news, Master Harley. Good news indeed." He held the door open for us to get into the limousine.

As I sat in the car, I looked at Garrett. I thought I saw a sparkle of wetness in the corner of his eyes. He lifted a finger to his lips and smiled. I nodded slightly in acknowledgement.

We left the hospital full of smiles. Everything was good again.

Chapter Twenty Six

"Happy birthday, Mari!" Harley greeted me as he threw open the door to his home.

I entered the foyer to be overpowered by a WOSL disc jockey off-key rendition of Steppenwolf's 'Happy Birthday' from their 'At Your Birthday Party' album. I stood paralyzed with overwhelming shock.

My closest friends popped up from behind chairs, tables, out of the cloak closet, and from doorways. They had the goofiest looks on their faces. Peg dressed like a clown. Hixson wore a gladiator outfit complete with a hatchet hanging from his side. Thomas was a leprechaun. March, the hippy of our group, looked even more so with his vibrant tie-dyed t-shirt of many colors. Judy and Lori dressed like Munchkins from 'The Wizard of Oz.' Flash was dressed like a mad hatter. Harley wore a high waist suit with ruffles down the front of the shirt and a matching top hat. He looked like a dandy from another century. Mike and Maryanne wore outfits making them look like Henry the Eight, and Queen Victoria respectively. For a minute I thought I was at a Halloween party.

"Surprise!" They yelled and tooted on paper horns. Everyone was wearing a children's birthday party hat. They launched into another rendition of Steppenwolf's 'Happy Birthday' song.

"Wow! Here I thought we were just doing a weekend get together," I said as I looked into the living room to see it decorated in party favors. "I thought the Halloween party is tomorrow."

"It is," Harley hugged me and planted a kiss on my lips. "Happy Birthday, Mari."

"And many more," the others chorused.

"You guys, are too much," I laughed.

Festive bows and streamers dangled from the ceiling and the drapes. A variety of pumpkins and ghouls for Halloween were scattered throughout the space. Plastic birthday tablecloths covered the floor. Stacks of paper plates, plastic utensils, and napkins. Gift-wrapped presents perched on the brickwork in front of the fireplace.

"We're having a birthday picnic in the living room." Harley clapped his hands.

"Dinner is rib eye steaks, salad, baked potato, corn on the cob, and rolls," Peg confided. "Garrett has been marinating the steaks for two days."

"And Flash made dessert," March rubbed his stomach.

I stared at everyone. My friends were all acting like nine-year-old children full of glee and excitement. It was almost as though they had never celebrated a birthday before. "I'm flattered. Whose idea was this?"

Everyone turned and pointed at Harley. He grinned sheepishly. "I had to have some way to celebrate your birthday."

"Come here, Mari," Harley beckoned. "You get the seat of honor in front of the fireplace."

Everyone grabbed a plate, flatware, and napkin before sitting on the tablecloth. Maryanne sat next to March with their backs against the couch. Hixson, Mike, Lori, and Judy took their respective places next to each other. Peg sat to my left and Harley to my right. Thomas sat next to Harley. That left two spaces, one for Flash and the other for Garrett.

The Steppenwolf album gave way to Hamilton, Joe Frank & Reynolds, followed in turn by Linda Ronstadt, Neil Sedaka, and Barry Manilow.

Flash entered the room carrying a platter of baked potatoes in one hand and a bowl of salad with the other. Garrett followed behind him with a plate of steaks and a pan of corn. Flash left the room and returned with a basket of rolls and butter.

"So, how long have you guys been planning this?" I asked as I savored a bite of steak.

It was so tender you could cut it with a fork. Each bite brought forth a burst of flavors. "Garrett, this is delicious."

"Thank Flash," Garrett replied as he buttered a roll. Every time we got together, Garrett ate a lot of rolls. Bread was one of his weaknesses. "It's his marinate recipe. All I did was follow his directions and cook it."

"Wow, Flash! You should be a chef!" I said. I took another bite and rolled the morsel around in my mouth much like a wine taster would do to determine the body of the wine being sampled.

"Thank you," he demurred while forking loaded baked potato into his mouth.

Harley looked around the room at this motley gathering and sighed with pleasure. He was surrounded by good friends and good food. I knew he didn't get this kind of camaraderie with his family and it felt good that we disc jockeys could provide that.

The music ended, and Maryanne went to the stereo to put on 45rpm versions of Nat King Cole's 'Unforgettable,' Jim Nabors' 'Somewhere My Love,' which in turn gave way to Etta James' 'At Last.'

"What?" she asked, "We need a little romantic music to celebrate with," she said.

She added Janis Joplin's 'Me and Bobby McGee,' 'Summertime,' and Creedence Clearwater Revival's 'Have You Ever Seen the Rain,' to the turntable.

"So what's new with everyone?" Harley asked. "I've been a little out of pocket, so catch me up." He stretched his legs out in front of him. He nudged me with his right hip. I returned the gentle bump.

"I'm thinking about doing my masters at Bowling Green University," Mike announced. "Judy is thinking about going with me."

Judy smiled shyly. "Yeah. We both graduate next spring and wanted to go to the same school for our masters."

"You guys getting married, too?" Peg asked. "Man, I'm jealous. First, you and Mike get together, then Hixson and Lori, Harley and Mari, then March and Maryanne. Where have I been? Out playing in left field, I guess. I need to seriously get busy."

"Nah...just planning to live together for awhile first," Judy giggled. "I thought you and Thomas were becoming an item."

"She's my backup. You know, if we're both still single when we turn thirty, we'll marry each other."

"Really?" I asked. "You both have backup contingencies?"

"Yes," Peg replied. "In the meantime, there's no harm dating each other on occasion."

"I got a scholarship to study culinary arts and one for broadcasting at The Ohio State University in Columbus," Flash piped up. "I haven't decided which I want the most. I'm trying to figure out if I can somehow manage to do both."

"That'd be so cool," Hixson said. "Flash the radio station engineer by day and chef of his own restaurant by night."

"Congratulations," Harley said and clapped Flash on the back. "Anyone want drink refills?"

"A Coke, for me, please," I replied.

"I'll take a Coke too," said March.

"Got any Pepsi?" Lori asked, "If not, make mine a Coke."

"Be right back," Harley sauntered from the room. He returned minutes later with the drinks.

"I was offered a publishing contract with a book promotional tour," I said quietly.

"Really?" Thomas asked, "I didn't know you were into writing. I write poetry, myself."

"I dabble," I said.

"Which story, Mari?" Harley settled beside me. "Is it that swamp story?"

"Yeah."

"Are you going to do it?" he asked, running his hand down my shoulders and back.

"I don't know," I shrugged. "I'd like to talk with you about it later."

"Mari," he persisted, "This is a great opportunity for you."

"It's a two year tour in the US and Europe. I don't want to put college on hold. And I most definitely don't want to put our wedding on hold for that long."

"Okay, love, we'll talk about it later." He smiled.

March went to the turntable and put on KISS's self-titled album, followed by Steppenwolf's 'The Second,' Bob Seger's 'Seven,' Gordon Lightfoot, and 'Green River.'

"Time for presents!" Harley reached out and grabbed a gift. "This one's from Hixson."

It was wrapped in plain brown paper. I tore it open to find an album of Hungarian Gypsy Music. "Can we play this next?" I asked, looking at the cover.

"I remembered how much you seemed to enjoy it last spring," Hixson said, his face aglow with delight.

"I love it, Hix. Thanks."

"Open mine next," Peg begged. "I made it myself."

Harley handed me an elaborately wrapped package. It was a macramé of an owl using wood twigs for branches, cotton batting for the eyes, woven rope for the body, and Buckeyes for the eyes.

"It's beautiful," Harley said.

"It is," I agreed.

Maryanne and March gave me a silver pen with a carrying case. "For when you get the urge to write the next great American novel," she said.

Thomas handed me a tiny box. "It's an American Indian arrowhead."

"Cool." I examined it carefully. "Obsidian?"

"Yes." I remember how excited you were when we had to identify artifacts in our anthropology class. You said something about being interested in archaeology."

Mike gave me the latest Stephen King novel. Lori and Judy each gave me Gordon Lightfoot's 'Cold on the Shoulder,' and Steppenwolf's '7' album.

"I want to hear 'Foggy Mental Breakdown,'" I said as I opened the album jacket. I cast a sly grin at Harley and added, "and 'Ball Crusher,' the taboo song."

The guys chortled and slapped Harley on the back. He turned red and shot me a murderous glare.

"Why? What's wrong with that song? It's about flattening baseballs, right?"

"Oh, my dear, sweet, innocent Maryanne," March chuckled and whispered in her ear.

"GASP!" Maryanne turned beet red. "There's a song about men's...men's gonads?"

"Yup," everyone laughed.

Garrett handed me a package. "For you Miss Mari, happy birthday."

"Garrett, you didn't need to get me anything. Thank you."

I opened it carefully. Inside was the loveliest sweater I had ever seen. It was a dark green cashmere with my initials embroidered on the left side near the shoulder.

"Garrett!" I cried, "This is beautiful!" I put on the garment. It fit perfectly. "Thank you so much!"

"You're welcome, Miss Mari," he smiled.

Flash looked at me and grinned sheepishly. "My gift to you is dessert. I hope you like it." He stood and left the room followed by Garrett.

"Thanks, Flash. I'm sure I'll love it."

Harley shyly handed me a small rectangular box. "For you."

The wrapping was silver and gold. It was tied with an orange ribbon. Inside was a jewelry case. I slowly opened it. The box contained a simple silver chain bracelet with a pink heart. "It matches my necklace! It's lovely, Harley. Thank you so much."

"You're welcome, love," he beamed with joy. He clasped the bracelet around my wrist.

Garrett came back carrying a tub of homemade ice cream and scoop. Flash returned with a four tier cake. The icing was a chocolate vanilla swirl. Red roses decorated the top. Pink lettering said, "Happy birthday, Mari!" The candles formed a spiral with a single large one in the center.

Another round 'Happy Birthday' burst out with the gang singing even more off-key and out of tune than earlier. "Wish!" They shouted.

I closed my eyes, made my wish, and blew out the candles.

The cake and ice cream were heavenly. Flash could put all the frozen treat companies out of business with his concoctions.

"Flash," I said, shoveling a mouthful of ice cream. "This is wonderful. Thank you so much."

We sat around enjoying conversation and eating Flash's dessert. "March," Flash said, "want a rematch game of chess?"

"You're on!"

"Mari," Peg lifted an eyebrow at me. "How about the same for us and pinball?"

"Sure."

"Gonna, get slaughtered," Harley mumbled. "You a glutton for punishment, Peg? I'm telling you; Mari could be the pinball wizard from The Who album 'Tommy.' She's won contests."

"I've been practicing," she replied.

We all went to the game room and began a long night of fun. Flash beat March at chess. I won the pinball games. That was followed by a game of Monopoly. Around two in the morning, we retired to our sleeping arrangements which had not changed since the spring.

Harley and I sat in front of the fireplace. Each of us was wrapped in a blanket and had a pillow.

"About that publishing contract," he stated. "I think you should do it." He removed his blanket and picked up a poker. He stirred the ashes and turned the log in the fireplace.

"Would you be able to go with me?" I asked him.

"No," he shook his head sadly. "I have my business to consider. I'm training Edward to manage the company. He's the veteran I hired last year." He rewrapped the blanket around him and settled back down beside me.

"Two years is a long time," I said as I thought about it. I rested my head on his shoulder.

"I'd miss you terribly. Mari, this could be the chance of a lifetime for you."

"I don't want to be separated that long. If it's meant to be, there will come another chance."

"Mari," he began and looked at me.

"Harley," I warned. "I want to be here with you. When we're married, we can revisit that path if the opportunity comes around again. If it doesn't, I won't regret it. You are more important to me than any publishing contract."

He leaned over and tenderly kissed me. "Okay, Mari. You win."

"Thank you," I sighed, returning his kisses.

"Get a room," March's voice rang out.

"Yeah, you two," Thomas chimed in. "I have to leave in the morning. I need my sleep."

"I thought they were asleep," Harley whispered.

"So did I," I chuckled softly.

An evening of companionship, food, presents, and games drew to a close with the love of my life beside me. Who could ask for more? Thus ended the best birthday I had ever known.

Chapter Twenty Seven

That morning we ate a fabulous breakfast provided by Flash, who had become our defacto chef for our get together. Afterward, we started decorating the house and grounds for Halloween. Harley had planned a party for the students and selected faculty in addition to preparing for trick or treating children.

Some neighborhoods in Lima had elected to celebrate Halloween on Saturday that year while others went on Sunday or Monday, the official date. Harley had invited the children, their friends, and parents in his neighborhood to join us.

The gates were covered in gossamer webbing to look like giant spider webs. The driveway was lined alternating hay bales with barrels holding a ghost or goblin.

"These bales are heavy," March grunted as he swung one into place. Shirtless, his muscles rippled from his pectorals down to his abdominals and across his back. He winked and struck a saucy pose when he caught Maryanne looking. "Like what you see, babe?" He drawled in a lazy Midwestern accent.

She quickly resumed working on the spider webs. "Men!" She muttered to everyone's amusement.

"You get along now, little lady, and leave us men folk to the heavy stuff," Flash chided.

Pumpkins and witches lined the circular drive to the house. Lanterns lighted the road, casting eerie shadows upon the ground. The entrance was transformed into a haunted castle. Ghosts and goblins flew past overhead on razor thin wires. A sound system played spooky sound effects.

The foyer held huge black kettle pots with dry ice in a false bottom to create the illusion of smoke rising from potions. Inside the actual kettles were pots of popcorn balls, chocolates, soft drinks, juices, assorted fruits, and sweets. Tables lined the hallway filled with finger foods. The chandelier was replaced with a mirror ball that reflected light throughout the space.

The game room became an enchanted fairyland with gnomes, toadstools, and fairies intermingled with the games. The center of the room was set up for the old carnival game of bobbing with a tub full of water and apples floating in it.

The living room was left as a place for conversation. Halloween music pumped through the sound system, with The Who's' 'Boris the Spider,' Alice Cooper's 'Welcome to my Nightmare,' Blue Oyster Cult's 'Don't Fear the Reaper,' Black Sabbath's 'Megalomania,' Electric Light Orchestra's 'Evil Woman' and 'Strange Magic,' Donovan's 'Season of the Witch,' and the classics 'The Monster Mash' and 'Monsters' Holiday' by Bobby Boris Pickett.

A selection of VHS movies perched in a cauldron beside the television set. Included were 'Black Christmas,' 'Carnival of Souls,' 'The Haunting' by Robert Wise, 'Shivers' also called 'They Came From Within.'

"What a great collection," I said as I thumbed through them. "I didn't know you liked horror flicks."

"Sometimes," he walked over and placed a hand on my shoulder. "They're great to make fun of, except for 'The Haunting.' That one has some serious creepiness. Ever read the book by Shirley Jackson?"

"Have I? It's one of my all times favorites." I looked at the tape. "We have to watch this one tonight."

"Just as long as the room doesn't go waltzing with us trapped in it," Harley laughed.

"That'd be fun. After everyone is gone we can all pile in here and have a horror movie feast," Peg nodded her approval while rubbing her hands in anticipation.

"Hey," Thomas greeted as he walked in. "Wow! You guys have done a fantastic job. Sorry, I couldn't come back earlier. The family planned to do something and then changed it to Monday. So," he grabbed a popcorn ball from a cauldron in the foyer, "here I am." He bit into the treat.

With thirty minutes to spare before the first guests were to arrive, we rushed to change into costumes. Peg went as a witch; Maryanne dressed as a princess. I wore a red cloak with black lining similar to Little Red Riding Hood. Flash became a ghoul; March was a giant gnome, Garrett became Quasimodo, Thomas was a goblin, and Harley was the vampire count in a black cape. He carried a wooden walking stick with a silver wolf head.

The fog machine was pumping out a mist, covering the foyer floor, which added to the creepy ambiance of the entryway. The outdoor lights had been on mere minutes when the doorbell chimed. "Trick or treat. Smell my feet. Give me something good to eat." Kids greeted Harley as he slowly drew the door open accompanied by sound effects making the sounds of scraping wood, rattling chains, and moans.

"Come in," he intoned in his best Transylvanian accent. He theatrically bowed low and pointed to a black kettle. "Treats are served."

Parents followed the children. They craned their necks taking in the decor. "You went all out, Mister Davis," one of them commented.

"Thank you. Refreshments are in the foyer. Please help yourselves. You can sit in the living room and eat if you wish. There's games, dancing, and movies. Enjoy."

The next to arrive were students from OSU-L and the technical college. Wilma, a nursing student I had become acquainted with, came dressed as a hippy.

"This is so cool," she hugged me.

Soon the place was hopping with kids playing games and eating treats. Flash and Garrett were kept busy refilling the kettles and food trays.

"Pardon," could be heard as they brought in new trays of goodies. "Coming through."

March and Maryanne judged the apple bobbing and other games, doling out prizes.

"We have a winner!" March yelled.

"Pick a prize," Maryanne indicated a table laden with goodies and toys.

Thomas and Peg took turns greeting trick or treating children.

Harley and I circulated the premises making sure everyone was having fun, and no one was neglected.

The hours passed quickly, and soon the party was over. Each of us pitched in and helped clean up. A table with food, drinks, and snacks was placed outside the living room. Everyone changed out of costumes into sleepwear. We grabbed blankets and settled down to watch 'The Haunting.' Only Flash and Garrett were missing, claiming they wanted to finish up in the kitchen.

Flash periodically popped in to refill our snacks and drinks, send clear away refuse. The movie is in black and white which lends itself quite well to terror driven atmospheric scenes. We had just reached the one where Eleanor and Theo are trapped inside while the doctor and Luke are chasing a dog creature outside.

Harley sat reclined on the rug with his arm around me. March had Maryanne gathered on his lap as she hid from the scary events playing out on the screen. Thomas and Peg huddled together under a blanket.

BOOM! The noise was so loud we literally jumped. BOOM! The walls shook.

"Where is it coming from?" Harley muted the television sound and raced to the window. Finding nothing out of the ordinary, he turned back to the room.

The living room door slammed shut. We turned to stare in horror as the knob twisted with an audible click.

"No!" Thomas ran to the door. Grabbing the knob, he yanked it hard. "Locked."

BOOM! BAM! The sound was coming nearer. The movie played on, forgotten as we lived our own version.

"Sounds like a canon ball hitting the walls." Peg said miserably.

WHAM! The door shook as something pounded it. WHAM! The vibration caused the door to shutter. Any minute now whatever was in the foyer was going to come crashing inside. "MAKE IT STOP!" Maryanne wailed.

The temperature in the room got progressively colder. I felt like I was sitting in a freezer with a bright fire that gave off no heat.

Harley picked up the telephone and rang the kitchen on the house intercom. He put it on speaker so we could all hear.

"Yes, Master Harley?" Garrett answered.

"What's going on?" Harley demanded. He paced as far as the telephone cord would allow.

"I beg your pardon? I can barely hear you over the movie noises, Sir."

"The sound is off, Garrett."

The next pounding bounced right off the door. The entire frame shook. Then came the whispers and giggles.

"Garrett, I'm not amused," Harley glanced at Peg.

She was huddled in Thomas's arms and shaking from fear. Her lips had taken on a bluish tinge.

"Peg is scared out of her wits and might die from fright. Maryanne isn't doing much better. Mari is rubbing her arms like she's freezing. Plus, the dang door is locked."

"Oh dear, that's not good. We'll be right there."

Minutes later Garrett and Flash opened the door to be greeted by our shell shocked faces. Flash held a sledgehammer by his side.

"Surprise?" he said weakly. "Garrett showed me where to hit and not cause any damage."

"We used one of the sound effect tapes to create the noises and voices." Garrett added sheepishly.

"I'm surprised at you, Garrett, "Harley muttered. "How'd you guys make the walls shake?"

"We didn't. I kept looking in to check where you were with the movie. When the movie played that scene, we started the sound effects. Your imaginations made you see the walls shake. I only hit the door frame to add to it." Flash grinned disarmingly at us.

"Okay, you two, you got us," Harley chuckled. "Your idea, Flash?"

"Ahem," Garrett cleared his throat. "It was my idea, Sir. I remembered you telling me about following Miss Mari and Miss Peg to the haunted castle. I thought you'd enjoy a trick being played on you."

"Well, I didn't. Awe, heck. Who am I fooling? I did enjoy it after my heart started back up." Harley chuckled. "Okay, you guys really got us. Just remember, I pay back in kind," he winked.

"Uh, oh," I groaned. "You guys are in for it."

Thus our Halloween party ended with laughter. The following morning we cleaned up the place, leaving the decorations outside for Halloween Monday in case Harley had trick or treating kids drop by.

Chapter Twenty Eight

"Daiken Alba will present a discourse on Unidentified Flying Objects, Nazca Line, hidden bases on the moon, and the Men in Black and how the Bermuda Triangle ties into ancient alien civilizations. The discussion will be held this Wednesday in the lecture hall at 7," Harley read the flyer on the glass door. "Hey, guys. What'd you say? Let's go. The Bermuda Triangle is right up my alley. Always wanted to know if Roswell was real. The Bermuda Triangle, now that spells secret alien base."

"Sure, Harley. I'm game," Thomas replied.

"Me too," the rest of us said.

March, Maryanne, Peg, Thomas, Harley and I met at Kewpee Hamburgers after classes and radio show ended. The burger joint on Elizabeth Street is an old time mainstay in Lima and is home to some of the most delicious hamburgers in Ohio. It had a homegrown diner atmosphere.

I got the chocolate malt and cheeseburger with fries. Harley ordered a bowl of chili, a slice of chocolate pie, and 7-Up. March went for two hotdogs, fries, two slices of sugar cream pie, and Coke. Maryanne had a cheese sandwich, onion rings, and Dr. Pepper. Both Peg and Thomas ordered hamburgers, fries, and tea.

"Um, um, good," Harley forked a bite of chili into his mouth. He savored the morsel as though it was the last forkful on earth. How Harley always managed to make his food look so mouthwatering good, I never understood. It was like he was a connoisseur of American diner food.

"Have you two picked a date yet?" Maryanne asked as she took a sip of her soft drink.

"Spring of 1978. That's as far as we got date-wise," I replied. "It depends on whether or not his parents can come. So far, they've shot down every date Harley has asked them about."

"Why?" Peg asked.

Harley shrugged. "I don't think they believe we're engaged. Mother keeps saying the ring isn't a real engagement style. Father keeps coming up with meetings and conferences he's supposed to attend for every date suggested. They don't want me to marry Mari."

"Why not?" March looked like he was about to blow a gasket. I never saw him angry before. "Mari is a fine girl. Anyone would be proud to have her at their side."

"You got that right," Thomas said as he chewed his burger thoughtfully. "She's pretty, smart, talented, loyal, and completely dedicated to Harley. What more could they want?"

"Beats me," Maryanne said.

I remained silent, if a little embarrassed. It hurt that Harley's parents could reject me so outright without actually getting to know me. Sometimes I worried they might convince him to drop me in for one of their high society girls. When I felt that way, all I had to do was look at him. I knew better. Harley, himself, said he was a black sheep. Although the family was important to him, he did not let them dictate his life. That resolve to live life on his terms, according to his religious beliefs, would not let anyone decide for him whom he would love and marry. For that I was grateful.

"Hey! If we're going to the lecture, we'd better get. It's after six." Harley exclaimed, glancing at his watch.

Hundreds of students packed the lecture hall. Ringing the outer perimeter of the room were several men. Two stood at each door and eyed everyone coming in. Each person looked identical as though they all shopped at the same store or used the same tailor. They wore black pants and jackets, white shirt, and a black tie. Even their sunglasses were black. Why they wore sunshades in the evening was anyone's guess.

"Who are these guys? Security?" March leaned towards us.

"Gestapo?" Peg ventured.

"Looks more like the men in black to me," Thomas spoke, keeping his voice low.

"The what? What does that mean?" I asked, thoroughly confused. "Who are the men in black?"

"The MIB or the men in black are those guys who supposedly show up at suspected UFO crash sites. According to some ufologists, they are either aliens, government agents, or agents of Project Blue Book." Harley's eyes lighted up, and I knew I was in for one of his 'talks.' He ushered us down the auditorium style hall to our seats. We sat up front center stage.

"The MIB allegedly follow guys like Erik Von Daniken, Harold Dahl, Albert K. Bender, and John Keel. They claim it is to make sure they don't spill secrets," Harley said as he slouched down in his chair and propped his feet up.

The stage lights came on. Daiken Alba strode confidently to the stool and podium. "Good evening. First, let me say," he spoke in a thick Swedish accent. "It's nice to see so many people here who want to know the truth. Aliens are real and have been visiting Earth for eons. Second, I must warn you," he paused dramatically.

The auditorium was so silent you could hear every movement in the room. A few nervous twitters could be heard.

"I do not wish to alarm you, but if you look around you will see men dressed in black," he paused again while people glanced around.

"These men are here to make certain I do not disclose specific government classified documents and secrets about the existence of UFOs. Therefore, should a question be asked that I do not answer, it is because I am bound not to by the men in black." Daiken turned on the slide projector.

The picture here shows geoglyphs of the Nazca lines in the Nazca desert of Peru. To me, they resembled a bunch of circular and squiggly lines.

"I told you," Harley whispered. "Can you say conspiracy theory?" he chuckled, garnering a frown of disapproval from Daiken.

"You there in the middle, do you refute what I am saying?"

Harley put his feet down and sat upright. "No, Sir, I don't. I'm very interested in learning about UFOs and how they might tie in with the pyramids, the moon, Nazca lines, and the Bermuda Triangle."

"Magnificent. That's what we're here to discuss." He appeared mollified.

Daiken explained how he thought the circular patterns on the slide indicated landing site chambers to transport ancient aliens from the Nazca base to Atlantis, which he claimed was the Rock of Gibraltar, to Bermuda, the Artic, and the Antarctic.

Harley raised his hand. "So, are you saying aliens landed at Nazca and hyper-jumped to Bermuda, or Gibraltar?" He leaned forward and rested his hands on the back of the seat in front of him. He was totally captivated by the subject.

"That is my current theory, yes."

"Does this include the face on Mars? How does the Project Blue Book come into this?"

"The face on Mars is a Sphinx-like structure similar to the one in Egypt." Daiken ignored the question about Project Blue Book. Instead, he began pacing the stage and glancing at the men in black as though he was afraid. I couldn't tell if his concern was real or part of the theatrics he seemed to enjoy.

"What is this Project Blue Book?" I asked.

"It was a team dedicated to studying UFO sightings to determine if there was a threat to national security. The United States Air Force ran it and Project Sign until 1968 or 1969 when it was officially disbanded. Some conspiracy theories say it is still in operation under a black budget operation." Thomas spoke quietly, keeping an eye on the speaker to avoid drawing further attention to us.

Daiken continued talking about the Nazca lines, spaceports and the pyramids. One of his slides showed a series of numbers that were supposed to be longitude, and latitude for each area and how they corresponded. Daiken completely lost me when he started in on the mathematical equations between the pyramids of Giza, the Mayans, the Aztecs, and the Toltec's tied into the location of a constellation in deep space and Orion's Belt. I never was any good at math. Both Harley and Thomas tried to explain it to me to no avail.

"That's well and good, but I have no clue what you're saying. It's just giving me a migraine." I complained, rubbing my temples.

After the lecture, we returned to Kewpee's for soda floats, pie, and soft drinks. As we waited for our order, conversation turned to the Daiken Alba lecture.

"Was Daiken Alba for real?" Maryanne asked as she dug into a slice of chocolate cream pie.

"I dunno. I thought Daiken was kind of into overdramatizing things," I sipped my coke.

March looked up from his second helping of sugar cream pie. "There's only one way to find out. We do our own investigation."

That caught all of our attention. We stopped eating, drinking, and talking to stare at our long haired pot smoking friend as though he was an alien dropped into our laps.

Harley sat back against the booth seat and pondered the suggestion. He even pulled at an imaginary beard as he reviewed the merits of March's statement. "Let's suppose we endeavored to take on such an ambitious project. Where would we start?"

"We'd need to secure funding first," Peg volunteered.

"That's not a problem, " Harley commented absently.

"I forgot, you're rich," Peg sighed. "Must be nice."

I looked at each one and settled my gaze on Harley. For the first time, I wondered how wealthy he was that he could be so caviler about the cost of such an expensive undertaking.

"We'd need an ocean worthy research ship like Jacques Cousteau's," Harley finally commented.

"Or, we could always do it the college student way," Thomas added. "You know, buy two little sail or motor boats."

"We could tie the boats together," March said.

"How much rope do you think we'd need?" Peg asked.

"A ton," Thomas said. "We'd need to make sure we had enough rope that one of the boats would remain out of the danger zone at all times."

"And what is the perimeter of the danger zone?" Maryanne asked as she signaled the waitress for a drink refill.

"Just east of Miami, Florida, off San Juan, Puerto Rico, to the mid-Atlantic off Bermuda." Thomas looked to Harley for confirmation.

"Sounds right. That'd be about 500,000 to 1,510,000 square miles. That's a lot of rope," Harley grinned. He loved challenges that appeared impossible to attain.

"If we can get close enough, the boat in the safe zone can pull us out when that mist thingy appears," March was getting into the idea.

I couldn't believe we were sitting in a diner seriously discussing the merits of hooking two boats together by rope in the middle of the Bermuda Triangle.

"Guys, have you thought how much rope that would be? Even if we only needed a fourth of the distance and we used the lowest safe zone number that'd still be around 75,000 to 125,000 square miles of rope, right?" I asked.

"Not quite, Mari," Harley replied. "Still, we'd need more rope than two boats could carry. Going to have to think about that some more. Right now, I need to get Mari back to campus so she can get her car. We'll see you guys tomorrow," Harley said as he snatched the bill off the table. "You guys get the tip, okay?" He sauntered to the counter and paid our tab.

"I'll follow you, to make sure you get home safely as usual," he kissed me lightly on the nose.

Chapter Twenty Nine

"Mari?" Harley said when I answered the telephone.

"Yes?" I wondered why he sounded tense.

"I just found out my folks are coming for Thanksgiving. I was wondering what your plans are."

"Well, let's see, my guess is not having a weekend get together at your place," I teased. "So, that would also rule out an overnight road trip."

"Mari," he growled.

I could hear the desperation in his voice. "I'm having Thanksgiving lunch with my family. Then later tonight, we're playing Rummy or Pinochle."

"What time do you eat lunch and when do you start playing cards?" Harley sounded very anxious.

"Lunch is somewhere between ten and one. We play cards around seven or eight. Why?" I pondered his questions. The fact his family was coming to visit had to be the reason for his attack of nerves.

"Do you think you could get away for a few hours? Have an early dinner with me?"

"And your family?" I squeaked.

"Would you?"

"I can probably do that. Should I bring anything? What do I wear?"

"Nothing to bring. Garrett's handling that. Wear your dark blue striped dress. You know, the one I love. Bring that black shawl and a black clutch purse."

"Blue striped dress, black shawl, and clutch purse. What time should I be there?"

"I'll pick you up around two thirty. Is that enough time?" Harley sounded relieved.

"Plenty. My family can eat a Thanksgiving dinner in thirty minutes or less."

"Wow! We take a few hours."

"Don't expect me to ride on the back of your hog in a dress. Mom would never let me out of the house if she saw you pull up on your motorcycle."

"No worries. The car it is," he laughed, sounding jovial. I could imagine him picturing me riding on the back of his bike in a dress.

Thanksgiving Day arrived. My home was a mad house with Mom cooking the turkey, making two types of stuffing, one cornbread, and the other oyster, making candied yams with marshmallow, mashed potatoes, cranberry sauce, green bean casserole, salad, dinner rolls, and chilling wine. Our kitchen was small and not suited for two people, let alone three, to be working in it at the same time. My task was to put the table leaf in to extend the dining table, cover it with seasonal cloth, and set the plates.

It was twelve thirty when we sat down to eat. The food smelled wonderful, and I was hungry but ate sparingly, so I would not be full when I dined with the Davis's.

"Maru," Mom could never quite pronounce my name correctly. Mom looked at me. "You need eat more."

"I'm going over to a friend's house later, Mom. I'm expected to eat with them too."

"Who is this friend? A boy?" she frowned.

"Yes, Mom. Don't worry. There will be others there too." I took another slice of turkey. "And I'll be back in time to play cards."

"You're gonna get fat," Mom said. My Japanese mother was always concerned about us having enough to eat, yet, if we did eat she told us we were going to gain weight. There was no winning with her.

"Yes, Mom," I sighed.

After lunch, I helped clear the table and wash the dishes. Looking at the wall clock, I realized it was almost two o'clock. I hurried to my room and pulled out the dress, matching slip, neutral pantyhose and the black shawl. I dabbed a little Jontue perfume behind my ears. Finally, I pulled the necklace out, put on the matching bracelet.

A Volkswagen Beetle pulled up in front of our home at precisely two thirty. Before Harley could exit the car, I rushed out. He hurried around to the passenger side and held the door open for me.

"Really? A VW Beetle?" I laughed as he settled behind the steering wheel.

"It's a fun car," he shrugged. "Good for traction when the roads get icy. Just chunk a couple of bricks in the backseat and some under the hood in the front. It's a 1961 model that I rebuilt."

"That's cool."

He carefully turned the car around and headed out to the highway. "Did you have a good lunch?"

"Yeah. We're going to be eating turkey until Christmas," I sighed. "Good thing I love turkey sandwiches."

Harley is a careful driver. He always went the speed limit or a little under. Today, he was going much slower, at least five miles per hour under the limit.

"You got a glimpse of my folks when Elizabeth and Dale were here." He muttered, "If you thought it was bad then, prepare for a full onslaught of Davis rudeness."

"That bad?" I winced.

"That bad." he nodded. "Mari, they don't exactly approve of our relationship."

"Oh." I could feel the lump growing in my throat. "Is it me? Or is it my middle-class background?" I asked sadly.

"It's not you, Mari," he hastened to explain. "It's social, economic status. To put it bluntly, you aren't rich. They are snobs. Try not to let them get to you. I love you just the way you are." He reached over and squeezed my hand.

"Wow, that is blunt," I looked out the window on my side. "Do I even stand a chance with them?"

"I'm afraid not," he said gently and pulled the car to the side of the road. He turned to look at me. I could feel his eyes on me as I continued to look out the window. "But, I don't care." He reached out and gently grasped my shoulder, turning me to face him.

I looked down at my hands in my lap. My fingers were intertwined. "Doesn't that make it hard for you? Your family not approving of your fiancée?"

"I'm marrying you, not them." He pulled my hands apart and lifted one to his lips. "I don't care what they think. You shouldn't either. They are ultimate snobs, Mari. No one would meet with their approval unless they had the same or more money than my family."

"How sad," I commented, finally looking at Harley's handsome face. His eyes were so kind and sweet; it made me smile. "I'm glad you're not like that, my Steppenwolf loving biker dude."

"Hey babe," he growled teasingly. "That's my girl. Chin up and howl with me."

We tilted our heads back and let out the worst wolf howl I have ever heard. "Let's go. Don't want to give them any more ammunition by being late," I said with a laugh.

"Got that right," he pulled the car back onto the highway.

After several long minutes, my curiosity got the better of me. "Just how wealthy is your family?"

The muscle in his jaw clenched. "We're billionaires, Mari." He continued to look straight ahead at the road.

"Billionaires? Wow!" My nerves jumped up two notches on the fear scale. "That much," I muttered.

"Yeah, that much," he grunted. "Does it matter to you? Is it the money or me?" Uncertainty filled his voice.

"What? No!" I gasped. "I don't care about the money. I care about you. I was just wondering how badly I appear to them; that's all. I guess I rank next to bottom on their social scale."

"Mari, I don't give a fig about social levels and whatnot." Harley glanced at me. "I fell in love with you, not some glamorized notion of 'My Fair Lady,' you know the movie."

"Really, Harley?" I asked. "How can I possibly win your parents' approval?"

"You can't. Nothing you can do will accomplish that. My parents want me to marry Ashley. Ashley doesn't care for me, nor I for her. So, don't worry about it. You are my choice. I love you."

"And I love you, not your money or your status, just you."

Vehicles lined his driveway. "How many people are here?" I asked.

"My parents, Elizabeth and Dale, Thomas and his date, a couple of my parent's friends from back east, and my cousins Alan and Nichole. Everyone rented their vehicle instead of riding together."

"Gee, and they all have expensive cars except for Thomas."

"Yeah, they wouldn't be caught dead in a vehicle costing less than a fortune. Only high-end cards like BMW, Mercedes, and Limousines qualify."

"And here you are driving a VW Beetle," I chuckled.

"They weren't happy," he admitted. "I even had to hire wait staff to suit them."

A man dressed in a butler's garb stepped to the curb and helped us exit the vehicle. We looked silly having a servant opening the door and helping us out of an inexpensive car.

"And whom shall I say is present?" The man asked as he opened the entrance door.

"Mister Harlan Davis and Miss Mari Forrester." Harley took one look at the man's surprised face when he realized he had just asked the master of the house who he was, and burst out laughing.

"I'm sorry, Mister Davis, my mistake," he stuttered.

"Don't worry about it," Harley clapped him on the back. "No harm was done."

Inside the foyer, the butler took Harley's overcoat and hung it in the coat closet. I elected to retain my shawl. We were then guided to the living room and announced.

"Mister Davis and Miss Forrester," the butler said and bowed out of the chamber.

"Harlan," His mother crooned. "You look a little thin."

What is it about mothers that they always think their kids are too light or fat? Somehow, children, even grown children, are never just right.

"Mother," Harley took her hands and air-kissed both of her cheeks. He stepped back and smiled. "It's good to see you. Mother, the last time you were here, I didn't have an opportunity to introduce Mari to you. The lovely lady beside me is Mari Forrester. Mari, this is my mother, Barbara Davis."

"I'm very pleased to meet you," I said, sticking my hand out only to be met with a stare.

"I'm sure you are, dear," she said and turned away.

Harley scowled and shoved his hands into his pockets. "I'm sorry, Mari. I hoped she'd be at least polite."

"No problem, love." I slipped my arm through his. He adjusted our arms so it would be considered proper by his hoity-toity family.

"Mari!" Peg rushed over to me. "You made it!"

"You're Thomas's date?" I asked dumbfounded.

"Yep. His family went on vacation, and he didn't. My family celebrated Thanksgiving last night. He asked, and here I am." She twirled around.

"At least I have one friend here," I mumbled.

A wait person came over to us with a silver tray on her arm. Flutes of champagne were arranged beautifully around a lighted candle.

"Champagne?"

"No thanks," Harley said and looked askance at me.

"None for me," I replied.

"I'd love one," Peg giggled. "I've never had champagne."

Harley walked over to the sideboard and lifted a crystal goblet and spoon. He lightly tapped the spoon on the glass. "May I have your attention, please?"

He waited until the conversation died down and all eyes turned toward him. "First, I want to welcome everyone to my home. Thank you for sharing this Thanksgiving Day with me. Second, I have an announcement to make. Many of you already know, but I wanted to make it official. Mari Forrester has graciously agreed to be my wife." He held his hand out to me. "Please welcome her into our family."

Thomas and Peg complied even though both already knew. "We are so happy for the both of you."

Dale stepped up and slapped Harley on the back, "You old dog, you!" Turning to me, he lightly kissed my cheek. "Congratulations. Harley is a wonderful man, a very fine man."

"Thank you." I blushed.

Harley's cousins introduced themselves. Nichole cupped her hand to the side of her mouth and commented, "I hope you're ready for this."

"How'd you two meet?" Alan asked.

"At OSU-Lima," Harley replied. "She's a popular disc jockey at WOSL radio."

"Hello," a couple approached us. "We're Stephen and Dorothy Vickman," the gentleman shook Harley's hand. "We understand congratulations are in order."

"Thank you, Mister Vickman," Harley nodded.

"Yes, thank you," I added.

His wife studiously ignored us. Mister Vickman nudged her, and she walked away. "I must apologize for my wife. She was disappointed our daughter, Ashley," he indicated a blonde girl standing by the fireplace, "was not selected to be your wife."

Harley looked shocked. "I never even knew she was interested in me. The last time I saw her, she told me to go freeze my bum off. That was after I proposed to her."

"Mister Harley!" Vickman gasped, "Such vulgar language."

"I beg your pardon," Harley nodded politely and looked relieved when Garrett entered the room.

"Master Harley, dinner is served. Please follow me." Garrett looked dashing in a dark blue tuxedo as he ushered the guests down the hall.

"Where will I sit?" I asked Garrett nervously.

"Do not worry, Miss Mari. Usually, you would sit at the head of the table opposite Master Harley. He has requested you be seated to his immediate right instead. The end of the table will be left open. His parents are going to throw a fit."

"Why?"

"Master Harley is not only breaking protocol with your seating but also with me. He insists I join everyone at the table." He winked at me.

"Oh my! That's marvelous!"

"Indeed, Miss, indeed." Garrett took the seat to Harley's left.

Festive seasonal trappings decorated the room. Poinsettia plants were tastefully placed around the abode. Pine cones and boughs along with fresh roses created lovely table center pieces. The china was Noritake in a pine pattern with matching silverware, crystal goblets, and glasses. The fire had been lighted and cast a rosy glow throughout the room. The sideboard was draped in white lace cloth and held an assortment of desserts including pumpkin custard,

Crème Brule, pecan, apple, and cherry pies, chocolate, carrot, and ginger cakes.

"Shall we offer a prayer of Thanksgiving?" Harley asked as he bowed his head. "Heavenly Father, we thank Thee for the bounty we are about to consume. Thank you for the people who prepared and served this repast, and for the food that nourishes our bodies. Father, we thank thee for our families and friends and ask that you bless us in the coming year. Amen."

Staff flitted in and out bringing in numerous dishes and placing the morsels on our plates. We started with a butternut squash soup. There was turkey, carved ham, yams, potatoes, salad, cranberry sauce, crushed cranberries, bean casserole, three types of stuffing including cornbread, oyster, and chestnut, glazed carrots, gingered fruit compote.

Harley picked up his soup spoon and sipped the squash soup. Not accustomed to formal dining etiquette, I watched carefully and copied his every move. If I was about to make a mistake, a discreet 'Ahem' from Garrett stopped me.

"Dale, how is your recovery progressing?" I asked.

"Much too slowly. If you ask me," Elizabeth cut in, "he should have been through with therapy in two months. We had to postpone our wedding until next year. I had so wanted to have a Christmas wedding in the park with snow all around us."

"Freezing cold for the ice princess," Harley mumbled lowly; only Garrett and I heard him.

"I'm sure the kind of injury Dale suffered takes time to heal." I tried to placate her.

"It's been over five months. Dale's not working hard enough. I don't think he wants us to marry."

"You could be right." It was my turn to mutter. Did she have no concern for the well-being of her fiancée? Did she really think the world revolved around her?

"Harley," Ashley spoke up suddenly. Her voice was strident. "Why her?"

"Who?"

"Your, um, friend."

"She has a name, Ashley. It's Mari."

"Whatever," she drew the word out so much it sounded like a speech affectation. "Why that gold digging harlot?"

Harley stood up, placing his hands on the table and leaned forward. "I'm warning you, Ashley. Keep a civil tongue in your head." His face flushed purple with anger. He has a vein running between his brows that becomes prominent when he is angered. That vein looked like it could pop at any second. "Mari is my fiancée, and you will treat her with the respect she deserves as my intended. You are a guest in my home. I will not tolerate such rude behavior. Do I make myself clear?"

"Perfectly," she said archly.

"Harlan Christian Robert Davis," his mother gasped. "You will not speak so harshly to Ashley Vickman. You know how delicate her constitution is."

"Mother, she was rude to my fiancée, which means she was rude to me. This is my home. I. Will. Not. Tolerate. It. Not from Ashley or you."

"Uh oh," I murmured. "Now she's done it."

Anytime Harley split his sentences into single words meant he was beyond angry.

Peg jumped up yelling, "I'm on fire!" She brushed at invisible flames and spun around. "Oh wait. I'm not burning. Must be the champagne." She grinned impishly at me. Leave it to Peg to come up with a hair brained reaction to defuse the situation.

"Is she drunk?" Elizabeth asked with disdain.

"Nope. I've always wanted to be a clown," Peg laughed.

"That's not funny." Elizabeth snapped.

"I think it is," Harley roared with laughter. The tension drained from his body and he sat back in his chair. "Dessert, Mari?"

"Yes, please. I'd like to try the pumpkin custard."

"That's a good choice. It's more like Pumpkin Crème Brule than custard."

"That's good. I'm not especially fond of custard."

"I made it like a Brule for you, Miss Mari," Garrett commented. "Master Harley told me you enjoyed cream pie and pumpkin. So I tinkered with the custard recipe. I hope you like it."

"If you made it, I'm sure I'll love it, Garrett." I smiled at the thought that Garrett went through all that trouble for me.

"If not, there is the carrot cake. Master Harley said that is your favorite."

"You two sure know how to spoil a girl." It made me feel special that these two men cared so much about me.

All dinner long I noticed how Barbara Davis frowned at Garrett any time he spoke. "Harlan, why is your manservant eating with us?" she asked coolly.

"Because I invited Garrett. He's more than a manservant to me. He is my friend, and I consider him family."

"He is no more family than that so-called fiancée of yours."

"Master Harley," Garrett rose. "Perhaps I should retire to the kitchen."

"You will do no such thing, Garrett. I invited you to join us."

"Mother, my so-called fiancée is named Mari. I expect you to show both Mari and Garrett the respect they've shown you. If you can't, feel free to take yourself to your room or home."

"Harlan!" his father barked. "You will not address your mother in such a manner."

"I'm sorry, Mother. Forgive my bad manners," Harley grumbled.

Thomas looked around the room and stood up. "I think Peg and I are at the wrong table. Shall we retire to the kitchen?" He held his arm out to her.

"Why, I do believe you are correct, kind Sir," she responded in her best fake Boston accent.

"I will join you," Garrett folded his napkin and followed them out of the room.

"Mari?" Harley looked quizzically at me. "Shall we join them?"

"If you wish." I felt miserable for him. He had tried so hard to make this dinner pleasant.

"If you will excuse us," Harley nodded to the remaining people.

We enjoyed the rest of the dinner with the hired help. It was a pleasant change from the hostility experienced in the room with the family. Garrett regaled us with stories about Harley's childhood. Peg teased him unmercifully about his penchant for getting into trouble.

True to his word, Harley had me home before six o'clock in time for my family traditional card game.

He pulled the car to the side of the road and faced me. "I am so sorry about the fiasco dinner turned into. I lost my temper and shouldn't have."

"Don't worry about it. Your family goaded you in that direction with snide comments. You care a great deal about Garrett. He should have been at the table. It is your home. You can invite anyone you please."

"Whew! I'm glad you feel that way," he sighed. "Now, what are your plans for Christmas Eve?"

"Uh, I guess I'm spending it with you and your family?"

"Would you?" he asked. His eyes widened in that little boy way of his. "I'll have you home in time for your family card game."

"That's not a problem. We generally watch Christmas shows on TV that night. What time Christmas Eve? I'm working until noon; otherwise, I'm open."

"Can you get a ride to work?"

"Mom will take me."

"Good. I'll pick you up at K-Mart. Mother wants to have a Christmas dinner party. I'm inviting the veterans who work for me and their wives, and of course, Thomas and Peg will be there. They sure are getting chummy. Do you think anything's developing between them?"

"I don't know. Peg hasn't said anything, but, then again you never know with her. I don't think Thomas is her type, though. She likes the bad boys. The worse they are the more, she likes them. That would leave Thomas out. I think they're just friends."

"That makes sense." Harley came around to my side and held the door open.

"Want to come in and play cards?"

"I suck at cards, except for poker. Anyway," he spoke reluctantly, "I need to go mollify people. Have to calm down the crap I set in motion."

"I'm sorry." I didn't know what else to say. Sorry seemed trite, but it was the best I could come up with.

He gathered me in his arms. "Thanks for being there for me." He kissed me tenderly. "Love you." He released me and walked back to the car.

I felt sorry for him having to deal with the fallout from his family. Suddenly, my family with all our quirks didn't seem so terrible.

"Love you more," I said as I watched him drive away.

Chapter Thirty

Christmas Eve fell on Friday. That meant the shoppers were out in full force looking for last minute sales. Staff had been working crazy hours. I worked from seven to noon that day. Others worked from ten to five, and eleven to six. Our store closed at six o'clock to allow a store wide Christmas party for the staff.

Harley pulled up on his hog. He flipped the visor up and grinned. There was a twinkle in his eyes.

"Hi, beautiful," he greeted.

"Harley," I took my helmet from him and straddled the bike. "What are you up to?"

"Who? Me?"

"Yes, you," I lightly tapped him on the shoulder. "Is there anyone else on this bike besides us? An invisible alien, perhaps?"

"Nope. Not up to a thing," he laughed. "Thought we'd go to a Christmas play."

"A matinee?"

"A Christmas Carol."

"I love the Dickens book!" I clapped my hands. "Or are you trying to escape your family, hmm?"

"Why Mari, you know me too well," he chuckled. "Escape is a nice way to put it. Running away is more accurate. A little time with my love to soothe my battered soul, is what I need."

"Then let's get to that play. Ride on, my weary knight."

Our local theater group performed the play. Many of the performers went to OSU-Lima.

"Ah! There's nothing like watching a classic tale come to life on stage." Harley sat back in his seat and propped his right leg on his left knee. "I love how the stage actor's on pour energy into their

204 Harley & Me

performances. They know there's no retakes, so it has to be right each time they go on."

"See a lot of plays, do you?" Every time I'm with Harley, I learn something new.

"They're the only thing I miss about back east."

"Other than high school drama class trips to see college plays, I've only been two others."

"What'd you see?"

"I saw 'Cleopatra' with my Mom when I was seven. The other one was 'Man of La Mancha' in Seattle, Washington when they took it off Broadway."

The curtains rose, and the lights dimmed. The audience chatter died down. Soon we were lost in the story of Ebenezer Scrooge and how the ghosts of Jacob Marley and the three ghosts of Christmas past, present, and yet to come, made him see the error of his greedy selfishness. I loved watching Harley react to every scene. He was completely immersed in the play. It was like he had been transported from this age of the recent Vietnam war, gasoline rationing, and people's burgeoning greed and frantic gifting and forgetting the true meaning of the season. This was an era where Happy Holidays was taking the place of Merry Christmas. Harley's attention was so focused on the play it was as though he was back in that simpler time. Yet, even back then people did not treat others with compassion as evidenced in how Scrooge acted with Bob Cratchit.

All too soon the play came to an end. The curtains came down and the lights up. We stood in front of our seats blinking. Harley slipped his arm in mine and grasped my hand.

"That was superb!" I exclaimed.

"You honestly liked it?"

"I did. I loved it." On impulse I pulled him to me and kissed him. From the way his eyes grew large, it was like he'd never been kissed before. "Surprise," I gently tousled his hair.

"Unfortunately, we better get to my place. Don't want to disappoint the folks. I wonder if we can provide more entertainment for them. Maybe throw in a knock down drag out fight with you winning?"

"Harley!" I gasped, appalled at his suggestion until I saw the twinkle in his eyes and a hint of a smile on his lips. "Oh, you! You're incorrigible."

"You mean uncontrollable."

"Oh, you!" I groaned. "You're impossible!"

"But you love me anyway."

The foyer was transformed into a winter wonderland. A giant tree reaching from the floor to the ceiling of the second floor graced the center of the entryway. Bows and ribbons of every pastel color imaginable covered the entryway. Gold, silver, and green tinsel, and garland hung from every branch. White lights and tiny glass encased candles twinkled and flickered merrily. Big and small, stars, balls, and angels mingled with peppermint canes and gingerbread men. Popcorn and holly berries twined around the pine. A crystal angel topped the tree. A blanket of faux snow hid the mounting planks and water bucket from view. It was very lovely and unlike Harley.

Harley would have had a smaller tree in the living room near a corner window. It would have been decorated with ornaments by local artisans and aglow with a single string of lights. He enjoyed simplicity.

A small orchestra played Christmas music from the second floor. People entering could see the musicians.

"I took the liberty of getting you a dress for tonight. I know you don't have a formal gown. It and a pair of shoes are in my room. We both need to change. You can have my bathroom. I'll change in the bedroom."

He led me to the back of the house and up the left side servants' stairs. The dress was laid out on his bed. It was an elegant, yet modest hunter green evening gown with matching shoes. The neckline was a gentle curve not the tawdry scoop cleavage so popular with many women. I carefully picked up the garment and entered the bathroom to change.

I looked myself over in the mirror. The dress made me look like a fairy tale princess. I picked up Harley's comb and ran it through my locks. On the sink counter was a mother of pearl comb for my hair.

"You ready?" Harley called through the door.

I opened the door and stood shyly in front of him. He was silent for a very long time. Harley looked me up and down. He stepped back and turned me around.

"You are beautiful." He whistled. He had dressed in a tuxedo that matched my dress. A dark green bow tie and black shoes finished his ensemble.

"Thank you."

"Ready?" He held out his arm.

I grasped his arm, and we again went down the back stairs. By the time we reentered the crowed foyer, it was a veritable who's who of western Ohio, including a few celebrities. The veterans wore their dress uniforms while their wives wore simple yet beautiful dresses. Thomas was in a gray tuxedo. Peg dressed in a pale blue gown worn off the shoulders with a lace shawl.

"Dinner is served, Master Harley." Garrett bowed and made a sweeping gesture toward the dining room.

Instead of sitting next to Harley like I did at Thanksgiving, I was seated at the opposite end directly facing him. Harley did not look pleased. Instead of causing a ruckus, he gave a slight nod of his head in the direction of his mother. His father sat to his right, and she was next to him. Next to them were his sister Elizabeth and Dale. His cousins sat to the left of him followed by the Vickmans. Then came those with political clout and the celebrities, leaving Thomas, Peg and the veterans to sit near me.

"It's okay, Mari," Peg said. "It's better this way. We can enjoy our dinner without feeling like saying gag me with a spoon every time they open their mouths."

"Thanks, Peg. They are being rude to us. That, in turn, means they are being rude to Harley. We are as much his guests as they are." I gulped. If this wasn't a slap in the face to me, Thomas, Peg and the vets, I didn't know what was.

"Maybe, Harley had us seated here away from them to keep us safe from their snobbery," Thomas suggested.

I turned to the veteran sitting next to me. "You are Edward Walters, right?"

"Yes, Miss Mari." He took a sip of water.

The wait staff brought a bottle of wine to the table and offered it to Harley for inspection. Harley passed it on to his father who nodded his approval. The waiter then proceeded to offer a glass to each guest.

"No, thank you," I said. "Edward, how do you like working with Harley?"

"He's the best. We have all been made to feel as though we are a family."

"Mister Davis," said a red-haired veteran, named Adams, "He pays us a fair wage, given us life, dental, vision, and health insurance. Let me tell you, with the nearest VA hospital being in Dayton, having additional health insurance is great."

"We also get paid sick and vacation time," Stuart, a swarthy, black-haired vet said.

"He started a retirement plan for each of us," said Adams.

"And paid holidays," Edward said. "He sends us to workshops to develop our skills, and has offered to pay us to go to college."

"Wow!" I exclaimed. "Sounds great."

"Just don't jack with him," Adams commented wryly. "Jimmy found out the hard way. Mess with Mister Davis and you end up fired."

The twinkling of a tiny bell made me look up. Harley stood at the head of the table. "I would like to welcome our veterans to my home. Good Sirs, thank you for your selfless bravery in serving our country during World War II and an unpopular war known as Vietnam. I salute you. Merry Christmas, gentlemen." He raised his water glass and offered a toast.

The people sitting at the other end of the table silently raised their glasses, while those at my end were quite rowdy. Garrett approached me and whispered in my ear. "Miss Mari, as the hostess, shall we begin to serve the meal?"

"What about a prayer?"

"I believe Master Harley has been asked to forgo his tradition due to the variety of people here."

"What? Politicians and celebrities?"

Garrett nodded solemnly. "Yes, Miss Mari."

"And what about you? Will you be joining us?"

He glanced down at the table and shook his head. "No, I will not this time."

"Well, I would like to offer a prayer first." I rose from my seat and lifted the tiny bell from the table. I rang it and cleared my throat. "Seeing as this is a holiday season, I would like to offer a prayer. Let us bow our heads please." I looked around the room. Only the veterans, the wait staff, and Harley had lowered their heads.

"Our Heavenly Father, we come to you offering a prayer of gratitude for the bounty we have received throughout the year. Father, we thank the people who prepared this wonderful repast, those who serve it, and for the veterans who fought for this country. May each person be blessed. We thank you, Heavenly Father, in the name of thy Son, Jesus Christ, we pray. Amen."

"Amen," Harley said looking at me with a smile. He mouthed, "Thank you."

The wait staff began bringing in the meal. The dinner started with a clear cold soup, followed by a small salad. A ham and a turkey were brought in, and Harley was asked to carve the first slice. Assorted vegetables including a green bean casserole, carrots, steamed broccoli, and squash, cranberries, potatoes, and assorted breads were set in the center of the table. The sideboard held various drinks both alcoholic and nonalcoholic along with ice cream pies, cobblers, pumpkin and pecan pies, figgy. pudding, bread pudding, custards, cheesecakes, chocolate, lemon, and sugar cream cakes. The staff lined the sideboard awaiting a request for service.

"You look lovely in that lavender gown, Mrs. Davis," I complimented her. "Is it imported from France?"

She ignored me and looked across the table at Ashley Vickman. "That should be you sitting at the hostess end."

"Oh, I know. How uncouth! Harlan had some nerve asking those people here tonight. It's your party, not his."

Harley frowned at their conversation. "Please pass the rolls," he said to no one in particular. He selected a slice of bread and broke it into pieces. He chewed each piece thoroughly while looking from his mother to Ashley. The vein in his head throbbed visibly. The last time I saw that, it resulted in an angry confrontation.

At the end of the meal, Harley rose and rang the tiny bell. "I have an announcement to make." He waited until everyone stopped talking and looked at him. "My company has performed quite well this year. As a result, I invited my employees here to join us in celebrating the Christmas season."

Garrett stepped forward and handed Harley some envelopes. "Because of your hard work, I can give out substantial bonuses. Gentlemen, please step forward when I call your name."

"Adams," Harley looked at him, pumped his hand and gave him an envelope. "Thank you for your service to this country and for your hard work."

Adams took the envelope and opened it. From the widening of his eyes, I could tell it contained much more than he ever expected. "I don't know what to say," his voice quivered. "Thank you, Mister Davis."

"Thank you," Harley smiled.

"Stuart," Harley held out his hand. "Stuart was injured in Vietnam and nearly lost his leg saving another soldier." He turned to face the man as Stuart slowly limped toward him. "Stuart, I thank you for the sacrifices you made and for your innovative ideas."

"Thank you, Mister Davis," tears welled up in his eyes as he looked inside his envelope. "You gave me a chance. For that, I will be forever grateful."

"Edward, you have performed exceptionally well during my absences. I hereby name you company manager."

"Thank you, Sir. You took each of us in when we were down. For that act of kindness, we each vowed to do our best."

Peg leaned over to Adams and asked, "what was in the envelope?"

"Peg!" Thomas gasped.

"What? So, I'm nosey."

"A check for ten thousand dollars, Miss Peg," Adams answered.

"Same here," said Stuart.

"That's a fortune!" Peg looked shocked.

"Mister Davis doesn't do anything halfway that's for sure," Edward said as he rejoined us.

"Finally, but not least, Garrett, please step forward."

When Garrett stood beside him, he clasped his hand. "You have been with me since I was born. You have picked me up and dusted me off when I fell. Garrett, you have stood beside me when no one else would. You encouraged me to go for my soul mate, Mari. You are my employee, my mentor, but most importantly, you are my friend and confidante. It is with great pleasure I present you with this meager token of my appreciation." Harley pulled an envelope from the inside pocket of his tuxedo. He handed the envelope and a kerchief to the older man.

"Thank you, Master Harley. Serving you is a joy. One I hope to enjoy for many years to come."

"So do I." Harley clapped Garrett on the back. "So do I."

Chapter Thirty One

"Hey, Mari," Harley came up behind me in the Ladies lingerie section where I was working.

K-Mart was chaotic after Christmas with people returning gifts and searching for bargains. The counter bins containing an assortment of bras was a huge piled up mess.

Harley slipped his arms around me in a brief hug. "What are you doing New Year's Eve?" He kept his arms wrapped around me as he nuzzled my neck.

"Uh, same as Thanksgiving and Christmas Eve?" I laughed. "And playing cards until midnight." I leaned back into his embrace.

"Would you?" He shuffled his feet. Once again he looked like a child hopping from one leg to the other hoping the answer was affirmative.

"Sure," I replied. "Another dinner party?" I thought; at least I'm getting good at using the correct silverware, sticking my pinkie finger out with the proper cups and glasses, and being polite to a bunch of stuck up snobs.

"No, not exactly," he paused. "It's a ball."

"A ball!" I sputtered. "So, I need another new evening gown?"

"I got it covered." His face flushed pink. "I keep doing this, and I'm going to turn into a fashion model dresser."

"I can see your resume now, a hog riding, biker dude, fashion model dresser." The image in my mind was ludicrous. A sandy-haired gorgeous hunk wearing black studded leather with chains and a feather boa as he strutted around fashion models picking out pink and purple florid outfits for them.

"Mother insists on having her New Years Eve gala." He rubbed his face as though he was tired. "With all this running around, I'm exhausted.

A sensation of fear gripped me. Every time Harley felt exhausted he seemed to become sick. I wondered if it was the stress of the holiday season getting to him.

"Are you okay?"

"Yes, why?"

"I'm concerned about you getting sick again like last year after the Steppenwolf concert."

"I'm all right," he dismissed the notion of illness. "Mother has me running around like crazy helping her get this ball organized." Harley frowned, "She does this every year. This time she mailed out the invites months ago. Yesterday, Mother told me to hire an auctioneer for the charity auction. Today, she wanted me to employ very specific chefs flown in two days before the ball. Then, there's the decorating. Can't have the Christmas stuff up. Has to be appropriate for the New Year. And the theme is 'Peace Throughout the World.' How in the heck do I find decorations for that? So, I spent the day locating event planners." Harley spoke rapidly.

"I haven't even had time for my company. Edward has been representing me at all client meetings. He calls me after dinner and fills me in. After everyone has gone to bed, I can work on my new designs. I'm not getting to bed before one in the morning." He talked using a lot of hand gestures, which was not like him. He looked worn out.

"Poor Garrett. He's bombarded with flying clothing designers in and arranging fittings. He gave the green dress to one of them. He said it fit you perfectly and asked them to design a simple gown and select a pair of matching shoes for you."

"How long has this been going on? It's not good for you."

"Since the day after Christmas."

"Can the fashion people get those outfits done in time?"

"They're staying at the house. They'd better get them done. "

"Wow! Mister wealthy Harlan Davis is showing up. I hope this is stress talking and not the real you," I commented.

"What?" Harley snapped. "Oh, no, Mari," he shook his head. "I'm sorry. I'm just frazzled and getting more so dealing with all those contractors and my family."

"Anything I can do to help?"

"Just don't let me go off the proverbial deep end. Okay? Keep me grounded." Harley draped his arm over my shoulders and tugged me closer to him.

"I'll do my best." I wondered if his family would put so much outlandish pressure on Harley if they knew what it did to him physically. I doubted it would change a thing. Harley already had a lot of stress from running a successful business, attending college, and helping me plan our wedding.

New Year's Eve dawned a cold minus two degrees with a light dusting of snow. By day's end, the snowfall total would reach an inch and a half. Harley had the limousine waiting for me when I got off work.

"Hi, Garrett." I slid into the seat. "Where's Harley?"

"He couldn't be here. Mistress Davis has him picking up some items for Miss Ashley Vickman." Garrett uncharacteristically rolled his eyes.

The lineup of cars was worse than Christmas Eve. There had to be a hundred people attending. The drive was bumper to bumper. Vehicles parked on the lawn. Garrett skillfully maneuvered the limo through to the garage in back.

There he led me through the rear entrance and up the service stairs. Once again, I found myself changing clothes in Harley's room. The new evening gown was a dark purple with swirls of blue, red, and black. There was a matching cloak, shoes, tortoise shell comb, and a clutch purse. A jewelry case was placed beside them. Inside was a silver chain with a teardrop gem. It all looked very regal. Instead of feeling like a princess, I felt like a queen.

I was brushing out my hair and placing the comb when someone knocked on the door. "Come on in," I called out.

"Are you decent?" Harley asked from the other side.

"I hope so." I cracked the door open.

He stood dressed a dark blue tuxedo looking quite dapper with a black silk tie and spit-shined shoes. The unruly way he wore his hair hinted at a touch of the rebel devil making its appearance. There was a glint of the carefree biker in his beautiful eyes. I loved it.

"You look lovely," he murmured as he looked me up and down, followed by a low wolf whistle.

Once again a small orchestra was on the second floor overlooking the foyer. The entire ground floor was transformed into a ballroom. All the rooms had been emptied of their traditional furnishings. Tables and chairs for dining had been placed along the outer perimeters, leaving the middle for dancing. Wait staff lined the walls waiting for instructions. The most notable guests were seated in the dining room while the rest were put into the living and game rooms, and foyer based on their social, economic status. His parents sat at the center of the table and took on the role of host and hostess. Elizabeth and Dale were on their left and Harley was on their right. As Harley's fiancée, I sat beside him.

The food was elaborate with a sweet potato soup, lemon-lime pannacotta, and an apple pomegranate salad served as the first course with a glass of wine. The second course was Foie gras torchon with pickled pear, oysters with caviar, shrimp cocktail, salmon pasta with goat cheese and herbs, and poached lobster with creamed celery root. The third course consisted of mustard crusted roast goose, lamb, Swiss chard and Beurre Rouge, roasted asparagus, Brussels sprouts with trumpet mushrooms and pickled beets with gooseberries served with champagne. The dessert course included German chocolate cake, amaretto cherry ice cream, eggnog crème Brule, Meyer lemon cake with bourbon glaze, and strawberry cream pie served with coffee.

I noticed Harley did not partake of any dish made with alcohol or their accompanying drinks. To honor him, I did the same.

"You don't have to do that," Harley spoke quietly.

"I know. I want to." I said. "They sure like their alcohol."

"Just wait until midnight." He frowned and fussed with his napkin.

"That bad?"

"Some of these guests are."

I looked around the room at each guest. Many of them were on their fourth or fifth glass of wine or champagne. Elizabeth appeared a bit inebriated. Dale did not seem happy.

"I wish you didn't drink so much at these formal affairs," Dale commented.

"Hush," Elizabeth scolded. "Do you want to tell the entire room?"

I returned my attention to Harley. He was fiddling with his napkin again.

"I still don't see why we had to seat them in three different rooms. This room could have seated a hundred if we'd removed the dining table and sideboard. This room could have held nine rounds and a head table comfortably." Harley rubbed his chin. "But Mother always has to point out who is in what class. Those whom she considers an equal sits with us. Next, comes the ones with slightly less followed by the people who are barely wealthy or are in the news a lot."

"Harlan," Barbara Davis stated. "Is the food not to your liking? You have hardly touched a morsel on your plate."

"Mother, you know I do not consume food or drink that has alcohol."

"That religion of yours is a farce. You should rejoin our church. At least you wouldn't have all those ridiculous rules to follow. You should be more like your sister, Elizabeth. She knows how to appreciate our gracious lifestyle."

"Mother," Harley's voice took a hard-edged tone. "What church I belong to is my business. The rules I follow make sense to me. As for Elizabeth, would you rather I run around having sex with anyone who wants to dish it out? Should I drink myself into a raging drunk at every party? Or maybe I need to take up smoking and chewing tobacco, so I stink and leave a nasty mess in ashtrays like Father does. Is that what you want?"

"Harlan!" His father snapped. "You will address your mother with respect!"

"I'm sorry."

From the look on Harley's face, I could tell he was not happy being publicly reprimanded. His eyes flashed with resentment. If there was one thing I knew about Harley, it's his love of independence. No one could control him unless he allowed them to do so. He also loved family, whether they were his biological or his expanded ones of friends and employees. It was this love and loyalty that created conflict within him.

"Harley?" I lightly touched his arm. "May I have a word with you privately?"

"Sure," he grunted. "Please excuse us for a minute." He took my hand and led me out of the dining room into the library. He turned to face me and crossed his arms. "What is it? Are you going to fuss at me too?"

"Nope," I said and gently tugged his arms apart. "I just want to give you some breathing room. This dinner has to be stressful. I see you clenching and unclenching your fists, playing with your napkin, or running your hands through your hair. Pretty soon you're going to snatch yourself bald." I pulled him into my arms.

As I ran my hands up and down his back and kneaded his shoulders, I felt him relax as the tension drained away. "That's right. Breathe deep, hold and exhale. Let the stress leave your body. Tonight will soon be over."

Harley bent down and rested his head on my shoulder. "I love my family, Mari. I really do."

"I know you do, love. Believe it or not, they love you too in their own way."

"I know they do. I just can't stand my family's high handed manner in how people are treated. Just because someone isn't as wealthy doesn't mean that person should be treated like dirt. In the end, we are all humans regardless of the color of our skin, gender, socioeconomic background, religion, education and so forth. Jesus walked with the poor and sick. He eschewed the greedy merchants he came across at one of the places of worship. Why can't we all treat each other equally?"

"I don't have the answers to your questions, love. I think we can only do what we can as individuals. If everyone did a good deed for someone and that person, in turn, did one within a month this world would be a better place."

"You so get me, Mari. If everyone did service to another, there wouldn't be wars. People wouldn't die of starvation or from dirty drinking water."

"I believe in you. I support your endeavors to make life better where you can. You bring great joy to many people, Harley. Look at Flash and how much he's changed since you gave him your room when we all got together. That one night of privacy provided him with so much comfort. The veterans working for you told me how much you did for them in an era when they are not appreciated for the service they provided this country. You, Harley, have touched the lives of so many."

"Awe shucks. You make me sound like a saint. I'm a bit of a devil, not an angel." He placed his hands on the side of my face and kissed me.

I don't know how long we stood there or how long Garrett watched us.

"Ahem," Garrett cleared his throat. "Master Harley, Mistress Davis sent me to find you."

"We'll be along in a minute," Harley replied as he continued to gaze into my eyes.

"Very good, Sir."

"Thank you, Mari." Harley hugged me. "I so needed that pep talk."

"Anytime. Shall we return to drama central?"

"I like that. Drama central," he laughed. "Will you honor me with the first dance of the evening?" He grinned. "Don't worry, Mother always has a slow uncomplicated dance first. I'll guide you through it."

"I'd love to, Harley."

We returned to the dining room to find our plates cleared from the table. People were walking around mingling. Ashley sedately approached Harley and grasped his arm.

"I claim first dance," she purred.

"I'm sorry, Ashley. I have already asked my fiancée to dance."

"But, then the second dance is with your mother." Ashley stuck out her lower lip in a pout.

"As per our family tradition. You may have the third dance if you wish."

"Fine," she huffed and flounced across the room to her mother.

"What do you mean, it's over?" Elizabeth screeched and slapped Dale.

"I mean, we're finished. I'm breaking our engagement," Dale kept his voice level. "I can't take any more of your petty, childish behavior."

"I'm not giving my ring back," Elizabeth shouted.

"Fine with me. It didn't cost as much as you told everyone it did." Dale strode from the room with Elizabeth close behind him.

"Well, he has a back bone, after all," Harley shook his head.

Barbara walked over to Harley. "Will you please talk some sense into Dale?"

"I'm sorry, Mother. That is something Dale and Elizabeth need to work out without interference."

"She's your sister."

"Who treated her fiancée no better than she treats servants," Harley replied. "I believe the dancing is about to start. I have a dance promised to Mari." He held out his arm.

"You are to dance with Ashley Vickman. She is an equal in your station of life, not this Mari you claim to like."

"Love, mother," he grated. "I love Mari. Proper etiquette dictates I have the first dance with Mari."

"Then you need to talk some sense into Dale."

"Which I have respectfully declined."

His mother sighed, "when did you become so rebellious? Was it that biker gang you hang out with?"

"You mean my employees? Since when did you start hating motorcycles? You told me I was named after your love for the bikes."

"People change."

"Not always for the better either," Harley mumbled.

I pulled him to the side and whispered, "if it means that much to her, go ahead and dance with Ashley. I don't mind."

"It's the principle of the thing, Mari. Mother has to realize I'm a grown man, not a child. She can't run my life."

"Very true, love. But, in the end, does it matter who had the first dance? If it keeps the peace, I think you should dance with Ashley."

"If you insist.

I watched as Harley walked across the room and asked Ashley to dance. She shot me a smug look before rising and following him onto the dance floor.

"She is better suited for him, you know," Barbara said.

"Money wise, probably. Temperament and interests, no," I said. My heart felt heavy as I watched them waltz around the room. Ashley knew the societal protocols. I only knew his heart. I wondered how long he could hold out against a full scale family onslaught.

"You are only living a fairy tale, child. You can't possibly believe he loves a person of your social strata, do you?"

"Why not?" I asked woodenly.

"Child. You know nothing of proper etiquette. Why I don't think you even bought your gowns. Harley bought them, didn't he? You do not have what it takes to run in his circle of influence. You are nothing but poor white trash."

I'd never heard middle-class or blue-collar folks referred to as poor white trash before. All my life, the people around me took great pride in achieving the middle-class status. Now, here I was being dismissed as though I was nothing but a gold digging wench.

"He will marry you because he asked you to be his wife. Over the years, he will come to resent you. If you care for him, you will break off this charade and encourage him to pick a wife more suited to his standing in society. He doesn't love you; he is in love with the notion of Cinderella."

"Excuse me, please." I dashed from the room, up the servant's stairs to Harley's room. I quickly changed into my regular clothes.

"Where are you going?" Harley asked when I came out. He was leaning against the wall.

"Home." I dabbed at my eyes with a tissue.

"What did my mother say to you?" He launched himself toward me, folding me into his arms.

"Nothing," I buried my face in his shoulder and tried to stifle the tears.

"Mari," he tenderly lifted my face and looked into my eyes. "What did my mother say to you?"

"She's right; Ashley is better suited to you. She's your equal, not me."

"Nonsense," his thumb wiped the tears from my cheeks. "Ashley cares for no one but herself. You, Mari, are my better half. You complete me." He kissed the top of my head. "Now, tell me, what did my mother say."

"She called me poor white trash," I blurted.

I could feel his muscles tense as a flash of anger shot through him. "She said, what?" He asked incredulously. "We'll see about that."

He stomped down the servant's stairs. I tarried along behind him reluctantly. Harley pushed into the dining room and strode over to his mother. She was happily chatting with the Vickman's and looked questioningly at him when he grasped her elbow.

"I want a word with you, Mother." Harley steered her out of the room into the library.

"What is this about, dear?" she asked and settled into a plush chair.

"This is about the pig-headed way you have treated, Mari." He ran his hand through his hair.

"Harley," I approached him, "Please don't."

"Not now, Mari," he growled. "Please sit down."

I walked across the room and sat near the door. It made me feel terrible to realize I may have caused an irreparable rift between Harley and his mother. This evening was turning into a nightmare to end all bad dreams.

"Mother," Harley faced his mother. "With all due respect, I must insist you refrain from making derogatory remarks about Mari and my friends."

"Me?" Her hand flew to her chest.

"Yes, you. This entire holiday visit starting with Thanksgiving, I've had to listen to you make disparaging comments. You have cast aspersions on Mari to no end. I will not tolerate such disrespect in my home."

"Son," Harley's father entered the room. "You will not address your mother in such as disrespectful manner."

"I mean no disrespect, Father. I merely wish to impress upon Mother my highest regard for Mari and my friends. Mari has gone out of her way to be polite and friendly. I expect you both to treat her in a similar manner. I am an adult, fully capable of making my own decisions. I suggest you treat me with the respect I deserve."

"Harlan, you will be addressed as an adult when you give up this Cinderella fantasy of yours," his father laid a hand on Harley's shoulder. "You would do good to listen to your mother. This Mari person is not for you. She is from a lower class and can not possibly do you justice in public."

"ENOUGH!" Harley roared. "You will either treat my fiancée and my friends with respect, or you may pack your bags and go home right now! Do. I. Make. Myself. Perfectly. Clear?" Harley's face turned a dark red. The vein on his head pulsed rapidly as his anger mounted. He clenched and unclenched his fists. "And I mean immediately."

"Well! I've never been treated so rudely by my own son," Barbara huffed. "Victor, do you see what I mean about this Mari person? She is a bad influence on Harlan."

Harley strode to the telephone and pressed the intercom button. "Garrett? Please come to the library."

Within seconds, Garrett was standing in the doorway. "You called, Sir?"

"Yes, Garrett. Please escort my mother and father to their rooms. They are leaving."

"Very good, Sir."

"Harley," I rose and went to him. "No, don't do this. It's New Years Eve. You don't want to act like them, do you? Let your mother enjoy the rest of the ball. We can spend the time in the music room listening to Steppenwolf."

He stared at me so long I thought he might have forgotten about his parents. "Are you sure, Mari?" he asked. "You're right," he sighed.

"I take it; I am no longer needed in here?" Garrett asked.

"Yes, Garrett. Thank you." Harley turned to his parents. "Please forgive my temper."

He then escorted me from the library to the music room. Thomas and Peg soon joined us there. We spent the remainder of the evening listening to songs and talking. Garrett periodically popped in with a tray of refreshments and drinks.

"Please join us, Garrett," I invited.

"I would like that," Garrett replied, "for a few minutes, anyway."

At the stroke of midnight, we cheered in the New Year. Harley pointed to the ceiling. I looked up and saw we were standing directly under a sprig of mistletoe.

He tilted his head and grinned impishly. I melted into his arms. The kiss was sweet, filled with love, and joy, I never wanted it to end.

Chapter Thirty Two

The Spring Quarter flew by rapidly. Harley was kept busy planning to expand his business. He spent a lot of time searching for larger facilities that could accommodate not only research and development but also manufacturing.

My class load doubled, so I was now taking courses from 8 am to 10 am. and from 3 pm to 5 pm. I continued disc jockeying at WOSL Radio and working in the K-Mart lingerie department. My schedule at K-Mart was mainly Friday and Sunday nights six to ten, and Saturday from ten in the morning to two in the afternoon.

The rest of the time we spent planning our wedding. We both wanted a simple ceremony with family and close friends in attendance.

"I don't think my family will be here," Harley said. "At least, that's what it sounded like the last time I spoke with my mother."

"I hope she changes her mind. It'd be sad if she missed out on her son's wedding."

"Yeah, but don't count on it." He shrugged the tension from his shoulders. "Anyway, there's going to be a lecture on serial killers tomorrow night. Want to go?"

"The talk about Edmund Kemper, Ian Brady and Myra Hindley, Donald Henry Gaskins, and Charles Manson?"

"Yes."

"I take it you want to go?" I asked skeptically.

"It'd be interesting to hear about the forensics and methodology involved in tracking down these criminals."

"Blood, guts, and gore," I smirked. "Sure, why not? Who's giving the lecture?"

"Vincent Franklin. He's made a career out of studying these cases."

"Are any of our friends going?"

"Of course, March, Maryanne, Thomas, and Peg will be there. We'll get a bite to eat at five and be back in time for the lecture at seven."

"I know, Kewpee Hamburgers or Zag's?" I smiled.

"That's a hard choice," he rubbed his belly and grinned. "Let's let the gang decide."

"Sure, Harley," I blew him a kiss.

He pretended to catch with his hand and hold the imaginary kiss next to his heart.

"How's the new facility search going?"

"I'm looking at two right now. One is in Van Wert, the other in Delphos. Delphos has more promise I think." Harley flipped through pages of wedding photos. "Do we want something in a church or a rental hall?" He snapped his fingers, "I know! How about having it here? We could use the gazebo."

"I like that idea. Okay, so we know the what and where. Now we need to pick the date."

"This is going to sound corny, but how about June 7th?"

"The date you proposed? That is so romantic."

"Now we have the what; wedding, the where; my backyard gazebo and the when; June 7th, 1978. We just need outfits, theme, menu, guests, and music. I guess that leaves Steppenwolf out."

"Yeah, I don't see 'Born to be Wild,' 'Just for Tonight,' or 'Another's Lifetime' as a wedding processional or recessional," I laughed. "Maybe we can have Steppenwolf music for dancing."

"I'd like that."

"What about Gregorian chant or some Bartók'?"

"Maybe. Kind of depends on what theme we choose. By-the-way, money is no object. I'm paying for this."

"Harley, that's not fair to you."

"Yes, it is. I can afford it. I want us to have the wedding of our dreams."

"Master Harley," Garrett poked his head into the room.

"Yes, Garrett?"

"I'm sorry to bother you. Edward is on the telephone."

"I'll be right there." Harley rose, "Please excuse me, Mari." He followed Garrett into the hall.

I could tell from the tone of his voice it was bad news. The only line I heard was, "What happened?"

Minutes later, Harley rushed into the room. "Mari, I have to go. There's a problem at the company."

"I'll come with you." I neatened the pile of papers we were working on.

Garrett met us at the entry door. He handed us our helmets and jackets. "Godspeed, Master Harley."

It took twenty minutes to reach his company. A cadre of fire engines, police cars, and ambulances surrounded the facility. Smoke poured from the open doors and windows. Flames danced in a puddle of gasoline. Firemen dragged hoses in every direction as they battled the blaze.

Harley flashed his identification card at the officer blocking traffic from entering. As soon as he stopped the motorcycle, Harley jumped off and ran toward a cluster of employees.

"Edward!" He shouted.

"Over here, Mister Davis," Edward coughed. He was covered in grime.

"How did this happen? Did everyone get out?" Harley glanced at each person as though he was taking a body count. "Stuart. Where's Stuart?"

"He didn't make it, Mister Davis," Edward said sadly.

"What? Oh Heavenly Father, NO!" Harley dropped to his knees. His hands rested on his thighs. He threw his head back and wailed. "NO!" Great racking sobs shook his body. "How many?"

I knelt beside him and gathered him in my arms. He fought me, shrugging out of my grasp. I let him go. This was an emotion he had to let out.

"Fatalities?" Edward stood with his legs spread; uncertainty was written all over his face.

"Yes," Harley hiccupped, "How many? Any others?" Harley swallowed hard. I could tell he was taking it personally. He felt responsible for each employee.

"A few minor burns, cuts, and scrapes, is all." Edward hung his head. "Adams and Zafar are being taken to the hospital for smoke inhalation."

"How? What happened?" Harley remained kneeling on the ground.

"When I got here I found the door open. I thought I'd check things out. Everything looked fine, so we started working on the newest build. That's when Adams noticed one of the hogs had been tampered with. The gasoline vapors were quite strong in the showroom." Edward waved his hands around.

"I immediately had everyone start shutting down. Unfortunately, Stuart was welding and didn't hear me. I don't think he knew what hit him. The fire ignited from his torch."

"A flash from the torch ignited the gasoline?" Harley's fingers combed through his hair.

Edward continued to keep his head bowed. "I feel I should resign. Stuart died on my watch. He has a wife and children. What are they going to do?"

"Nonsense, Edward. You were not at fault. Stuart's family will be taken care of. You have my word. No one that works with me will suffer." Harley rose and patted the veteran on the back. "Do you think we can make this place work until I can relocate us?"

"The place is salvageable with some elbow grease. I'm certain of that."

"Then that's what we'll do as soon as the police and fire departments are done with their investigations. In the meantime, everyone will continue to draw full pay."

Harley walked toward the building to survey the damage himself. He stuck both hands into his jacket pockets and scuffed his shoes on the pavement. The glass in the showroom littered the concrete. Big hogs sat in the showcase as though waiting for rescue. Huge scorch marks marred the show room where the flames had reached. Inside the workshop, the welding area was a blackened mess. Smoke still billowed from the hot spots. Tools and equipment lay scattered on the cement floor where the blast had flung them.

His staff milled around. These war-hardened men looked shell shocked. Edward walked toward him.

"Mister Davis?" A fireman and a cop approached.

"Yes?" Harley tore his gaze away from the disaster and studied the two men.

The fireman wore a yellow slicker and had a mask dangling around his neck. His face was covered in sweat that caused the soot to dribble down from his forehead to his chin.

"Do you have any enemies that might want to put you out of business?" The cop frowned as he pulled out a notepad.

"Not that I know of." Harley squinted at them.

"Do you have insurance on this place?" The cop scribbled furiously. "Any recent claims?"

"Yes, I have insurance. No recent claims. Never had any claims." Harley's voice hardened when he realized where the line of questioning was headed. "Am I under suspicion?"

"Just covering the bases."

"I think, you'd better contact my lawyer." Harley pulled out his billfold and took out a card. "Neither myself or my employees will be answering any more questions without legal representation." He spoke dismissively. Once again, I glimpsed a view of the wealthy corporate Harley I had seen previously. It was a peek into another persona that I didn't much care for. I preferred my gentleman, carefree biker to the corporate honcho.

Harley walked over to his employees. "Do not answer any more questions without an attorney. I am willing to pay all attorney fees. You pick a lawyer. Do not hold back anything, even if it makes me look guilty of wrongdoing. I want nothing but the truth."

"Mister Davis?" Edward interrupted Harley's train of thought.

"Which hog was tampered with, Edward?" Harley stood staring at the big machines.

"The 1976 FLH solid black model. Someone cut the lines."

"Cut the lines, huh?" Harley lifted a hand to the back of his neck and rubbed. "Whatever on earth for?" Harley looked back at the shop. He stared at the mess. "I'm going to find out who did this to us."

"Harley?" I queried as I stepped over and around broken shards of glass, ripped pavement, and sheet metal. "Anything I can do to help?"

"Yes, excuse me from attending the lecture tomorrow night. I'm needed here."

"I understand. I'll help."

"Sifting through the wreckage, cleaning up and restoration is dirty work, Mari." He looked at me.

"I don't mind," I replied.

The devastation on his face was hard to take. He was saddened by the loss of life, the injuries, and the utter maliciousness someone must have felt toward him, his employees, and his company.

"It will be okay. You can rebuild, bigger, stronger, and more successful. Don't let this get the better of you."

"I won't," he sighed. "I intend to find out who is responsible." He took one more look at the charred walls. "Now, I need to go pay my condolences to Stuart's family. I need to reassure my staff they will not go without."

"I'll go with you," I offered.

"Thank you," Harley's voice was flat; devoid of emotion. "He lived in Ada." He turned to Edward. "Has Stuart's family been notified?"

"Not yet, Mister Davis."

"I'll take care of it." Harley walked across the street to a telephone booth. "Garrett? Please send a car to the company. I'll need to take Stuart's wife and children to the hospital so they can say goodbye."

We walked back across the street and stood near his motorcycle. "Mari, how do you tell a wife her husband isn't coming home? How do you tell a six-year-old his father will not be back?"

"With compassion, Harley. You tell them with humbleness and compassion the simple truth. Stuart died in an industrial accident. You tell her, she need not worry about expenses and stuff. I know it's small compensation for the loss of her husband."

Minutes later, a car pulled in front of us. Garrett rolled down the window. "I take it, I'm to follow you, Mister Davis?"

"Yes, Garrett."

Harley waited until Garrett pulled the vehicle behind him before heading to Ada. The drive took twenty minutes. We parked in the driveway of a modest brick house. The wind had kicked up, and I tugged my jacket tighter. The gusts sent leaves and papers tumbling down the street as though fleeing a foreboding portent.

We trudged up the walkway to the porch. There were three steps to climb and ten to the door. Harley pressed the doorbell. The wait seemed to take forever before Stuart's wife answered.

She was a petite Vietnamese lady with shiny, straight black hair that matched the color of her eyes.

"Mister Davis," she said, her speech had a heavy Vietnamese accent. "Stuart is not home, yet."

"I know May Ling." Harley shuffled his feet. "May I speak with you, privately?"

"Yes, Mister Davis. Please come inside."

Harley and I entered the humble home. A small boy sat on the living room floor pushing a toy truck. The furnishings included black lacquered cabinets with gold trim in the Oriental or Asian tradition. A comfortable sofa, a wood coffee table, and a recliner comprised the rest of decor.

"May Ling," Harley began. "Stuart has been with me since I started my company here. He has been a valued employee. It is with great regret I must inform you about an accident on the job."

May Long looked stoically at Harley. "What you say, Mister Davis? My Stuart is hurt?"

"No, May Ling," Harley spoke softly. "He did not survive."

"Dead?" She cried, "Stuart is dead?"

"I'm very sorry to say it. Yes, Stuart is dead. I wish it were different. I'd gladly trade places with him if it were possible, but, it's not. I have a car waiting to take you to the hospital. Rest assured May Ling, I will make financial arrangements, so you do not have to worry. The police and fire department might want to talk with you. You do not have to speak with them without a lawyer which I will pay for. I want you to be completely honest with them."

The ensuing days went by in a whirl of activity. The police and fire departments conducted their investigations, ultimately coming to the conclusion it was an intentional action that resulted in the fire and Stuarts death. Eventually, Jimmy, a former employee was found guilty and sentenced to time in prison. True to his word, Harley established and funded a trust fund for Stuart's family.

The employees and contractors worked long, hard hours rebuilding the facility and completing orders they already had on hand. I pitched in and helped with the cleanup.

Needless to say, we never made it to the lecture on serial killers.

Chapter Thirty Three

With the company back in business, Harley decided to take the Summer Quarter off from classes and work. He needed some down time to recharge his batteries.

I also felt a need for some time off. So I elected to take only one-morning class and continue with my radio show. I asked to work only three evenings at K-Mart a week, none on the weekend.

This arrangement gave Harley and me more time together. We walked the grounds of his property as we enjoyed the gardens. We had a lot of picnics in those gardens. Other times we visited the surrounding towns. I never knew that part of Ohio was so rich in history. I learned that astronaut John Glenn hailed from Cambridge, Ohio about 170 miles from Lima and east of Columbus. We took day trips to Columbus where we enjoyed the museums.

We also visited Dayton home of Wright Patterson Air Force Base and reputed to be the location of an alien aircraft and bodies. Near there is the Adena Indian Mounds. While I was interested in the Adena culture, Harley's primary focus was on finding out if there really were alien remains stored at the base. Thomas, March, Maryanne, and Peg joined us in the minibus for that outing.

"Wouldn't it be cool if we could find a way onto the base?" Thomas said.

"I still have a valid military dependent ID card," I volunteered. "I can get us onto the base for commissary and post exchange."

"How is that possible?" Peg asked.

"I'm enrolled as a full-time college student." I looked over my shoulder at Peg.

"Groovy," March said. "Once on base, we can wander around. Pretend we got lost if we're caught."

"Just what I was thinking!" Harley pumped the air with his fist. "This is going to be fun." From the look on his face, I could tell Harley was having a great time.

"I'm not sure about this, guys," Maryanne said.

"Chill, sweetheart," March said. "We're just going to look around. Maybe see an alien body or two."

"That's what I'm afraid of," she grumbled.

"C'mon, Maryanne! Where's your sense of adventure?" Peg asked.

"On an alien ship bound for Alpha Centauri," Maryanne mumbled to our amusement.

"Uh, Houston, we have a problem," Thomas mimicked the astronauts heard through the Apollo years. "Maryanne has been hijacked and is on her way out of earth orbit. Her trajectory puts her on a direct course for Alpha Centauri. What is rescue ETA? Over."

"4.396 light years," Harley copied the voice of NASA's commentator.

"Ah, roger that, Houston. 4.396 light years."

We approached the gates to Wright Patterson. The guard on duty came to the driver side. I handed my identification card to Harley, who in turn, gave it to the guard. The guard studied it for a long time as he glanced at the card and then at me.

"What's your purpose for this visit?"

"The commissary and base exchange," I replied.

"Follow that road. There are signs posted that will take you there."

"Yes, Sir."

We drove off down the road. As soon as we were out of sight of the guard house, we turned down a road and headed toward the back of the base. Everyone knows that's where all top secret stuff in the movies is kept; at the back or hidden underground.

"In 1973 there were fifteen UFO sightings over Dayton," Thomas said.

"Don't forget the bodies and crash debris from the Roswell event in 1947 is supposed to be in Hanger 18 Area B," Harley added as he glanced in the rear view mirror. "No one following us, yet. Now, if only we can find Area B."

"But some reports say Hanger 18 is Hanger 4 Area A, B, and C. So, we should also look for those," Thomas added.

"I agree," March said. "Let's find out once and for all what secrets are hidden here. I bet everything is underground. Kind of a Cheyenne Mountain thing, you know?"

"What is it with you and Cheyenne Mountain?" Maryanne asked. "You're always yammering on about it."

"Really, Maryanne? Cheyenne Mountain, home of NORAD? North American Aerospace Defense Command?" Harley asked incredulously.

"Doesn't ring a bell," she shook her head.

"Me either," Peg shrugged. "Never heard of it. What's so important about NORAD?"

"Ah geez," March groaned. "Guys, we're gonna have to educate these girls."

"It monitors North American airspace for missile attacks and Russian ships."

"Oh!" From the way Maryanne's face lit up you could tell the light bulb had come on. "You mean that protection thingy where they tell those guys in the silos whether or not to launch missiles."

"Bravo, I believe she's got it."

"Uh, oh." Harley glanced in the rear view mirror. "Here they come."

Base security flashed their lights, and we pulled over. Harley kept his hands on the steering wheel in plain sight, only moving to lower the window when the officer indicated. "Yes, officer?"

"You are in a non-public sector of the base."

"We are? We're looking for the commissary."

"That's on Chestnut Street. Go that way," the officer pointed down the road, "and turn left. You can't miss it."

"Thank you. It would help if we had a map of the base." Harley put the vehicle in drive and pulled onto the road. A quick look behind told us the security officer was following us.

"Sorry. I do not have one with me." The officer continued to peer into the window at us.

We went down the road to Chestnut Street and made a left. The officer made the same turn. A few blocks further, we spotted the commissary and drove into the lot. Harley parked the minibus. Sure enough, the security car stopped. I sighed and got out. "What drinks do you guys want?"

With their orders in mind, I walked into the store. It took me twenty minutes to purchase the soft drinks, chips, and assorted snacks. When I returned, the security car was gone. "Here you go." I handed out the goodies. "Harley, I got you a root beer. I hope that's okay."

"It's okay." He took the drink, popped the lid, and took a huge swallow. "Shall we try again?"

"Oh, why not? What can they do to us other than throw us off the base or arrest us?" Thomas dug into a box of Cracker Jacks. "Hmm...the toy is a sticker. Do you guys remember when they used to have really cool stuff like toy soldiers?"

"Some kid probably swallowed one." Maryanne munched on a Frito corn chip.

"Okay, let's see if we can find Area B." Harley pulled out of the parking lot onto the street.

We meandered along roads turning left and then right as we headed toward a warren of metal buildings in the back. They were long rectangular shaped buildings with large doors that appeared to roll up and down. A regular door was to the left of the central entry. These buildings could have been hangers or warehouses for all we could tell. There was no way to know for certain unless we could look inside. Finally, we found one door slightly ajar.

Harley, Thomas, March, and Peg jumped out of the minibus and casually walked over to the door. I slid into the driver's seat prepared to act as the getaway driver. After looking around, Harley slipped an arm inside and opened the entrance completely. We were totally unprepared for the cacophony of sirens and flashing lights set off with that one simple action. The four marauders ran pell-mell back to our vehicle.

"Go! Go! Go!" Harley yelled as he pulled his door closed and reached for the seatbelt.

I stomped on the gas and peeled away from the building only to find our vehicle surrounded by a multitude of security cars. "Turn off the ignition and step out of your vehicle with your hands in the air!" The officers trained their weapons on us. Each time he repeated his instructions his voice rose an octave.

"We're coming out now," Harley used his most soothing tone in an attempt to diffuse the situation. "Our hands are over our heads."

We stood beside the minibus looking like scared college kids caught in a panty raid. All I could think about was how my Dad was going to react. Would he be blisteringly angry, or silent and angry? Either way, he was going to be madder than a disturbed hornet.

"Lay on the pavement face down with your arms stretched overhead and your legs spread." The officer instructed.

Three male and female security people approached us. They divided by gender and proceeded to search us. Finding nothing we were told to stand up.

"Thanks be, I left my tokes at home," March mumbled.

"Hush, March. Keep quiet," Harley glanced sideways at him.

"What were you kids, thinking?" The officer demanded as he flipped open a pad.

"We wanted to see the alien bodies," Maryanne blurted.

"One of those, huh? Hate to disappoint you but there are no alien cadavers stored here."

One of the other officers leaned into their vehicle window and spoke into a microphone. "Roger, that." He glanced in our direction. "Three males and three females. All about college age."

Within minutes a cadre of reporters rushed up. Where they came from, or how they got on the base, I never knew. Microphones were shoved into all our faces; even the officers were harassed.

"Don't say anything," Harley warned us. "Just in case we get arrested. We don't want anything we say used against us. If need be, I'll get my lawyer to represent us."

"No need for a lawyer, Mister Davis," the officer looked at him. "We're just going to escort you off base this time."

We were herded back to our vehicle. Security cars surrounded us. Once we were safely inside the minibus and driving toward the gates of the base, I realized something odd had happened.

"Whew! That was close!" Harley wiped his brow with the back of his shirt sleeve.

"Uh, Harley?" I watched the car in front of us as it made a right turn.

"I can't believe we almost got arrested," Maryanne dug in her purse and removed a tube of pale pink lipstick.

"Harley?" I tried again as the odd feeling increased.

"I wonder if we'll be allowed back on base some other day." Thomas twisted his watch around on his wrist.

"Um...Harley?" I looked pointedly at him. Why was everyone interrupting me? I wanted to scream at them to let me talk.

"Shut up, guys! Mari has something to say!" Leave it to Peg to get them to be quiet.

"Harley, how did that officer know your name? I mean, I don't remember you giving or showing them your license. None of us gave our names. The only one they would have had is mine since I had to show my military dependent identification card."

The silence was deafening as we sat in the minibus contemplating possible explanations and coming up blank. "How did they know who you are? You ever been here before?" I studied my hands.

"No," he shook his head.

We approached the gate. The lead vehicle dropped back until it was even with us. Harley rolled down the window.

"Mister Davis, we advise you to steer clear of non-public sections should you return in the future," the officer briefly lifted his shades to peer at us. "The consequences might not be pleasant in the future."

We left the base. No one talked until we were headed back to Lima. The nagging feeling still had not left me.

"Were those security personnel even military?" Thomas asked.

It hit me then. "Guys? Those people did not dress in military police uniforms. They were in plain clothes and wore dark shades. Sure military folks often wore sunglasses, but they always look like they were in the armed forces."

"Oh, my," Peg covered her mouth with her hand. Her eyes grew as big as saucers. "They were men in black?"

"I don't know who they were, but they weren't armed forces personnel. They didn't look like or dress like our men in uniform."

"Geez...let's get out of here." March scratched at his beard.

We got back to Harley's home to find Mike, Lori, Hixson, Flash, and Judy had arrived for our weekend get together. Flash and Garrett had fired up the grill and were fixing ribs and sausage links. Mike and Hixson were busy getting drinks, plates, flatware, and napkins. Lori and Judy were cutting fruit and making a salad.

"You guys are just in time," Flash called out as he basted the meat with a homemade sauce.

"Boy, do we have a story to tell you; but, you have to promise not to repeat it." Harley came over to help with the glasses for the drinks.

"Hey, guys!" Maryanne screamed. "Come here! They're reporting about us on the news!"

We rushed inside in time to see a shot of the minibus as it was escorted off base. The reporter was saying we were UFO hunters

"Six alleged UFO hunters were detained at Wright Patterson Air Force Base today for unlawful entry into restricted test facilities. The identity of the alleged hunters is unknown at this time." The reporter droned on about the escapade.

"Guess, I might want to have the minibus painted," Harley commented as the station turned to other news.

"Yes, Sir. I'll have Edward take care of it," Garrett entered the house.

Then there was a brief mention of the Big Ear SETI project. On August 15, 1977, a signal appearing to originate in the constellation Sagittarius was received by Ohio State University's Big Ear radio telescope. Astronomer Jerry R. Ehman is credited with the discovery earlier this week while he was reviewing recorded data. He dubbed it "Wow!"

"Whoa! What a coincidence!" Hixson grunted. "That happened earlier this week, and today you guys nearly got arrested for hunting UFO's."

"That was you guys?" It was the first time I ever heard Mike sound shocked. "Is that what you had to tell us? Did you break into the base and top secret facilities? Man, you have some guts."

"Actually, we entered quite legally. Mari has a base id card. As for the facilities," Thomas shrugged, "the door was open."

We carried the food to the picnic table. After a brief prayer, we began eating with gusto. Other than the snacks I had purchased at the commissary, none of the six of us had eaten since breakfast, and we were ravenous.

We rehashed the adventure, including our suspicions about the security detail. Everyone sat silently, as we thoughtfully chewed our food. Hixson finally broke the silence. "You think it was those people Daiken writes about?"

"The men in black?" March nodded and took a swig of his soda. "I need something stronger."

Hixson passed him his flask. Harley frowned but kept silent. I think we were all a bit unnerved by what had transpired earlier.

"Thanks," March took a swallow and wiped his mouth with his napkin. "Yeah, that's what I'd guess, the men in black. As Mari pointed out, they weren't armed forces; that's for sure."

"They were creepy." Maryanne shivered. "They wore black suits. Even the women. And black shades. They all wore the exact same outfit. I mean, who does that?"

Flash went inside and cued David Bowie's 'Space Oddity,' and 'The Rise and Fall of Ziggy Stardust and the Spiders From Mars' album. The music appropriately fit our mood and topic of conversation.

"Don't forget, they knew Harley's name. They probably knew all our names." The name thing still had me wigged out. It was seriously freaky. I could understand them knowing my name, after all, they had seen my id card.

"Now, you know why you guys can't talk about it?" Harley asked as he plucked a piece of fruit and examined it as though it might have come from another planet.

After dinner, everyone pitched in cleaning up before we went inside. Oddly enough, no one was interested in playing games or reading. Instead, we all gathered in the living room and listened to the music playing on the stereo. All the tunes selected fit our otherworldly mood. Even though it was summer, each of us seemed to take comfort in having a fire blazing in the fireplace almost as though the very nature of the flames doing their ethereal dance kept us safe from government secrets, underground bunkers, black operation projects, hidden aliens and spacecraft debris. We sat lost in our thoughts for extended periods of time before someone invariably asked another question or brought up a supposition.

"If they knew Harley's name," March ventured the thought foremost in everyone's mind, "what's to say they didn't know all of our names? And if they do know our names, does that mean they know about Mike, Lori, Hixson, Judy, Flash, and Garrett?"

"I don't know. I would guess so." I said slowly and settled back against Harley, letting his arms protectively encircle me. "If that's true, where did they learn about us? It's not like we'd ever gone UFO hunting."

"The Daiken lecture last Fall," March snapped his fingers. "Maryanne, Thomas, Peg, Mari, Harley and I went to it. We took a lot of interest and asked some questions Daiken wouldn't answer."

"That's right!" Thomas sat up and leaned forward. "We even tried to talk to him afterward, and he brushed us off."

"He pointed out men stationed around the room and claimed they were there to make sure he didn't reveal secret stuff." Peg placed her hands on her knees.

"What if," Harley looked around the room, "what he said about them is true?"

"We'd better hope not," Flash stabbed at the flames in the fireplace with a poker.

"If it's all true, then we are sunk," Hixson rubbed his eyes. "They would know everything about each one of us. We'd all be in danger."

We snuggled into our blankets and plumped pillows. No one wanted to go to their rooms. Eventually, we drifted off to sleep. Each of us clung to another as we sought solace in dreams.

The next morning, I woke up to find Harley drinking a cup of hot lemon water in the kitchen as he looked out at his yard. He wore faded jeans, a blue shirt, and hiking boots.

"Going somewhere?" I came over to him and ran my hands along his back. I nuzzled his neck and sniffed the fresh scent of Irish Spring soap on his skin.

"For a walk." He slipped his arm around me. "Care to join me?"

"I'd love to; just let me get my jacket." I quickly left the kitchen and got my outer garment.

We walked hand in hand out the back door, past the grill and pool toward the gazebo. Harley tugged me into the bower. The concrete had a puddle of water. "Must have rained sometime last night," he muttered as he took off his jacket and flipped it over the puddle.

"What are you doing?" His action was so old world it struck me as humorous.

"So your feet don't get wet," he looked wickedly at me. "Guess it didn't work. My jacket got soaked." He bent and picked up the garment, and hung it over the rail to dry. "So much for chivalry."

We sat for a while in the rotunda looking at his land. The rising sun and a slight misty fog cast an eerie solitude over the grounds. The dapple from the beams of light enhanced an otherworldly sense of serenity. "Let's walk through the gardens." He steered me away from the little building further toward the back.

The gardens were stupendous. Even in August, each garden had particular flowers in full bloom. They were exquisitely maintained. Elegant statuary and benches were strategically placed. We strolled arm in arm gazing at the beauty before us.

"Mari," Harley looked at me with pain in his eyes. His color was turning pale. "Let's sit for a bit."

"Harley, are you okay?" I gently guided him to a bench and knelt before him. His hands were ice cold. "Harley?"

He had a vacant look in his eyes and face that scared me to death. Never had I seen him like that in the past. He rubbed at his chest and gasped for breath. His left hand trembled so badly he slipped it under his leg.

"Harley?"

He peered at me through squinting eyes. "Don't feel so good." He coughed and inhaled. "Help me up."

I hurried to comply. As Harley rose, his left leg buckled and he dropped to his knees. "HARLEY!" I screamed. "GARRETT! HIXSON! MIKE! MARCH! Someone help me!" I struggled to lift him back onto the bench.

The guys came running in various states of dress. Some wore pajama bottoms and regular shirts, others wore jeans and no shirts. "What's wrong?" March reached us first. He grasped Harley under the arms and heaved him onto the bench.

"Harley's sick!"

Harley's head rolled back, and his eyes fluttered. He moaned softly. His hands continued to tremble. "We need an ambulance," March hollered to Garrett as the older man came out of the kitchen.

Garrett turned and went back inside. "Guys, help me carry him into the house." March lifted Harley from under the arms while Hixson and Mike raced to grab his legs.

"Geez, he's twitching!" Mike grunted. "Does he have epilepsy?"

"No," I shook my head. I was so frightened; I couldn't keep the tears back. "One minute he was fine, the next he was like this. Something is wrong. Seriously wrong."

Time seemed to slow and minutes felt like hours before we heard the faint wail of an ambulance as it turned down the drive. Everyone piled into cars and followed the emergency vehicle to the hospital. Harley was admitted for a series of tests and then transferred to the hospital in Toledo where he'd had tests done the previous year.

While he was between tests he tried to sign his business, home, and funds over to me as his fiancée. It took a lot of effort, but over the days I convinced him to sign the company over to Edward and the veterans; his home and funds over to Garrett.

"Make sure Garrett is financially secure and set him up to disperse some of your funds to the needy." I pleaded as I poured him a glass of water. "He's been with you since the day you were born. Garrett has been loyal; he's your mentor, friend, confidante, and practically raised you."

"Are you sure, Mari?" Harley closed his eyes. "I want to make sure you are taken care of too, my love."

"Positive. Set everything up, so it takes effect immediately if, heaven forbid, something happens to you. I'm young. I'll be okay. Garrett is what, in his fifties?" I sniffled. "I don't know what I'll do without you. Harley, you are my heart, my light in a world filled with darkness."

"I'll always be with you, love," he whispered.

"You're going to be okay, right?" I felt desperate to know he would beat this dreadful disease.

"I don't know. The doctor's running a whole battery of tests. That can't be good." Harley kissed my hand. I leaned forward and placed kisses on his lips. "I'll have my lawyer set it up." With a sigh, he settled back against his pillows. The little bit of effort seemed to wear him out.

Chapter Thirty Four

"Mari," Harley's voice sounded weak. He had been hospitalized for months. With each passing month, he seemed to lose more strength and vitality.

A large lump formed in my throat. Harley was so pale and haggard it tore my heart asunder. I looked around the hospital room. All the medical equipment, the IV pole, the narrow bed, the bland colors the room was nothing like the Harley I had come to know and love. It was so sterile and had a medicine stench.

"My parents want to take me back east. They said Columbia or Walter Reed hospitals would give me a better chance of beating this Rhabdomyoscarcoma. They also mentioned MD Anderson in Houston, Texas. They specialize in cancer treatment."

Rhabdomyoscarcoma is also known as RMS. Even the name of this cancer sounded terrible. It is a very aggressive malignant form of soft tissue cancer that generally affects children and young adults. Harley had the most aggressive form known as Anaplastic Rhabdomyoscarcoma. Back in 1977 the survival and cure rate was not high. Once the cancer has spread less than 20 percent of its' victims survive.

"What do you want to do?" I perched on the side of his bed and rested my hand on his. I spooned some pudding into his mouth and gently wiped his lips.

"It appears treatment might take awhile with surgery, chemotherapy, radiation, and something called immunotherapy. I understand that this therapy is relatively new and only became available in 1975. Insurance won't cover it because the consider it to be experimental. So, I would have to pay for it out of pocket."

"Is that what you want to do?"

"It gives me the best chance of beating this cancer. Not much of a chance, mind you, only twenty percent. Mari, it's spread from my leg to my lungs and bone marrow," he sounded depressed and scared. "I don't want to do it, but it's my only option."

"If it doesn't work?" I asked softly feeling as though my spirit was being ripped from my body. A dreadful sense that this might be one of the last times I saw Harley washed over me. I felt so terribly cold with fear.

"I want to die at my home in Lima surrounded by you, Garrett, and Thomas." His voice was barely above a whisper as he talked.

"Then that's what you should do."

"We'd have to postpone our wedding plans, possibly forever." A deep sadness overcame him twisting his handsome face into a mask of emotional pain.

"I know." I whispered, "just don't let us go because I won't let you. Even if we never officially marry, I will always be yours, and you mine." I paused for a long time trying to find the right words. "Harley, I want what is best for you. If you think this treatment will help you get well, then I'm all for it. I will wait for you for however long it takes, forever if necessary." I gently held his hand. Even the slightest touch seemed to cause him pain. "You are my love for eternity. The first time I saw you, I never thought someone like you would be so kind, generous, caring, and loving. What I saw was a biker dude. But something in your eyes and your demeanor said I didn't see past the facade. I never thought I could love anyone as much as I do you."

He smiled and puckered his lips. I bent forward and gently kissed him. "You turned my life upside down Harlan Christian Robert Davis. You made all my days bright and sunny. You helped me become a better person."

"Awe, shucks, ma'am." Pleasure spread across his face. "I fell in love with you the moment I saw you, Mari." His eyes never left my face as he spoke.

We spent the next few hours quietly. I gave Harley sips of ice water to soothe his parched throat. I tenderly wiped the sweat from his brow, tucked blankets around him, and adjusted his pillows to make him more comfortable. When he said his back hurt, I helped him roll onto his side and gently massaged him. I placed many kisses on his lips, his hands, and his cheeks while murmuring, "I love you."

The door to the hospital room opened and in strode his parents.

"Mari," his father said dismissively. "Harlan, we've come to take you home. The hospital has completed the transfer papers for Columbia University Hospital in Manhattan. An ambulance is waiting to take you to the airport."

"Father," Harley struggled to sit up. I pressed the button on his bedside to raise the head of his bed. "I think MD Anderson in Houston is a better option. They specialize in cancer treatment. I'd rather go there."

"Columbia is a fine hospital. They keep abreast of all new medical treatments."

"Mister Davis, please excuse me for interrupting." I bristled at the authoritative tone of his voice. "This is Harley's life we're talking about. Don't you think he should have the final decision on if and where he gets treated?" I rested my hand on Harley's shoulder.

"Who do you think you are to address me in such a rude manner?"

"She is my fiancée, father. I'll not have you speaking to her this way."

"I believe I know better than you, Mari, what is better for my son. You are young and Harley has authority issues."

"If you mean, he doesn't like being bossed around, you're right. I'm just saying, it's his life. He should be the one to select what his options are."

"I am his medical power of attorney. Harlan is too ill to make such an important decision."

A cadre of nurses and attendants entered the room. "Well, Harlan, everything is set. We're going to put you on a gurney and take you to the ambulance. We wish you the best and hope for a full recovery." The nurse said cheerfully.

With practiced ease, the attendants lifted Harley off the bed and placed him on the gurney while keeping the IV lines from tangling.

"Walk with me, Mari?" He looked so lost. "Hold my hand?"

"Of course, my love."

As he was wheeled down the hall, Harley's gaze never wavered from me. "Do not be sad for me. I've lived a full life made even better with you at my side." He softly squeezed my hand. "Nothing can ever separate us, not even death. I will be with you always."

"And I will do the same for you, my love."

As we reached the ambulance, he pulled my hand to his lips and kissed each finger. "I will always love you with all my heart and soul. I will always watch over you."

I felt dampness running down my face and reached up to touch the tears. When they started, I have no idea other than somewhere between his room and the vehicle.

"If I should die, Mari, you will not be alone. I will be the leaf tumbling across your path on a windy day. I will be the stray hint of the sunshine that kisses your face on a cloudy day. I will be the moonshine smiling down at you. When you are feeling scared or down, I will be the soft unseen touch on your shoulder or the hint of a familiar voice calling your name."

"I will love you forever my Steppenwolf loving prince." I leaned forward to place one last kiss on his lips before they took him away.

I stood in the ambulance bay watching as they took my heart away. I don't know how long I remained there.

"Miss Mari?" Garrett walked toward me. "Master Harley requested I make sure you got home okay. Come with me." He gently guided me down the sidewalk to where he had parked the limousine. I have no idea when he moved it from the visitor parking lot.

"After I take you home, I will be leaving Lima to join Harley at Columbia. You have my solemn word I will take care of him as best as possible during these trying times. I will do my best to make sure his wishes are honored."

"I know you will do your best, Garrett. You are more of a father to him than Mister Davis ever was. He loves you."

"Thank you, Miss Mari. I will keep you updated and try to find a way for you and Master Harley to talk."

Garrett was true to his word. Every week he got my work schedule and arranged for Harley to call me. The calls often came after eight at night and were brief but filled with remembrances of our escapades. We laughed a lot during those telephone conversations.

Months passed, then came the call from Garrett telling me Harley would be coming home in two days. He gave me flight information and asked if I could be at Harley's home when they arrived. Those were the two longest days of my life.

Finally, it was time. I raced over to the house and let myself in with the key Harley had given me. Even though I was scared out of my wits, I managed to light a blaze in the fireplace. I turned the furnace on so the rest of the house would be warm. During Garrett's absence, he had hired maids and groundskeepers to keep the place presentable.

Thomas arrived, bringing Harley's favorite Chinese take out meal. "I thought he might be hungry." He carried the bags to the kitchen. "They aren't here yet?"

"No," I replied miserably.

"I'll call the airport. Maybe the flight's been delayed." Thomas walked into the foyer and dialed. I could hear snippets of conversation.

"Well, okay. Thanks." Thomas came back into the living room scratching his chin. "The plane landed two hours ago. There was no record of Harley or Garrett being on that flight. Maybe they had to take a later flight. I'll call and check that out."

I felt a creeping sense of dread coming over me. I just knew the answer was not going to be pleasant.

Thomas returned looking dismayed. "Garrett was on a flight that landed a half hour ago, but Harley wasn't. I wonder what that means."

"It means," I fought to keep the tears and disappointment at bay. "He isn't coming home." I wrapped my arms around me and paced the floor.

"But his parents said he was doing better and the doctors were giving him a respite from treatments."

"They lied," I said flatly.

Thomas gently guided me back to the sofa. "Come, sit beside me."

We sat silently on the couch in the living room. Both of us were so wrapped in our thoughts we didn't hear the car approach the mansion.

"Miss Mari? Mister Thomas?" Garrett called out as he entered the foyer.

"Garrett!" We jumped up and ran to meet him.

"Where's Harley?" Thomas demanded.

"What happened?" I asked.

"I'm sorry. Master Harley had a sudden relapse late last night. He passed away at eleven this morning. I was tied up making arrangements to transport him to a funeral home. I didn't want to break the sad news over the telephone, so I took a later flight." Garrett peered at us with red, puffy eyes.

Thomas abruptly sat on one of the Ottomans lining the foyer walls. He stared vacantly at his hands. His fingers kept twining around forming knots.

Time seemed to come to an abrupt stop. I could hear the ticking of the grandfather clock, the rhythm of the pendulum swinging back and forth was irritating. The crackling of the wood burning in the fireplace was obscenely loud.

I felt terribly cold as though I was standing inside an ice palace. I stood there taking in the scene as though I was frozen in place. Everything seemed to move in slow motion. Then suddenly time came rushing forward bringing with it a multitude of searing, heart wrenching pain.

I ran from the house into the driveway, repeatedly screaming, "NO!"

I dropped to my knees on the pavement and shook my fists at the sky. "WHY MY HARLEY?"

"Why?" I sobbed. My entire body was wracked with my cries.

I have no memory of time passing, or of Garrett lifting me and carrying me back inside. He wrapped me in a blanket and settled me in front of the fire. Thomas had turned on the stereo. 'Another's Lifetime' was playing softly.

Garrett brought me a cup of hot herbal tea. It was the only tea Harley drank. Chamomile with lemon and honey. "Drink this, Miss Mari." He lifted my face with the tip of his finger. "Master Harley would not want you to be so sad." He pulled the blanket tighter around me. "I will call your parents and explain you are staying with friends tonight."

At some point, I was led from the living room into Harley's room where I curled into a ball on his bed. As I lay on the bed, I could see the back yard and gardens from the window. Garrett gently covered me with Harley's comforter as I remained motionless looking across the room and out the window to Harley's favorite place. The gazebo looked lovely; painted in white with a light dusting of snow around it. It was peaceful. How I wished Harley was there with me now to enjoy the view. He would have loved it like he enjoyed the many simple things in life.

Two days later I was able to go home. As I walked in the door, I saw my Dad sitting at the kitchen table reading the newspaper.

"Hi, Dad." I still felt numb and couldn't believe it had only been two days. Garrett was leaving later that afternoon to attend the funeral services back east. I doubted I would ever see him again. During the past couple of nights, I heard his sobs when he thought everyone was asleep. Thomas had refused to leave either of us alone. I think we three just needed each other to get through those first days.

"Morning, Mari. I read that Harlan Davis passed away. He was your young man, wasn't he?" Dad looked up from the newspaper. He had a cup of coffee in his hand. My father always seemed to be holding a coffee cup. I wondered how many he drank in a day. Such an inane thought to have, but there it was. How many cups of java did Dad consume in a single day?

"Yes, Dad."

"I'm sorry to hear he passed. Was it sudden?" He stared intently at me. "You were very close."

"Yes," I sobbed.

My Dad isn't very demonstrative, but that day he hugged me close until I stopped crying. "He must have been very special."

"He was, Dad. Very, very special." I hiccupped. "He was the most special man I ever met, and now he's gone." Tears streamed down my face again. From where was all this wetness coming? I never knew a person could shed so many tears and not get dehydrated from loss of water and salt.

"Then be glad you had him even for such a short time." Dad used his thumb to flick the tears away. He pulled me back into his embrace. "Be glad of the time you had with him, Mari."

"I am." My Dad's words brought a strange sensation of peace to my aching heart.

Epilogue

Many years ago an angel once whispered softly in my ear. He wrapped me in his arms and held my fears at bay; and taught me to be a motorcycle mama loving the open road.

He had a reason for loving me and used to talk about how I was his soul mate. He always said he felt at home in my arms. He said holding me closely soothed his bedeviled wandering soul.

His was a warm and tender love. He always looked out for me even when he was a bit of a devil. He showed his affection not so much in words, but in deeds.

The gentle touch of his hand on my arm as he led me around a puddle, the way he cocked his head and gazed into my eyes, and the sheer joy that spread across his face when he saw me waiting for him in the parking lot.

He watched over me by trying to keep me safe when I did something foolish, but he never suffocated me. He gave me freedom and wings to fly high and experience life in all its glory.

Even when he was being wheeled to a waiting ambulance to take him to a hospital his parents selected for a last-ditch treatment, he tried to comfort me. He lay on the gurney deathly ill; yet, his thoughts were on making me feel his love.

"I will watch over you forever, Mari, until we are together again. I will be your guardian angel, and nothing will ever stop that," he whispered.

I was thinking about that day so long ago when I walked toward a local juice bar. The growing colors of spring, the sparkling dew, the fresh scent of grass, the chirping of birds, brought bittersweet memories to mind.

The pleasant coolness of the awakening day feels serene. A sense of being at peace with the world overcomes me. As I walked and watched the new day dawning, memories of Harley flow sharply through my mind. It has been thirty-nine years since I lost him.

I know it's not possible but I still long for his kisses, and I still want the future we had dreamed about. I swiped at the dampness on my cheeks as a tear leaked from my eye. I will always miss having his arms around me, feeling his sweet breath as he whispered in my ear.

The juice bar is my favorite place. It reminds me of the old diner Harley loved in Lafayette with booths lining one wall and a counter with stools on the other side. Antique table top jukeboxes sit in each booth. I flipped through the selection until I found 'Another's Lifetime' by Steppenwolf, 'Trying To Live My Life Without You' by Bob Seger and 'Hold On' by Tom Waits.

Having made my selections, I perused the menu. A turkey sandwich and a long tall glass of Born Wild, a juice concoction of cranberry, grape, strawberry and lemons, looked good.

My thoughts turned about to those halcyon days and the WOSL-Lima gang. Hixson and Lori moved on to complete their Masters and Doctorate degrees. Mike and Judy went into radio management and eventually got married. Flash obtained his degrees in radio engineering, and also managed to open a small restaurant in Columbus, Ohio.

Peg went back to Dirk and died at the age of thirty-six, March and Maryanne married and adopted four children and had two of their own thereby creating their version of the 'Brady Bunch.' Garrett dispensed Harley's funds to help the needy while keeping just enough to keep him comfortable throughout his lifetime. He either settled in another city or moved back to his home country. I do not know what became of Harley's company or his home. Neither exists in the locations I knew.

Thomas disappeared two years after Harley's death. His car was uncovered in ditch during the first spring thaw. The authorities claim from the way the vehicle sat buried; there was no way he could have gotten in or out. There were no signs of him leaving the car. The windows were rolled up, the key was in the ignition, and the doors locked from inside. The interior was littered with empty chip bags, drink bottles, and a wadded up blanket. There was no sign a person had been in the vehicle otherwise. The only other peculiar thing was a scorched mark on the headliner over the driver's side. Could it be Thomas finally had an alien encounter and was taken to their home world? Did the men in black tote him away to some secret base?

WOSL-Lima quit broadcasting sometime during the 1994-1995 school year. There are no records as to what caused the demise of the iconic radio station.

Having made my choices, I sat back with my eyes closed and listened to the growling voice of John Kay.

During all the treatments that stole time from him, he never cried out. When he was going through so much pain and misery, he never complained – not even once because he knew what awaited him on the other side.

There were many nights when I awakened certain I heard his beloved voice calling my name, "Mari." I lay there listening, hoping to hear him once again before sleep overcame me. It seems I always heard him when the time was blackest. His voice was like a guide bringing me from the brink of darkness into the light. Oh, how I miss him, even now decades later.

I will do as he wanted me to. I will live the rest of my life seeking adventure, and I won't be caught hiding in the shadows full of sorrow and heartbreak because life is filled with discovery and joy. Harley taught me how to love unconditionally, kindness and generosity can lift up those people less fortunate and will earn you respect, spiritually is important for the soul, and living life without regret is essential to happiness.

There's no one looking over my shoulder or giving me a hug; no one to take away my fears; no angel whispering softly of love. It's so peaceful and so lonely. And should he find me some morning, my thoughts will have taken me far, far away from here.

There comes a time when you feel the want to leave, to see the world, indeed, the universe, outside of here. And should he see me as the sun sets, he will look deep into my face and see the longing to know and visit the places he has been and held so dear. He will see a desire to have those adventures we had dreamed of but have only read about.

Oh, how I wish I could go to the places he had, to see the sights as he viewed them. It would bring a calming influence to my soul to know that I walked along the same paths, trails, and markets where he once trod. What joy I would experience just knowing I sampled the same foods, cultures, and environs he loved.

"Hey," the rich tones of a familiar baritone voice caressed me as I listened to the music. With eyes closed, I could almost picture Harley standing beside me like he did so many years ago at Zag's Pizzeria. "You're a hard person to keep up with."

Harley's voice came softly through the strains of the music. "May I sit here?"

I opened my eyes and stared into the face I thought I'd never see again. Harley looked much like he did back then. "It's not possible," I shook my head. "When they told me you died, a part of me went with you." A tear leaked from my eye. "I even read about it in the paper."

Harley reached out and took my hand, "Mari, not everything you read in the paper is truth." His hair was a deeper shade of sandy and dark brown and now had streaks of silver. He wore a black leather jacket, black shirt, and jeans, and carried a motorcycle helmet in his hands. He flipped the aviator glasses up on his head, and I stared into the wildly innocent eyes that have haunted me all these years.

"I went through a lot with cancer treatments, some of them I told you about when we talked on the telephone late at night. Others, I didn't care to rehash, they were so brutally draining. I never called you after those days, but I dreamed about being with you. Even though they never found the right combination, I never quite went away. I've been looking after you ever since."

I cried, and he slid beside me in the booth. It felt as though time had stopped and rolled back to 1975 and the Lafayette diner where our first date began. "Trying to live life without you is the hardest thing I've ever had to do, Harley. I miss you so much. Not a day goes by that I don't wish you were here with me to kiss away my fears, to protect me, teach me, and to love me."

"Even though I am not here physically, I never went away Mari. I'll be here forever, watching over you and waiting for the day we can be together again."

I wish, perhaps, to call upon some kind angel who will hear my plea and want to help. Maybe, I thought, the sweet angel would like to bring him back to me. I tried to hold back the mist gathering in my eyes and keep the quiver in my voice unheard as I whispered, "I miss you so much."

He gathered me into his arms, and my angel whispered, "I told you we would find each other again because love means never saying goodbye."

###

Author's Notes:

The music mentioned in this novel can be found online. Unless otherwise noted, the music can be purchased at:

Amazon.com:
https://www.amazon.com

Steppenwolf:
http://steppenwolf.com

- Another's Lifetime on Hour of the Wolf
- Just for Tonight on Hour of the Wolf
- Born to be Wild on Born to be Wild
- The Pusher on Born to be Wild
- Monster/Suicide/America on Monster
- Foggy Mental Breakdown on 7
- Jupiter's Child on At Your Birthday Party
- Annie, Annie Over on Hour of the Wolf
- For Ladies Only on For Ladies Only
- Magic Carpet Ride on The Second
- Disappointment Number on The Second
- Lost and Found by Trial and Error on The Second
- Hodge Podge Strained Through a Leslie on The Second
- Hey Lawdy Mama on Steppenwolf Live
- Don't Step on the Grass, Sam on The Second
- Ride With Me on For Ladies Only
- Justice Don't Be Slow on Slow Flux
- Ball Crusher on 7
- Snowblind Friend on 7
- Tenderness on Steppenwolf Gold
- Gang War Blues on Slow Flux
- Children of the Night on Slow Flux
- Smokey Factory Blues on Slow Flux
- Berry Rides Again on Steppenwolf
- Skullduggery Album/CD Skullduggery

- Rest In Peace Album
- Happy Birthday on Album/CD At Your Birthday Party
- Say You Will on Album/CD All In Good Time

Steppenwolf Performance December 8, 1975
Providence Civic Center, Rhode Island. Savoy Brown opening act.

Set list:
- Born to be Wild
- Gang War Blues
- Hey Lawdy Mama
- Children of the Night
- Jeraboah
- Monster/Suicide/America
- Smokey Factory Blues
- Fishin' in the Dark
- The Pusher
- I'm Movin' On
- Straight Shootin' Woman
- Get into the Wind
- Magic Carpet Ride

Encore:
- A Fool's Fantasy
- Berry Rides Again

Bob Seger:
- Beautiful Loser on Beautiful Loser
- If I Were A Carpenter on Early Seger Vol 1.

Bob Seger and the Silver Bullet band June 26, 1976
Pontiac, Michigan Pontiac Silverdome:

Set list partial:
- Bo Diddley
- Nut bush City Limits

- Back in '72
- Travelin' Man
- Beautiful Loser
- Katmandu
- Roll Me Away
- Turn The Page
- Heavy Music
- Ramblin' Gamblin' Man
- Night Moves
- Mary Lou
- Get Out of Denver

John Kay:
- I'm Movin' On from the Forgotten Songs and Unsung Heroes Album/CD

Boston: CD Boston
- More Than a Feeling

Aerosmith: CD Toys In The Attic
- Sweet Emotion
- Walk This Way
- Dream On on CD: Aerosmith
- Lord of the Thighs on CD: Get Your Wings

Sailcat: CD Motorcycle Mama
- Motorcycle Mama on Motorcycle Mama

Steely Dan: CD Can't Buy a Thrill
- Reelin' in the Years
Daddy Dewdrop:
- Chicka-Boom (Don't Ya Jes' Love It) on One Hit Wonders Vol 2

America: CD America The Complete Greatest Hits
- Sister Golden Hair
- A Horse With No Name

Journey:
- To Play Some Music on Journey
- Topaz on Journey
- It's All to Much on Look Into the Future
- I'm Gonna Leave You on Look Into the Future

The Carpenters: CD The Carpenters Singles
- (They Long to be) Close to You on Close to You

Porter Wagoner: CD Essential Porter Wagoner
- Green Green Grass of Home

Tom Waits: CD Mule Variations
- Hold On

Moby Grape:
- Moby Grape
- 69
- Wow
- Grape Jam

Creedence Clearwater Revival:
- Creedence Clearwater Revival
- Green River
- Bayou Country
- Willy and the Poor Boys
- Cosmos Factory
- Pendulum song Have You Ever Seen the Rain
- Mardi Gras

The Godfather:
- Speak Softly Love The Theme from the Godfather by The Sound Orchestra

Johnny Cash:
- Folsom Prison Blues

- Daddy Sang Bass

Roberta Flack:
- The First Time Ever I Saw Your Face

Alice Cooper (on Amazon)
- Welcome To My Nightmare

Nat King Cole:
- Unforgettable

Percy Sledge:
- When A Man Loves A Woman

Jim Nabors:
- Somewhere My Love

David Bowie:
- Space Oddity on David Bowie Album/CD
- The Rise and Fall of Ziggy Stardust and the Spiders From Mars Album/CD

The Who:
- Pinball Wizard on the Tommy Album/CD

Etta James:
- At Last

Bruce Springsteen:
- Rosalita Come out Tonight

Janis Joplin: Greatest Hits
- Summertime
- Me and Bobby McGee

Grateful Dead: American Beauty
- Ripple

• Truckin

KISS: KISS
• Nothin' to Lose
• Kissin' Time
• Strutter

Schubert: Leonard Bernstein available on Mp3 and CD
• Symphony No. 8 Unfinished
• Symphony No. The Great

Aaron Copland: The Copland Collection˙
• Appalachian Spring

• Chopin: The Chopin Collection by Frederic Chopin and Arthur Rubinstein

Hungarian Gypsy Music:
• The Bartók album traditional Hungarian gypsy music by Muzsikas

Tchaikovsky: The Ballets Andre Previn
• Swan Lake
• Nutcracker
• Sleeping Beauty

Other bands mentioned in this novel are listed below.
Unless noted otherwise availability is unknown.
Point Blank Nichole, Distances, That's the Law
Elvin Bishop
Todd Rundgren (on Amazon)
John Fogerty (on Amazon)
Gordon Lightfoot Cold on the Shoulder (on Amazon)
Charlie Spand
Speckled Red
Johnny Cash
Clara Smith
Mamie Smith

Barry Manilow
John Lee Hooker (should be available on Amazon)
Glenn Frey (The Eagles available on Amazon)
Sonny Bono (Sonny and Cher should be available on Amazon)
Aretha Franklin (on Amazon)
Ted Nugent (on Amazon)
Commander Cody and His Lost Planet Airmen
Del Shannon
MC 5
Grand Funk Railroad (on Amazon)
Elton John (on Amazon)
Captain & Tennille
Linda Ronstadt (on Amazon)
Hamilton, Joe Frank & Reynolds
Neil Sedaka (on Amazon)
Jigsaw
Ozark Mountain Daredevils
KC & The Sunshine Band
The Monkees
The Who: Boris the Spider
Alice Cooper: Welcome to my Nightmare
Blue Oyster Cult: Don't Fear the Reaper
Black Sabbath: Megalomania
Bobby Boris Pickett: The Monster Mash and Monsters' Holiday
Electric Light Orchestra: Evil Woman and Strange Magic
Donovan: Season of the Witch

Books:
- Steppenwolf by Hermann Hesse
- Siddhartha by Hermann Hesse
- The Haunting by Shirley Jackson
- A Christmas Carol by Charles Dickens

Plays:
- A Christmas Carol
- Cleopatra
- The Man of La Mancha

Movies:
- The Great Gatsby 1974 starring Robert Redford
- Easy Rider starring Jack Nicholson and Peter Fonda
- The Way We Were 1973 starring Robert Redford and Barbara Streisand
- Black Christmas 1974 version
- Carnival of Souls cult classic from 1962
- The Haunting 1963 version directed by Robert Wise
- Shivers also called They Came From Within 1975
- The Wizard of Oz starring Judy Garland
- My Fair Lady

Television Shows:
- Alice 1974 starring Linda Lavin
- The Brady Bunch

Places:
You can double check these listings for more accurate information on the internet.

The Victorian Loft Bed & Breakfast
216 Front Street, Clearfield, PA
814-290- 6565

Kewpee Hamburgers
2111 Allentown Road
Lima, Ohio

Kewpee Hamburgers original downtown location is on Elizabeth Street at the corner of Market Street in Lima, Ohio

Visit Wolfpark.org at: http://wolfpark.org/
They are a very worthy organization and I hope you will consider donating to them.

Wolf Park
4004 East 800 North
Battle Ground, Indiana 97920
765-567-2265

Rocket Restaurant:
1375 Baldwin avenue
Pontiac, Michigan
248-335-6464

Tecumseh Nature Areas is part of the Ohio State Lima University. During the time frame of this novel there was a cook out section a group of student volunteers helped to develop. I do not know if this area of the Tecumseh Nature Area still exists.

Clegg Gardens (Clegg Botanical Gardens)
1782 N 400 E
Lafayette, Indiana
765-423-1325

Prophetstown State Park
Mailing address:
4112 E. State Road 225
West Lafayette, Indiana 47906

Mapping address:
5545 Swisher Road
West Lafayette, Indiana 47906

I love hearing from my readers. Please feel free to email me at: cassandraparker753@gmail.com

Visit my Amazon page at:
https://www.amazon.com/-/e/B019CT2XMW

Facebook:
https://www.facebook.com/CassndraParker/

Copy and paste the links in the above pages into your email client or web browser.

An honest review is appreciated.

Made in the USA
San Bernardino, CA
19 April 2017